He moved his hand up her arm, tickling her skin along the way.

At her shoulder, he curled his fingers and brushed them along her jawline. "Why don't you stop being a detective for tonight?"

The beginning of resistance faded with the fresh wave of desire he initiated. Jamie ran his thumb over her lower lip. The passion felt different than their first night. Less impulsive. In fact, he didn't seem to act on any impulse now. And since she hadn't anticipated him touching her this way, neither did she. No, this felt deliberate. Like a thought-out choice.

While part of Reese warned her choice should be to stop, the more sensual one wasn't listening.

He slid his hand behind her head and coaxed her forward. As she leaned toward him, he stood and closed the distance. Maybe it was the long day. Maybe it was the explosion. She might be overtired and susceptible. But she wanted this. Him.

* * *

Be sure to check out the other books in this series.
Cold Case Detectives:
Powerful investigations, unexpected passion...

TAMING DEPUTY HARLOW

BY
JENNIFER MOREY

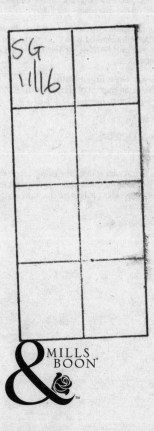

MILLS
BOON
&

First Published in Great Britain 2016
By Mills & Boon, an imprint of HarperCollins*Publishers*
1 London Bridge Street, London, SE1 9GF

© 2016 Jennifer Morey

ISBN: 978-0-263-91950-9

18-1216

Our policy is to use papers that are natural, renewable and recyclable products and made from wood grown in sustainable forests.The logging and manufacturing processes conform to the legal environmental regulations of the country of origin.

Printed and bound in Spain
by CPI, Barcelona

Two-time RITA® Award nominee and Golden Quill Award winner **Jennifer Morey** writes single-title contemporary romance and page-turning romantic suspense. She has a geology degree and has managed export programs in compliance with the International Traffic in Arms Regulations (ITAR) for the aerospace industry. She lives at the foot of the Rocky Mountains in Denver, Colorado, and loves to hear from readers through her website, www.jennifermorey.com, or Facebook.

For Mom, who claimed her independence.

Chapter 1

"How did you find me?" Jamie Knox asked the big man wearing the cowboy hat. He took great care to not be easy to find. The fact that this man did spoke to the depth of his resources.

Kadin Tandy walked across Jamie's New York City studio apartment. "One of my detectives tracked you down. He said you were instrumental in closing a case he worked in Alaska." He inspected the big-screen TV in the corner and then the queen-size bed in an alcove off the living room. "Something about creating a distraction with a helicopter and helping to save his client from the killer?"

"Brycen Cage and Drury Decoteau?" Jamie wasn't fooled that this man didn't know exactly what had happened that day. He sipped from his bottle of water as he sat on the sofa.

"They'd be the ones." Kadin strolled back toward him and stopped beside the kitchen island, the only table Jamie had.

Jamie stretched his arm out along the back of the sofa. "You came here to discuss my involvement in their case?"

"No. I'm here to offer you redemption."

That got his attention. "How do you know I need redemption?"

Kadin made a show of looking around Jamie's studio apartment. "What made you decide to live here?"

"It's close to Central Park, public transportation, and places to shop and eat. But the boutique elevator really hooked me."

"Deep-city living appeals to you?" Kadin didn't find his humor amusing, apparently.

"It's noisy and overpopulated." He was beginning to regret letting the man in. He'd let homeless people in before, so maybe that meant he'd let anyone in. The homeless people he fed. This man… What did he need? Something significant if he went to such lengths to arrange this meeting.

"Does that fill the void of rescuing people from insurgents in Third World countries?"

"You've done your homework." Jamie put the bottle of water on the coffee table.

"I always do when I want to recruit someone."

As Jamie leaned back, he tried not to show his surprise. He'd expected something significant, but not this. "Been doing that a lot lately?"

"I'm a start-up and I happen to be expanding to the international market."

"International?"

"My company is growing. I need someone to develop a security program. Risk management and mitigation. That type of thing."

Risk management and mitigation? Buzzwords that meant something different to this man and to his business. Jamie knew all about Kaden's past, how he'd come to be the man standing in his living room. He also knew what kind of security program he needed. One that mitigated with weapons and countermeasures. Maybe a little corporate security sprinkled in.

"I'm not a homicide detective."

"No, but you have a security background. Not all of my investigators are trained like you. Some are a bit on the vigilante side, but most have cop backgrounds that may not equip them against criminals like the one you worked for. It's not just about physical security in foreign countries. I also need my people secured in my building."

Jamie took a moment before he asked, "Why me?" That was the question he really needed answered.

Kadin smiled; not an all-out smile, more like an I'm-glad-you-asked smile. "You weren't the only good person who was snared by Dexter Watts and his boss. They all had a highly respectful opinion of you."

Admitting he was good at protecting or rescuing people from dangerous places and situations wouldn't be conceited. He was good because he had experience. But he still didn't understand why a man like this would single him out. So he'd helped one of Dark Alley's detectives. He hadn't done it for anyone but himself. To free himself from the clutches of two very bad men.

"Are you interested?" Kadin asked.

"You chose me because I came highly recommended?" He needed more of an explanation.

"I'm getting more and more requests to look into international cases. So far I've personally taken them." Kadin bobbed his head from side to side in a contemplative way. "Mostly for an excuse to take my family on vacation. The victims always come first, of course, but some of the places are paradise. My wife wouldn't stand for it if I didn't take her and my son along. But the workload is getting to be too much, and there have been some instances when the danger gets too risky with my family in tow. I'm putting more detectives in the field. Their lives are my top priority. I need someone I can trust to ensure their safety. Part of my decision was based on recommendation, but most of it was based on your history in security services. You've worked both sides. Military and private military. When the private side didn't work so well you made the right choice by stomping Watts out of your life. Nothing got in your way of doing that, either, and you did it alone. That's proof to me you're not only capable, you're someone I can trust."

He'd qualified by demonstrating his expertise and moral compass. That, Jamie believed. "All right. Then how will I redeem myself if I agree to work for you?"

"You'll be working on the right side of the law. My law. Your law. And, when it suits the case, whatever law applies to the country you or my detectives are in."

The man knew what the importance of being on the right side meant to Jamie. Jamie wouldn't have done what he'd done in Alaska otherwise. "I thought I was on the right side when I joined Aesir International."

"Catchy name. *Ice-ear.* Multiple gods. Race of gods. Too bad Loki ran it."

"Still runs it from what I hear." Jamie stood from the sofa and faced Kadin. Something made him seriously consider his offer, but the risk of impulsiveness kept him cautious.

Kadin brushed the lapels of his jacket aside and rested his hands on his hips, exposing his pistols. "What kept you with Valdemar Stankovich for so long? There has to be a reason. What did he have to hang over your head? A man who agrees to work for the likes of Dexter Watts and then helps take him down isn't a thug who does as told."

Jamie's respect for the man increased with his recognition that Stankovich had leverage to force him to work for Watts.

"I refused to do what he wanted and told him I was quitting," Jamie answered honestly. "Let's just say he didn't respond well to that and came up with a witness and evidence that had me doing something incriminating. I went to work for Aesir thinking I'd have the opportunity to fight terrorism. Make a difference. I couldn't allow him to destroy my reputation. So I waited for the right opportunity. I couldn't make my move until I had every shred of false evidence he created against me. That all came to a head with Watts. Stankovich has nothing on me now."

"What about the witness? Isn't he still a threat?"

"I took care of him. He can't talk anymore." He watched Kadin for any kind of reaction and saw only understanding and a growing kinship. Here stood a man who knew what it took to take justice in his own hands—against seemingly insurmountable odds.

"Maybe you've already had your redemption," Kadin finally said, dropping his hands.

"In some ways, I have." Demons still haunted him, though. He wasn't sure he'd ever be able to exorcize them. "Redemption for me would be living an honorable life, getting married, having children. Feeling normal."

Kadin glanced around the apartment again and looked through the window. A siren could be heard on the street below.

"This is normal? You'd raise kids here?"

Jamie had to agree the studio apartment and cramped city living wasn't part of the fantasy. After Aesir, he wasn't quite ready for suburbia. Or was he?

"Come work for me," Kadin said. "I need someone like you on my team. I can't promise you *normal*, but I can promise you an office and as much or as little travel as you want."

Professionally, Jamie didn't know what he'd do with his future now that he had Stankovich off his back. His immediate need drew him back to his roots, close to his mother in New Hampshire, and deep-city living, as Kadin had put it. He planned to take some time off, find a woman and settle down. Other than that, he had a clean slate.

Would joining an elite team such as Dark Alley Investigations give him the kind of life he needed?

"Think it over," Kadin said.

When Jamie nodded once, he headed for the door.

There, Kadin opened the door and stopped with his hand on the doorknob. "Consider moving to Wyoming, would you? This city-living thing is just a Band-Aid. The boutique elevator gave that away."

As the door shut, Jamie let out a breath of a laugh. Although highly intelligent and perceptive, Kadin acted as though Jamie had already accepted the job. Maybe he had. And without realizing it, he had moved to the city to still feel the connection to danger. Busy streets. Sirens. Gunshots. The noise gave him a sense of familiarity. But he was ready to settle down. He wanted that. Needed that. Craved it. Kadin's visit only sealed that desire tighter. Kadin had one thing right. No more transition time. No more living in constant danger. Stankovich was part of the past now. Jamie had to make a move for the future.

Sitting at her kitchen table, Reese Harlow picked up the internet news article with trembling fingers. Hammers pounded and demolition work vibrated around her as she stared at the photo of a powerful man wearing a cowboy hat. He leaned on the back of a pickup truck parked at the head of an alley, shoulder harness exposed, two guns, one on each side. Steely gray eyes met the camera. Without even meeting him, she sensed an extraordinary man looking back at her from the photo.

Her biological mother had emailed her the link to the article titled Cold Case Hero Expands Business. She'd searched herself and found this photo attached with other articles as though it had become a marketing piece. Former New York homicide detective, founder of Dark Alley Investigations. Father. Husband. She ran her finger over the man's name printed beneath the photograph.

Kadin Tandy. Her father.

And he didn't know about her...

She had known since she was a young girl that she
was adopted. She had good parents who loved her in
their own way and were town fixtures, but as she grew
older, she couldn't stop wondering about the identity of
her biological parents, as though their identity meant
something to her own. Last week, she'd met her biological mother for the first time. While that had been
strange and awkward and fascinating, and had consumed her thoughts all week, her mother hadn't been
able to tell her much about her father. She'd lost touch
with the teenage boy who'd fathered the child she'd
been forced to give up at the age of sixteen. Today
she'd sent Reese the link to this article.

If she went to meet Kadin, how would she approach
him? She'd read he'd lost his young daughter—to
murder, of all things. Reese couldn't imagine enduring such profound tragedy. Blurting out she was his
daughter might come as a bit of a shock. She should
tell him, though. She had to tell him. Someone should
have told him long ago. How could she do that in a
tactful way? She didn't think there would ever be any
good time or any easy way. Maybe she'd get to know
him first.

But did she really *want* that? She'd accomplished
what she'd set out to and found her biological parents.
She had their names and where they lived. That didn't
mean she had to have them in her life from this day
forward. Did it? Maybe she wasn't quite finished with
her exploration.

Exhausted from her lengthy pondering, she bent
her head to look down at the article again, not really
seeing it as her long blond hair fell forward in its con-
fined ponytail. She had contemplated cutting it into a

shorter style, but liked letting it down every once in a while. She retained her feminine side while satisfying a more aggressive one that way. Her best friend in school had called her Cinderella, with her brandy-colored eyes, thick wavy hair, tiny waist and shapely breasts. She had fond memories of her friend's well-meant teasing. And her friend hadn't exactly been frumpy. More men went after her than Reese. Probably because Reese had always been more interested in school and her career than boys or men.

The noise stopped and the sound of excited male voices pulled her attention back to the renovation. All the carpenters were in what would soon be her finished bedroom. What were they all in a fuss over?

Reese stood and went down the freshly drywalled hallway. Stopping at her bedroom door, she saw three carpenters hunched over pried-up old floorboards. She moved closer until she saw a faded 1970s tin *Star Wars* lunchbox that had been removed from beneath the flooring. When the carpenter opened the metal latch to reveal stacks of hundred-dollar bills inside, Reese drew in a startled breath.

A buried treasure? In *her* house? Nothing this exciting ever happened to her. She was just a small-town girl who'd gone to college and came back to get a job at the sheriff's office.

"Jeffrey Neville lived here before you," one of the carpenters said.

She'd discovered that when she'd bought the house. Jeffrey had died and had no family. The home had been escheated to the state and finally sold. He was the last of his line. Thinking about all the losing lottery tickets she'd bought, never in a million lightning strikes guessing she'd stumble upon someone's primitive retirement fund, she took the lunchbox from the one who'd dug it up.

"How did it get here?" she asked aloud, not expecting any of them to know. Life had certainly stirred up some surprises lately.

"Maybe somebody used the house to deposit their savings," another one of the carpenters said.

"Jeffrey must not have known about this," she said.

He lived in this house for more than forty years. Why would he not have used the money for something if he'd known about it? He had no family to pass it on to. He had lived modestly up until the day he died. The way the money had been hidden suggested it hadn't been meant to be found, and then something had happened to the person who'd put it here. Had it been stolen or otherwise obtained in some other nefarious fashion? Had Jeffrey known the person? A wife, perhaps? Strange, after living in this town her whole life, she didn't really know much about one of its residents. She'd never thought to ask, either.

"What are you going to do with it?" one of the carpenters asked.

She looked down at the man who'd discovered it, realizing that they were hoping she'd be generous.

"I don't know, but a small thank-you for finding it is in order." She tipped the carpenters handsomely and received a thank-you from each. She'd like to find out where the money came from, but first she'd put it somewhere safe.

She looked at each of the carpenters' excited faces. Nothing productive would get done after this today.

"Why don't you all take the rest of the day off?" In

a couple of hours, it would be five, anyway. And she needed to be alone.

They thanked her again and began to gather their tools.

Reese returned to the kitchen, putting the tin lunchbox on the table, her gaze landing on the news article. Even finding the money didn't overshadow the significance of what she contemplated regarding Kadin. Maybe his fame intrigued her. Maybe his love of law did more, lending a kind of a connection to him. Even though she'd never met him and he'd never seen her or known of her existence, she'd gone into the same type of work. How amazing was that? She'd like to know more about her biological father.

How would he react to learning he had a daughter?

The next morning, bags packed and in the car, Reese stopped at the bank on her way to the Durango airport a county over. She'd fly to Rock Springs, Wyoming, later today. She'd made reservations after the carpenters had gone and she'd thought for a while about the consequences of her making contact with Kadin Tandy. Good and bad. First and foremost, he deserved to know he had a living daughter. Even though she was incredibly nervous and had serious reservations about how it would change her life, she felt morally obligated to tell him. She'd deal with the fallout as it hit her.

"Hello, Candace." Reese put the lunchbox down on the counter in front of the redheaded teller. "I'd like to open a safe-deposit box."

"Reese. Congratulations on your windfall!" Candace's green eyes danced with enthusiasm. Not much over five feet tall, her elbows rested easily on the counter.

Reese laughed a little. "Thanks. I won't even ask how you found out."

"The whole town is talking about it." The teller gave her a form to fill out and then eyed the tin lunchbox as though it was a relic. "One of your carpenters told me. He made a deposit of his own yesterday. That was awfully nice of you to give them money."

"It's what I would have wanted." Reese handed the form to Candace. "And I'll never get used to the rapid lines of communications in this town."

"That tin is pretty old. Too interesting not to talk, I suppose." Candace handed her a key to a safe-deposit box and tucked some of her bobbed red hair behind her feather-jeweled ear. "You found it hidden in the floor?"

Reese took the key. "Yes. Quite the mystery, huh?"

"I'd say. Did Jeffrey's wife hide it?"

Reese went still. "His wife?" Why did she think his wife could have hidden money? And where was she now?

"She was murdered some forty years ago. That would explain why Jeffrey never knew about the money. I wonder why she hid it? Everyone is wondering that in town. We haven't had this much excitement in years." She laughed lightly.

Murdered...

Reese was still trying to catch up to the significance of that as Candace rambled on.

"Been so long, not many remember her. She was strangled to death and dumped on the side of Highway 149 on the way to Durango."

Reese reeled with the revelation. Then she looked

down at the tin lunchbox. This money could mean more than a forgotten fund. Reese lifted the lunchbox from the counter and lowered it to her side.

"Not even Sheriff Robison told me." She supposed he hadn't thought to, and she had no reason to dig through old evidence.

Candace leaned over the counter on her elbows. "Crime was never solved. I forgot all about it till you bought that old Neville place and my dad mentioned it the other day."

"Why isn't anyone still trying to solve the case?" Reese asked.

"Almost every sheriff in office has tried. A few deputies, too," Candace said.

"Well, maybe it's time for someone new to try." So much time had gone by since the woman's death that everyone had stopped talking about it and that led to no one caring enough anymore. Well, Reese bet if the woman could talk, she'd still care.

"What happened?" she asked. "How was she murdered? She was strangled, but what was she doing the last anyone knew?"

"Ella worked at the library," Candace said. "Just moved here the year before. Met Jeffrey and six months later they got married. She worked the night she was killed. The last person to leave the library was the last to see her alive. She was questioned and cleared. Ella closed the library and vanished. No one saw anything. Someone must have pushed her body out of a vehicle because it fell down a steep slope. To this day, no one knows what happened to her or why she was killed. The sheriff at the time questioned Jeffrey, but he had an alibi. He had a company dinner that night. His wife was supposed to meet him there but she never showed up."

Candace sure knew a lot about the case. Everyone in town likely did. "Where was her car found?"

"She walked to work every day." Candace took lipstick out of her purse and put on a fresh coat.

Ella had been taken somewhere between the time she locked the library and home. "That's terrible."

"Yeah. Wish her killer would be caught, even if it has been so long."

Reese wanted to be the one to grant that wish. "Thanks, Candace." She went to the safe-deposit boxes and found hers, Ella Neville's murder heavy on her mind.

Wish her killer would be caught, even if it has been so long...

Kadin Tandy solved cold cases. What if she went to him with Ella's case? She didn't have to tell him he had another daughter. Not right away. She could get to know him first. Somehow that made her impending trip easier to bear. Call it procrastination. Call it breaking the news gently. She just felt better with that approach.

Locking the tin in the safe-deposit box, she left the bank with a livelier spring in her step than when she'd entered. She'd stop at the sheriff's office and pick up the Neville case file. She would also ask Margaret, their office manager, to send Ella's clothes in for more modern testing. Then she'd head for the airport.

Kadin had moved his office to a bigger building. Jamie read about his first office, an unassuming downtown building with barely one office and a place to hold meetings—he and his wife had lived on the floor above. The new building was a restored mercantile building, the old sandstone exterior walls covered with white glazed brick. Three rows of six casement windows ran the length of the front. He could see a chandelier hanging in the middle of the upper two rows, revealing the open architecture of what must be a nice home with lots of light. A stone railing on each upper corner indicated the location of rooftop balconies. The building sat on high ground, with open space in the back.

The covered front walk on the first level shaded tinted windows and a double-door entrance with an inconspicuous and prettily written Dark Alley Investigations on the right door. Jamie stepped inside, ready for his first day of work.

An artsy lobby housed a young and beautiful, dark-haired woman behind a white marble-topped counter that matched the floor. A few plants warmed up a seating area and several paintings hung on high walls.

"Jamie Knox," he said to the woman.

She smiled, baring a mouth of pearly white teeth. "Go on back, Mr. Knox. Mr. Tandy is waiting for you. He's in the far right corner office."

The inner door buzzed, unlocking for him. He stepped from the lobby into the office-lined interior. Four conference rooms took up both sides of the front. A square area in the middle was filled with cubicles. People walked the halls and stood at printers or worked away at their desks.

Jamie went down the middle aisle, the smell of new carpet and leather accompanying him on the way. Everyone dressed business-casual, some of the men in ties with no jackets.

The far wall had a row of windows like the front, and as he turned to the right, he enjoyed a view of White Mountain and Pilot Butte. Before moving here he'd read that wild horses still ran in those hills. Nothing he'd see in a city, and the notion intrigued him.

Kadin emerged from his spacious office and greeted him. "Let me show you to your office."

Jamie followed him to the opposite side of the building and into the opposite corner office with the same view as the boss. He went to the window. "This gives me an adequate idea of your expectations."

Kadin smiled wryly. "You're taking on an important role in this organization. The safety and protection of my detectives and the victims' families are of utmost importance. The more notoriety I get, the more of a threat we are, and the more high risk the case, the more danger we attract."

"Risk is my résumé." This new role would present plenty of challenges, but Jamie would thrive. This was exactly what he was looking for—a way to get his life back on track, for the good.

"Mr. Tandy."

Jamie turned with Kadin to see the beautiful receptionist at the door.

"Sorry to interrupt. There's a Ms. Reese Harlow here to see you. She says she's a sheriff's deputy from Ute County, Colorado, and she's got a forty-year-old cold case she'd like to discuss with you."

"Put Roesch on it. I can't seem to give that guy enough work."

Kadin had a lot of top-notch detectives working for him, Jamie thought, but the one named Roesch must be one of the best if he completed his cases so fast the work didn't keep up.

"She insisted on speaking only to you, sir."

Many must request him personally, but he couldn't possibly solve every case that came to DAI.

"She said it was personal."

Speaking to Kadin or the forty-year-old case? Her insistence on speaking only to Kadin must be the personal part. But why?

Kadin stared at the receptionist for a moment. "Bring her back."

Evidently he wondered the same.

Chapter 2

Holding the Neville case file binder, Reese followed the receptionist through the cubicles to an office on the far side. At the door, the slender woman let her pass. She caught the name sign and grew confused until she spotted two men standing in the middle of a seating area, waiting for her. She hadn't expected two detectives. Both big men, the one with sexy blue eyes and short black hair captured her attention first.

What was Captain America with dark hair doing in Rock Springs, Wyoming? He stood with his hands at his sides, tall and unflinching, rippling muscles beneath a tight Henley shirt tucked into black jeans. This must be his office. Apparently he ignored company dress code. He seemed out of place in such elegant surroundings. Something more rugged would suit him better, like a battleship or a city riot. She gobbled up the sight of him, so hardened and forbiddingly handsome.

Why did he magnetize her so completely? He wasn't even wearing a cowboy hat. She'd have thought a man more country than him would be the one to catch her eye as undeniably as this man had.

The receptionist closed the door, jolting Reese out of her sudden affliction of man hunger. She looked to the man next to him and recognized him instantly. Kadin. Her father.

Her heart beat so heavily a lump formed in her throat.

You're here to explain the case...

She cleared her throat and swallowed. "Um, hello." She stepped forward, tripped on her shoe heel and had to take a few extra quick steps to catch her balance, nearly dropping the binder. She'd worn her only suit jacket and skirt today, gray with a white blouse underneath.

The man beside Kadin reached out for her at the same time he moved toward her. But she caught her balance before he touched her.

"Are you all right?" he asked.

His deep, raspy voice transfixed her. She melted into his blue eyes. "Y-yes." Feeling as though her breathy, stuttering answer revealed too much, Reese fought a flush and turned to Kadin with an outstretched hand. "I'm Reese Harlow."

"The deputy sheriff from...?" Kadin shook her hand.

She found herself transfixed again, this time for different reasons. Now she studied her biological father. The hugeness of the secret she carried pushed her awkwardness away. She looked for similarities. He must be where she got her five-nine height from. Other than that, she didn't see much resemblance.

"Never Summer, Colorado, which is in Ute County," she finally said, trying to gather the rest of her wits.

Kadin smiled politely. "I've never heard of it."

"Not many have. It's a small mountain town in southwestern Colorado."

"Ah. I have detectives from that area." He turned to the other man. "This is Jamie Knox, my new security officer. Today is his first day on board."

Reese reluctantly moved her gaze to him. Immediate smoldering attraction swept over her. "Mr. Knox." She sounded all breathy again.

His mouth rose with a hint of licentiousness and his incredibly blue eyes reacted in kind. "Please—Jamie. What brings you to DAI? You said it was something personal?"

She'd said that to get Kadin's attention. She hadn't lied. She had a whopper of a personal reason for being here. "A murder. Isn't that what brings everyone here?" She laughed at her attempt to be funny, wondering if she sounded as nervous as she thought.

While Kadin eyed her with some suspicion, Jamie's smile expanded ever so slightly. "Why don't we have a seat?"

Having to pass him to sit down, she fed on the sight of his muscled chest and felt tingly as she sat on the sofa.

Eyeing Jamie, Kadin sat on a chair across from her. Jamie boldly lowered his big, sexy body next to her, eyes still glinting.

"What about this murder that brought you all the way here, Ms. Harlow?" Kadin asked.

"You can call me Reese," she said. "I learned of your agency and, given the length of time that's passed in my case, I thought you'd be able to help me more than anyone else." She placed the binder containing copies of everything on the Neville case on the coffee table. "That's why I've taken a personal interest."

Kadin slid the binder toward him and began flipping through pages.

She didn't have to read along with him. She knew what it said. The coroner's report stated the inspector arrived at the scene and noted the time. The weather was indicated as sixty-one degrees, along with the humidity and position, location and condition of the body. Lifeless. Female in her twenties. Injuries on the body indicated the victim had died prior to her tumble down the embankment. Fully clothed in a big-collared, long-sleeved, sapphire-blue, knee-length shirtwaist dress with big white buttons up the front. Dirt collected from the fibers had come from the slope. Ligature marks on the neck indicated strangulation as the cause of death. Rigor mortis had been established throughout the body. Estimated time of death was twelve to fourteen hours prior to the coroner's examination.

Notes on the crime scene indicated tire tracks on the side of the road—both from a driver with a flat tire and another vehicle. The tires may have been from a 1973 Volkswagen Passat. Photos were taken of the body and the surrounding area, including the slope up to the road.

The first sheriff's follow-up report said he hadn't

done any extra testing on the evidence. The second sheriff in office looked into the case and questioned more residents, particularly hotel and motel staff. One witness had reported seeing a blue Passat but couldn't identify the driver, including whether it was a man or woman. The second sheriff had looked into the case again in the early 1990s and that had been the last time anyone had paid any attention to Ella Neville's murder.

While Kadin read, she stole a look at Jamie, catching his eyes doing a roam up her legs and slowly lifting to her chest and then finally her face. He grinned ever so slightly and made her feel a fresh burst of delighted tingles.

When she turned back to Kadin, she saw he'd finished and now observed them.

She cleared her throat. "As I'm sure you've ascertained from the report, no one knows what became of Ella after she closed the library. She never showed up to her husband's work-related dinner party. Less than twenty-four hours later, a man with a flat tire saw her body and called the police. The evidence is limited. There were tire tracks and not much else. Lots of pictures. Her clothes and shoes were bagged correctly, each labeled Dress, Underwear, Pantyhose and Bra."

"How were they rebagged?" Kadin asked.

Relieved that he'd dismissed her and Jamie's steamy moment, she said, "Not taken out of their original packaging, just sealed better from what I can tell. I sent the clothes to a lab."

"Good thinking. Can you stop them from going to your lab?" Kadin asked.

Taken aback, she recalled her conversation with

Margaret. "I think so, our office manager said she'd take them Monday when she runs her other errands."

"Send them to me. I have a lab that will do the best job. If there's trace evidence, they'll find it, and if anything has been contaminated, they'll know how to handle it."

"All right." But Reese felt suddenly cornered. This could be the beginning of a connection and she wasn't sure she was ready for that. Plus, he had a take-charge attitude. Would giving him her evidence be wise? Yes, for the case, but maybe not so much for her.

"This case is very cold," Kadin said, probably picking up on her hesitation. "You need all the expert help you can get if you want to solve it."

She did want to solve it. How badly began to take over. If she had to have an extended relationship with Kadin to do that, she would. But why did he offer to help? Was it passion for what he did—avenge victims of heinous crimes? Or did he sense something in her? Her personal reason for coming…?

He looked over more of the pages, coming to the pictures and taking special time to go through those. In the lapse in talk, she slid a glance toward Jamie and caught him checking her out again, sending more delicious tingles fluttering through her. He looked younger than Kadin but not by much. Kadin had to be well into his forties. She'd put Jamie at around thirty-one. Of all the things she imagined would happen while she was here, meeting a hunk wasn't one of them.

"Have you talked with any neighbors or family and friends—if any are still alive?"

Reese turned back to Kadin. "There is no family."

Jeffrey had no living relatives and the report said Ella had no family, either. That had come from talking to neighbors and friends, who'd claimed Ella had told them she had none.

"Pay particular attention to the husband. Nine times out of ten, they're the killer."

"Not Jeffrey." She couldn't even picture him holding a rope around someone's neck. "He was the most harmless man I've ever met."

"The most demented ones usually seem that way," Jamie said. "They're good at blending into society, even to the point of being likable. Take human traffickers for example. They lure innocent foreigners to the US with the promise of honest work and force them into slave labor, or worse."

He seemed to have firsthand experience with that kind of person. "But…what if he's as innocent as he seems?"

"You said his wife was supposed to meet him at a dinner party," Kadin said.

"Yes."

"Sounds like a perfect alibi to me."

Too perfect. What he implied hit her. No one had considered Jeffrey had gone to the dinner party on purpose, knowing his wife would close the library alone, knowing she'd never show up for dinner.

"Forget what a quiet, nice man Jeffrey appeared to be and look into any motive he may have had to kill her."

Reese thought of the hidden money. "My God."

"Already know of something?"

"The carpenters doing the renovations on my house found some money hidden under the floorboards of my bedroom. That's how I learned of the murder. Jeffrey and Ella lived there. Jeffrey lived there until he died two years ago. If he killed his wife over the money, why hide it?"

"Maybe he didn't know where it was."

"Obviously, he didn't. So, why kill her before knowing?"

"You must be a good deputy," Kadin said. "Those are all the questions I'd ask. The key is asking them all, no matter how unlikely the motive seems. Even if he knew of the money, that could be enough motive. He may not have found it, that's all. People have killed for less."

She glowed and felt strange for doing so, because the way he instructed her felt like father-daughter advice. He shared from his vast experience. That she appreciated, but seeing him as a father figure gave her a panicky feeling. She did not want to be close with her biological father, did she? How drastically would that change her life? Her plans?

She had parents. Biological parents she didn't even know couldn't take their place. And she had plans of her own for her future. She was just curious. That's all. Besides, her life had no room for obligatory relationships.

She uncrossed her legs and switched to her left one on top, a movement Jamie caught with manly appreciation, much more pleasant than her uncertainty over Kadin and what he represented.

"Let me have some more time with these documents," Kadin said. "How long are you in town?"

"Just for the night. I have a flight late tomorrow afternoon."

"Good. Let's meet in the morning. Do you have a car?"

"I took a cab."

"I'll have one of my drivers take you to wherever you need to go, and to the airport tomorrow."

"Thank you." She felt special. He had drivers and cars. This operation was much more sophisticated than she thought. She glanced at Jamie, and he was the new security officer. A truly capable-looking man, if one judged by form. Few, if any, could likely overpower him. If the intelligence in his eyes was any indication, few, if any, would outsmart him, either.

Turning back to Kadin, she saw him take note of their exchange again and grew flustered.

"I should get going." She stood.

Jamie stood right after her, and his looming body, even against her height, stimulated her pheromones.

"I'll leave you two to…whatever it is you're doing." Kadin eyed them, teasing, as he stood.

She faced him, smoothing her shirt even though it needed no smoothing. "What time tomorrow?"

"Whenever you get here. I'll clear my schedule. It's not every day I get a forty-year-old murder case."

She smiled back, feeling his passion for solving cases, especially those that didn't haunt him. He'd offered to help for that reason, and that reason alone. He hadn't picked up on any father-daughter vibes.

"Good to meet you, Reese."

She shook his hand. "You, too." She watched him leave and then the energy in the office changed. She was alone with this hot, sexy man. His presence engulfed her senses. If she touched him he'd burn her.

Where had this instant attraction come from? Was

it the slope of his nose, the line of his jaw? His tall, muscular build? Or was it what she'd seen in his eyes? He was intelligent, yes, but he also exuded uncrush-able confidence. Most likely what aroused her was the entire package. He physically stimulated and mentally intrigued her.

"Will you join me for dinner tonight?" he asked.

What an irresistible invitation. His lightness in flirting with her contrasted sharply with darkness lurking somewhere behind his magnetizing eyes. His mystery drew her as much as his physical perfection. How could she refuse? She wouldn't. Dinner with him excited her.

"I'll meet you in the Butte Hotel lobby at six. There's a restaurant there," she said.

"There's also a restaurant across the street. I'll meet you in the lobby and then we can walk there together."

She'd seen that restaurant, the nicest one in Rock Springs. And something about him made her feel free to say, "Looking forward to it."

A man like him wouldn't fence her in. She had no desire for commitment at this point in her life. Their geographical distance assured her he'd be a pleasant encounter and nothing more.

Jamie wasn't prepared for Reese in a dress. She emerged from the elevator with a jacket draped over her arm, blond hair up in a stylish bun and a light ap-plication of makeup accentuating her golden-brown eyes. She'd had her hair in a ponytail earlier. The black sleeveless jersey dress flared from the waist down and swayed as she walked toward him in spiky ankle boots. The modest bodice covered her chest to the rounded neckline. A simple silver cuff bracelet and silver hoop earrings finished the outfit. But he didn't pay much heed to that. He'd like to get her hair down and see her only in those boots. He might let her wear the bracelet.

She stopped before him with a coquettish look.

"You look beautiful." He had to say it. She did. And he was glad he'd worn a suit and tie.

Her luscious mouth curved in a smile. "I went shopping. I didn't pack for a date."

He offered his elbow, unable to stop looking at her.

She slipped into her jacket and then slid her hand under his elbow and onto his forearm.

Jamie's blood heated as he walked with her across the street to the steak house. He couldn't tell if his eagerness to start fresh with a normal life overshadowed his attraction to her. The first encounter with her had sizzled with chemistry. She'd felt it, too. He had seen it in her eyes. But he'd be making a mistake if he grabbed the first beautiful woman to step into his life if it turned out later she wasn't The One.

With Dexter Watts dead, Jamie had no further obligation to Stankovich—the terms of his service were complete. Valdemar may not see it the same way, but Jamie had done all he'd asked, and Jamie had ensured his nemesis had nothing more to hold over him. That part of his life was over. He looked forward to the next part, the best part, but he intended to get it right this time.

His days of pushing the envelope and working for the wrong people were over. He'd take his life back working for Kadin, a good man with an honorable cause. He could still travel and see the world the way he loved, but he'd have his integrity intact. And a family with the right woman.

He didn't know if Reese would be part of that journey. It sure felt promising, though.

"How does a town get the name Never Summer?" he asked as he opened the door for her.

"It's surrounded by fourteen-thousand-foot mountains." She stopped inside the restaurant lobby. "And ten thousand feet above sea level doesn't allow for a lot of warming."

"Why would anyone want to live in a freezer like that?" he asked while they waited for the hostess to greet them.

"The beauty. The silence." She sounded matter-of-fact. But then she softened as she thought further. "The smell of snow falling through a forest of coniferous trees, the wildflowers in summer and that first dampening of mountain soil." Her eyes raised heavenward as she drifted, inhaling as though smelling the mountain air right now. "The air is so cool and crisp and fresh after a big snow." She breathed in again, eyes closed.

He couldn't stop an erotic image of her.

At last, she lowered her gaze to look at him. "Cities are stressful."

He grunted because he had the exact opposite feeling toward cities. Cities comforted him the way her chilly, remote mountain hideaway did her. "I still don't see the reason for the name Never Summer."

"We have a summer but it never really gets hot. Mid-July to maybe early September are the warmest."

That sounded more stressful to him than cities.

"Right this way," the hostess said.

At their table, Jamie pulled out the chair for Reese, unable to recall the last time he'd done this for a woman. Long before the military. The girl after high school. He'd broken up with her to join the Army.

She smiled up at him, seeming to enjoy this as much as he was. The first date. The excitement of meeting someone who hit the mark. Or maybe he misread her. She did live in Colorado and his office was here in Wyoming. If she was all he felt she could be, then she was worth risking a long-distance affair for a while. He'd worry about logistics later.

He sat across from her. They spent the first few minutes in small talk, reading the menu, giving the waiter their order. The wine came and they sipped.

The air between them hummed electrically whenever their eyes met, as they connected on a subliminal level. He almost couldn't bare the intense physical attraction and suspected she struggled with the same affliction. While he knew what he'd do with that magic, he didn't think she'd be ready this fast. Besides, creating his new life would take time. He wouldn't rush into it like he did his job with Aesir.

"So…deputy sheriff, huh?" he asked, breaking the silence. Just how serious was she about devoting a lifetime to Never Summer?

She rubbed her hand up her arm, forearms resting on the table, a slow, comforting caress that made him wish he could rub it himself. "There's not much crime in Never Summer. Nothing compared to what your company sees." Except the Neville cold case. That definitely compared.

"How did you get into law enforcement?"

She looked away in consideration. Had no one ever asked her that before?

Finally she met his eyes again. "I've always had an interest in law enforcement. As a kid I loved cop cars and uniforms and watched shows about good guys catching the bad guys. Now I have a degree in criminal justice and passed the police academy at the top of my class." She smiled genuinely. "I love it. I can't tell you why. I've served as deputy in Ute County for four years now."

"You plan on staying there?" he asked.

"Why would I leave? My family is there." She sipped her wine.

He didn't like how certain she sounded, but her commitment to family counted as a plus. "Would you move somewhere else if an opportunity arose?"

"I've never considered that, other than leaving to go to college. Never Summer is a close-knit community." She paused in thought. "There's really nowhere else I belong. Besides, 'Sheriff Harlow' kind of has a nice ring to it."

She had aspirations of becoming sheriff. He liked ambitious women.

"Sheriff Knox does, too." He didn't stop himself in time. "Sorry. That just came out." He didn't mean he'd propose marriage, only tested out the sound in anticipation of being married—someday.

Would she be ready to settle down? She looked young. Twenty-five or twenty-six. He kept that question to himself. *Don't move too fast.*

He'd met women like her before, career-driven, tenacious, independent. They didn't pick controlling men. He wasn't looking for a woman to control. He was looking for a woman who meshed with him, a friend and a lover, someone who'd spend the rest of her life with him.

He must have looked at her in an intense way, as the passion he felt for his goal came out strong and freely. She fell into a long gaze with him, as they had several times now.

Then she seemed to jar herself back to the date, sitting straighter and putting her hands on the table. "Tell me your story. How'd you end up working for Kadin?"

"After the military, I went to work for a private company, but that ended up not being good for me."

"Who did you work for? Why did it turn out not good?"

"I don't want to talk about that now. The important thing is, now I work for Kadin."

"All right." She smiled.

Instead of pushing her away, his preference of remaining a mystery appealed to her. He found that a little suspicious. Did she like to avoid serious subjects? Would she not share her story to keep things casual? Her beauty and lively energy made him discard the flash of warning that this woman may not be in line with his vision of a future.

Except for Jamie's slip when he'd said, "Sheriff Knox," Reese liked how he kept serious talk at bay. He didn't talk about his past, what had led him to Kadin. It was too personal. While the reason he didn't might be something she should know, she didn't have to find out tonight.

She felt safe with him, safe to explore the desire this man—this stranger—stirred. He seemed so dangerous, and yet he treated her so romantically. All through dinner they'd talked about likes and dislikes. Movies. Food. Politics. He liked action, meat and potatoes, and laws that helped the little people and kept greedy corporate leaders honest and fair. She liked the occasional chick flick but she also liked action. Meat and potatoes were okay but she preferred seafood. The two complemented each other in an inexplicable way.

With dinner finished, she didn't want the night to end just yet. He presented her with temptation but… should she dare?

"There's something I'd like to show you. Are you up for a drive?"

Drive? Alone with him? "Where?"

"I'd like to keep that a surprise. Something incredible, something a small-town girl like you would love to see."

She wasn't sure she should go anywhere with a man she'd only just met. But the fact that he worked for a man with Kadin's reputation and she could defend herself as a trained cop, she agreed.

Now he pulled to a stop on a dirt road where it crested an incline. Moonlight gleamed over a grassy field atop the flat surface of the butte she'd seen from his office window.

"What's here?" She saw nothing.

"Just wait. It's usually around this time they show up—if they show up. They don't always."

She could see his enthusiasm for whatever would appear and it struck a chord in her. She met few people who had this kind of zest for life, more than aspirations to succeed, but for simpler things.

"There." He pointed.

She looked but saw nothing. "Do you come here every night?"

"I have been. It's curing me of city life."

"You prefer big cities?"

"I thought I did, before Kadin offered me a job."

She saw something deeper in that response and would have asked, but suspected it related to the serious topic he'd rather avoid.

"Come on. I'll keep you warm." He got out of the truck and came around to her side. Her boots were spiky and might sink into the soil. She put her hands on his shoulders as he helped her down from the truck. Exciting prickles of pleasure ran a current from everywhere she felt him. Chest. Hips. Thighs.

She stared up at him, seeing the dark swirl of passion come over him, too.

He lowered his head and then his eyes caught sight of something. "There."

She turned and he stood behind her, his arms going around her, heating her body to the point where she almost didn't see the herd of wild horses. They made their way up the hill to the top of the butte, some grazing, some looking majestically off into the horizon as though enjoying the moonlit view. She picked out the lead stallion. He walked with his head high and ears perked, sensing their presence before the rest of the herd.

Rearing up, pawing the air, the horse whinnied loud and stomped and clawed the ground with one hoof. The herd scattered a bit, but calmed when they saw no danger, resuming their moonlight leisure.

Nothing like this existed in Never Summer. The sight stole her breath and her heart.

The stallion ran the flank of his herd, getting them to move farther down the mountain, and soon they were out of sight.

Wordless, filled with awe, she turned to Jamie. "That was incredible."

"Yeah." He faced her. "Almost as incredible as you."

He slid his arm around her, drawing her to him. "Tell me you feel this, too."

Still breathless from the inspiring sight of the wild horses, she said, "Yes." He didn't have to explain he meant the passion that had begun the moment they saw each other.

The suddenness of this nudged a feeble warning just before he touched his lips to her. Soft and patient, he kissed her with warm reverence. Any hesitation fled as desire flared into roaring flames.

Chapter 3

Reese floated in an infatuated current all the way back to her hotel. Jamie's big form sitting across the truck from her engulfed her senses. His strong thighs parted, his muscular arm extended as he gripped the steering wheel, his shadowy profile masculine and sexy. His blue eyes turned to her, zapping her with that electric attraction. Her whole body throbbed with desire. She tightened her hand on the door handle.

What about him so allured her? Was it his distance from her—his address, so far from hers? She had to admit, she felt safe opening up to him, especially sexually. He presented no danger of trapping her into commitment. After college, she'd promised herself the freedom to explore her life goals, without anyone— any man—holding her back.

He stopped the truck.

Not wanting the night to end, she didn't move.

Killing the engine, he got out of the truck and walked around the front. Even the way he moved turned her on, with that long stride, unhurried and sure. Opening the door, he held out his hand.

"You didn't strike me as the old-fashioned type," he said.

She put her hand in his. "I'm not. I just don't know what to do with how hot you make me."

Taken aback at first, he stepped back as she got out.

"Come again?"

"Again and again." She smiled along with her teasing. What more of an invitation did he need? She felt bold, maybe too bold, but she also knew if she didn't act now, this night would be gone forever.

"Not old-fashioned at all."

"Not easily drawn into bed with a man, either," she said. "But you…" She let her gaze roam down his broad chest, at eye level.

He shut the door behind her, a definitive thud. Decision final. She heard the fob beep, indicating he'd locked the truck. All the while, he held her eyes in a long, heated look.

"Let's see where this leads us," he said in a deep voice that revealed his interest.

She walked beside him up to the double front doors of the three-story Victorian hotel, white brick with recently painted black shutters. Soft lighting added to this real-life fantasy. Her intense attraction to this man only added to the excitement that stole her caution. Something about him made her feel safe to be impulsive.

Inside, the sole clerk turned to greet them as they

passed to the antique elevator. The smell of old wood and sound of cables protesting joined the fiery chemistry electrifying the air. Jamie put his hand on her lower back, further inflaming her. She looked up and back. He looked down, and as the elevator stopped, he lowered his face to kiss her.

She turned and slid her hands up his deliciously hard chest and pressed herself to him. With a gruff sound, he kissed her deeper as the elevator door shut. She didn't care how long they stood there. Arrows of pleasure pierced her from her core outward. She'd experienced nothing else like it. Ever.

When the elevator began to move again, Jamie lifted his head and she laughed along with his chuckle.

"Oops," she said.

And then all traces of smiles vanished as passion took over again.

He held her head and kissed her again. She thought she'd go out of her mind with ecstasy right then. But the elevator stopped and the doors began to slide open.

Jamie stepped back from her and she quickly moved to stand beside him. Back on the main level, a man and woman in their fifties looked from Jamie to her before entering. Reese tried to conceal her breathlessness. Jamie didn't appear affected. He concealed the mad desire they ignited for each other rather easily. She fleetingly wondered where that ability came from before the older woman glanced over at them and distracted her.

The elevator rose to the third floor and stopped. She waited for the older couple to get out first. They went one way down the hall and Reese walked with Jamie in the opposite direction.

At her room, she unlocked the door and then pushed it open. Jamie held the door while she entered and followed her inside. Now that they were alone in her hotel room, the energy became much more personal and significant. What was she doing? The last time she had sex was in college, so maybe she could blame the long drought for this impulsiveness. That and the deep ache she had for Jamie.

She removed her jacket and draped it over one of two chairs on each side of a table in front of the window. The drapes were still open and during the day she had a view of the street. He walked toward her, passing the dark mahogany cabinet with a television on top.

Removing his suit jacket, he put it on top of hers and then turned to face her, his incredibly blue eyes communicating intent that hadn't dimmed since the elevator. He lifted his hand and cupped her face. Just that touch alone stoked the fire to a hot burn. She closed her eyes, in a state of awe and wonder that he could do that to her.

It's the fantasy.

Feeling his warm lips cover hers, she lost all thought of questioning whether she wanted this. She did. Oh, how she did.

Pressing against him as she had in the elevator, she sought more of him. He held her tighter and gave her what she asked and more. Time slipped away as she savored the contact and caresses of his mouth and tongue.

Jamie tugged at the pins holding up her hair. They fell and she shook her hair to release the rest. He sank his fingers into the strands and kissed her.

She pulled his shirt free of his pants and he loos-

ened his tie. Pulling the tie over his head, he watched
her begin to unbutton his shirt, letting her push it off
his shoulders. Shrugging out of the shirt while she ran
her hands over his smooth, hard chest, he unzipped
the back of her jersey dress. The dress sagged off her
shoulders and dropped to her feet. She stepped out
of the pooled material as he stared at her breasts and
underwear.

"Something else you bought today?"

"Yes." Even before he'd dropped her off at the hotel,
she's secretly prepared for this. At the time she hadn't
really thought anything would happen, but imagining
it had sure been a delight. The lacy black panties and
matching bra proved to be worth it.

He removed his shoes and unfastened his pants.
Down to his underwear, she admired the protrusion
before he moved forward, guiding her to the bed.

"My boots."

"Leave them on."

She scooted back on the bed as he crawled over her.

"All I want you in are those and that bracelet," he
said.

She opened her legs as he lay on top of her, his erection pressing against the lacy underwear.

A fire so potent that she stopped breathing for a
second scorched her. She arched as he took her breast
into his hand and ran his thumb over the hard nipple
through the material. Reese pushed down the hem of
his underwear, getting impatient for what she'd longed
for ever since he'd kissed her that first time.

He unclasped her bra and the contraption sprang
open, releasing her breasts from the frilly binding.
Instead of removing his underwear, as she'd hoped

for, he put his mouth on her breast, licking and then sucking with sensual care.

Reese tipped back her head and moved her hips to grind against him. He loved her other breast, making her wait longer. When he finished tasting his fill, he ran his tongue down the center of her torso to the top of her underwear. She was going to erupt if he didn't hurry.

Taking her panties in his fingers, he pulled them off, removing them all the way over her boots and dropping them to the floor. She lifted her knees, digging the spiky heels of her ankle boots into the mattress, and put her hands over her head.

Jamie made a gruff sound as he saw her pose and then quickly removed his underwear. Not too large and definitely not too small, he made her thirst for him more. Now.

As breathless as her, he slid his hands up her legs as he positioned himself between them. Then he guided himself to her opening.

"Yes," she rasped.

He filled her and drew back before pushing in again. Everything fell away except him, his ruggedly handsome face, passion-filled eyes, his breathing, and the ripple of arm and chest muscles as he moved back and forth. Wild sensation took her mind away with unbearable pleasure.

She cried out as she reached her peak almost instantaneously. He may have been surprised, but she didn't notice in the grip of such an intense explosion.

As he continued to thrust back and forth, another wave of pleasure began to build. Gradually he increased his tempo and she could tell he was close. So was she. She ground herself against each penetra-

tion and as he reached his limit, she cried out again,
writhing with him.

Several tumultuous seconds later, he rolled off her
and they both lay on their backs awhile, catching their
breath. Then he turned his head and opened his arm
for her. Uncertain over what she felt about this, she
curled to his side. He said nothing and she said nothing. If he felt anything like her, no words could ad-
equately explain what had just occurred.

When she'd invited him into her hotel room, she
thought she'd be safe getting a little reckless. Now she
wasn't so sure. Upon reflection, maybe she should
have paid attention to the strength of her attraction to
this man. Now she felt strongly that she'd like to see
him again. She'd learned the hard way that that didn't
work so well for her. She had plans, short-term plans
for her life that she would not, and could not, alter. She
had to stay true to herself. She couldn't allow her feelings to sway her. She wanted to be sheriff someday.

What feelings were these, anyway? She'd just had
fantastic sex with a drop-dead gorgeous man. What
woman wouldn't love a night like this?

Tomorrow she'd be gone. This would fade into
a pleasant memory. Maybe when she achieved the
sheriff position she'd be ready for something serious.
Even that amendment churned inside with dread. The
thought of sharing a checking account frightened her,
and not just the financial part. She didn't think she'd
be able to relinquish control, to have someone else
managing that for her—or with her.

Stay focused on telling Kadin your news.

That should be plenty to keep her mind occupied
and off how much Jamie made her feel. But it paled
in comparison.

* * *

Jamie woke with a smile lighting his heart. He couldn't have dreamed a woman would feel better than Reese. This fit exactly what he envisioned for his new life. Rising up onto his elbows, he didn't care about his sappy grin as Reese stepped out of the bathroom. Expecting her to still be naked, he was surprised to see her fully dressed.

"You should have waited," he said. "I'd have taken a shower with you."

She eyed him warily. "I…didn't want to wake you."

His smile dropped away. Something was off about her. He threw off the covers and stood, still naked. She averted her gaze as he approached. "If you're uncomfortable about last night, don't be." He slid his hand to the back of her neck and kissed her chastely.

She moved away and then stepped back from him.

A sense of warning doused what remained of his elation and prospects of a great future with her. "Is something the matter?"

"I need to go talk to Kadin."

That wouldn't take long and they'd already gone over most of the case yesterday. He supposed she might be anxious to solve her four-decade-old murder case.

"All right. I'll get ready and take you there."

"I think it would be best if you went home to get ready. I'll drop in your office before I leave this afternoon."

She seemed eager to get rid of him. How could she so easily push him away? This was not what he expected at all, not after the magic they'd generated together. He wrestled his disappointment under control.

Maybe the intensity scared her. And they had only

just met yesterday. He shouldn't rush her. He may be ready to take that plunge, but maybe she wasn't.

"All right."

"Good." A flicker of a smile curved up her mouth, but seemed rather forced. "I'll see you there, then."

With that, she left him standing nude in the bedroom, unmade bed to his left and the smell of her shower wafting from the bathroom.

She might be running scared, but he wasn't about to let go so soon. One night wasn't nearly enough.

Sitting in the bright lobby at DAI, Reese stared out the front window. Last night tracked through her head, from the treat of seeing the wild horses to the moment she fell into contented sleep, wrapped in Jamie's strong arms. Any more of that and she'd be lost. She'd belong to a man who'd sweep her away from everything she'd worked so hard to achieve. He didn't realize it, but getting messed up with her would only lead to a broken heart. She'd be doing him a favor by leaving as casually as possible.

If only her knotting stomach would agree.

The front door clicked open and the sight of Jamie in tan pants and a dress shirt with a tie and a leather jacket came with a familiar electric zap. She could see his glowing blue eyes from all the way across the lobby. She began to get hot just watching him stride toward her. Even her subtle rejection this morning hadn't dimmed his inexhaustible supply of confidence. She might have gotten herself into a fine mess with this one.

He stopped in front of her.

The receptionist had gone in the back office and hadn't returned. They were alone.

"I can see now we should have had a much more in-depth conversation about our expectations," he said.

"It's too soon to talk expectations," she replied.

"I was in the military before I joined a private military company. I didn't have time for serious relationships. I had a couple, but they didn't last and didn't come near what we had last night."

"Jamie…" She stood.

"What about you? You're pretty young, so I'm guessing you haven't had many, if any, serious relationships."

Why was he going into this now? He seemed to have a habit of getting right to his point. He knew precisely what he was after, and right now that was her. Maybe he was operating on unfamiliar ground. He'd never gone after a woman this seriously before.

She decided his tactic was wise. Just come out and lay it out for him right now. "I've dated and been with two men fairly long-term. They lasted a year and two years. I'm not looking for anything serious right now. You said it—I'm young. I'm not ready for that yet."

In his silence, she couldn't tell if that crushed his hopes or not.

"Of course," he finally said. "We only just met yesterday. It's far too early to be talking serious relationship."

Did they have an understanding? Why did she get the feeling he'd strategically set his course in action?

"Ms. Harlow?"

Grateful for the interruption, Reese said to Jamie, "I'll stop by your office on my way out."

"Mr. Tandy will see you now."

Reese stepped around Jamie and followed the receptionist through the back offices. The receptionist let her pass at Kadin's door.

Her heart thumped harder and faster. How would Kadin take the news she was about to drop?

He approached the door and, seeing Jamie walk toward the opposite office, called after him, "Jamie. You might as well join us."

Reese smothered a gasp. "No, it's all right. You and I can just talk."

"Don't be silly. Jamie was here yesterday. He might as well listen in now. I don't have much anyway, not more than we already discussed." He turned and walked back into his office. "How was your evening together?"

So, that's why he invited Jamie. He didn't know how tortured she would be with him near her, much less given what she was about to tell him.

Jamie grinned as he passed her, winking in a way that warmed her to the point of awkwardness. She couldn't resist him. Her body wanted to smile and so it did.

Reluctantly, she went to the seating area, where Kadin waited.

Jamie sat next to her on the sofa and she wished she had taken the chair adjacent to Kadin. His mere presence, with his big body and fresh scent, sent a pleasurable shiver through her.

"Your cold case is quite interesting," Kadin began. "The notes are all very small-town, but the sheriff did a thorough job collecting evidence."

"Small-town?" Should she be insulted?

A flash of a smile lifted his lips. "It was like reading a mystery. I could follow his thoughts like the character in a book. He made comments about the people of Never Summer that made it rather entertaining."

When she'd read it she hadn't picked up on that. But then, she lived there.

He stood and went to the whiteboard on the wall beside the seating area. "Even though it seems there wasn't much to collect, I'm confident we'll find some trace evidence." He picked up a marker and wrote *Ella*, *Tourism* and *Highway 149* in a row and spaced apart. "There are a few areas I'm not sure were examined close enough." He turned to look at them, marker in hand. "Ella is from California. No one checked there for family because she told everyone she had no family." He drew a line from the word *Ella* and wrote *Family?* "That includes checking out Jeffrey's alibi. Also, why did Ella move to Never Summer? When did she move there? These are all questions that were never asked at the time of her murder." He drew a line from the word *Tourism*. "Never Summer survives on its tourism industry. Since no one in town was a suspect, it seems likely a stranger passed through and may have committed the crime. I found nothing in the report to suggest any tourists were questioned." He wrote *Locate and Question Tourists.* "And the highway. Why dump the victim's body on that road? Sure, it's remote, but it's also close to Never Summer and no attempt was made to hide or conceal the body…" He wrote, *Why this highway in this direction?*

Reese sat transfixed and in awe. He'd just laid out the course of her investigation for her. She could learn a lot from this man…*her father.*

"I can help more if you'd like."

The offer chased her awe away. If he helped with

the investigation, she'd have to see more of him. He didn't even know she was his daughter. That had to be addressed first. She had to tell him before any of this went any further.

"Yes, well…" She cleared her throat and adjusted her position on the sofa, clasping her hands on her lap. This was harder than she thought. Not only for her, but for what it would mean to him.

"There's something I need to tell you."

Kadin's brow rose a fraction and Jamie looked sharply at her.

"I…I didn't come here to talk about the case. I…I mean I did, but…but there's another reason."

Kadin looked from Jamie to her, clearly perplexed.

"Maybe you should sit down for this." Oh, God, she was nervous. Did she really want to do this? What choice did she have? He deserved to know. He had a right to know.

She licked her lips and looked down at her clasped hands, which were turning white in her tight grip.

"Whoa." Kadin put the marker down on the metal shelf below the whiteboard. "This is serious, then." He faced her but didn't move to sit.

She looked at Jamie. He really shouldn't be here for this.

"What is it?" Kadin asked. "Just tell us."

Lifting her head, she looked up at Kadin. "It's personal."

"Personal."

"Yes. Between you and me."

"Me and you."

"Yes."

"I would have remembered an affair and I never sleep with women as young as you."

"No." She shook her head, lowering it again and then catching a glimpse of Jamie's rapt expression. "It's not that."

The quiet hummed. She heard Jamie's exhale. Kadin just waited.

At last she looked up at Kadin and said, "I'm your daughter."

Jamie choked on what must have been a midswallow with her shocking announcement.

Kadin's face remained impassive. Wearing no cowboy hat, nothing shaded his bright gray eyes or hid thick black hair, trimmed but unruly. She'd gotten her blond hair and brown eyes from her mother.

"I read all about you," she said. "You had another daughter you lost to a terrible tragedy. I didn't come here to be what she must have been to you. I want that said up front."

Still, Kadin only stared at her.

"I was adopted by my parents, Mya and Nelson Harlow, in New York when I was an infant. My mother was too young, just sixteen, when she had me. She never told you she was pregnant or that she gave the baby up for adoption."

"That's impossible," Kadin finally said. Then he jabbed his thumb at the whiteboard. "Is that case real or did you use it as a ruse to get in here?"

"No. It's real. Yes, I did use it, but…I…I didn't know how to tell you. I only thought you deserved to know."

"Why are you really here?" Kadin now demanded.

Reese sat back, not expecting this kind of reaction.

But then she realized he would be shocked at first, and then skeptical.

"Giselle Yates," she said. "I'm not sure if Yates was her last name when you knew her. She moved from Massachusetts before she gave birth. She didn't tell you because her parents forced her to give up the child—me. I only just met her. Giselle. My biological mother. She told me what happened and about you. I didn't know you were my father until she came to see me."

Kaden just stared at her again.

"I decided to meet you because I think you have a right to know," she repeated. "M-maybe I was mistaken."

She started to stand.

"No." Kadin put up his hand and then ran his fingers through his hair. Then with a curse, he walked away from the seating area and leaned over his desk.

"I know this must be difficult for you." Reese stood.

"I'll leave the two of you." Jamie stood and went to the door, closing it softly behind him.

After watching him go, Reese went to the desk. "With your daughter's murder... I'm so sorry."

"She never told me," he said, still bent over the desk. "After all these years. She never told me."

"She was afraid you'd talk her out of giving up the baby and at the time it was more important for her to repair her relationship with her parents. What they thought of her took priority. And then time passed and she decided it was too late."

"Too late?" He straightened, anger storming his eyes. "She should have told me."

Reese nodded. "I agree. That's why I came here. You needed to be told, and now I have."

"How long have you known?" he asked.

"I've known I was adopted since I was a young girl. I was raised in a good home. We lived in New York for a while and then my dad wanted to go back to his hometown, Never Summer. We've lived there ever since. My mother couldn't have children so they adopted me. It wasn't until I was in college that I began to get curious about who my biological parents were. I started to search for them...for you. I found my mother first. She traveled to Never Summer to meet me last month. She told me your name and didn't know what had become of you. Then just a few days ago she sent me a link to an article about your agency. That's when I learned about you."

She watched him take in her facial features while haunting memories must have been swirling inside his brilliant mind. Did he wonder if his murdered daughter would look like her had she lived? That twisted her heartstrings.

"I'm going to need some time to absorb all of this."

"Of course."

"Please don't take offense. This is quite a shock for me."

It must be, especially after losing his second daughter to murder. "No, I completely understand. I didn't come here to force a father-daughter relationship. You don't have to worry about me injecting myself into your life. You can keep in touch if you like, but no pressure from me."

He didn't seem to register what she said. Giving

him the space she could see he needed, she turned to go, quietly closing the door behind her.

She almost forgot to stop by Jamie's office. In the hall, she spotted him getting up from behind his desk. He stopped just inside the doorway.

She walked to him. After she entered, he closed the door.

"You sure can deliver a bomb." He whistled. "Kadin Tandy's daughter, huh?" His words were light but his tone was leading. "That's incredible. The media is going to go berserk. Why didn't you tell me?"

"The media doesn't have to know." They had an intimate dinner that had led to sleeping together. She could have easily told him over dinner, but the magnitude of meeting her real father had kept her from saying anything. It was still too personal.

He waited a few seconds as though expecting her to explain. When she didn't, he didn't seem put off, which touched her deep down.

"They won't hear it from me," he said. "But eventually, word is going to get out."

"Thanks for the warning." She did not look forward to that. "And your discretion."

He nodded and moved a step closer.

This would be goodbye now. She didn't evade him when he put his hand on her lower back, fingers caressing her rear before gliding up to pull her to him. He made her hot for him just like that. Breathless yet again, she ran her hands up his chest as he lowered his head and kissed her. He moved his mouth with hers, gently, reverently at first, but the hot desire they had for each other couldn't be quenched with just that. In an instant, she opened to him and he to her. The kiss grew fevered and out of control.

"It wasn't a dream." Jamie pressed her to the door and kissed her again.

Unable to stop herself, Reese reached for the clasp of his pants. He kissed her ravenously and then withdrew, taking her hand in his to stop her from continuing.

"Not like this," he said.

Both of them breathing heavily, Reese tipped her head back.

"It has to mean more," he added.

She feared he'd deliberately left off the rest of his thought—*to you*. This had to mean more to her.

She pressed with her hands on his chest until he moved back a step. "I should get going. I'm going to miss my flight."

"You'll have plenty of time." He released her hand and stepped back some more.

She turned and started to open the door.

"You know what this means, don't you?"

She looked back over her shoulder.

"I'm going to be seeing a lot of you."

A flash of apprehension shot through her. "You're in Wyoming and I'm in Colorado."

"That isn't going to stop me. Besides, a man like Kadin Tandy won't allow you to walk out of his life. His daughter."

She stared at him as the implications became clear. She wouldn't be able to avoid running in to him. While her pheromones cheered, her mind had other plans.

Chapter 4

Jamie couldn't concentrate on the résumé he held in front of him on his desk. Reese had returned to Never Summer two days ago. He planned to give her some time before he began his campaign to win her heart. He wasn't sure he could. His mind kept wandering back to when he'd awoken around 2:00 a.m. to find Reese still sleeping against him. Her eyes had fluttered open, drowsiness clearing and that mysterious, potent chemistry taking its place.

He'd rolled onto her and saw a flash of vulnerability. The first time they'd done this, lust had ruled. The second time meant something.

He would never forget that look in her eyes, as though he'd penetrated so much more than her body. He would have stopped if she'd told him to, but he knew she'd fallen under the same spell.

Capitalizing on her sweet vulnerability, he'd run his hands from her inner thighs up to her knees and spread them. She'd inhaled with an impassioned sound and arched her chest, head back and eyes sliding shut.

"Look at me," he'd told her.

She'd opened her eyes and the vulnerability intensified as he'd pushed into her, exquisitely slow, nearly going out of his mind to find her so ready for him. She'd inhaled again, sharper, softer after that, startled breaths with each inward stroke of hardness against softness. Perfection mating.

He'd kissed her the way a man would kiss the woman he loved as they both climaxed. Hard, deep pulsations that touched his soul. Her soul. He could believe they'd communed with the forces of heaven just then, the universe, the great energy and giver of life and love.

Three knocks made him drop the résumé he still hadn't read onto his desk and look toward the door.

Kadin stood there. "Have a minute?"

"You're the boss."

He didn't look happy as he shut the door and came to sit on one of the chairs in front of his desk. "Reese said something peculiar before she left my office the other day."

Why talk to Jamie about this? He surely had people closer to him that he could talk to, like his wife.

"She said she didn't come here to force a father-daughter relationship or to inject herself into my life. No pressure. Keep in touch if you prefer."

Yeah, that pretty much sounded like Reese. The way she ran away that morning had been a real eye-opener.

"She gave you quite a shock. Hell, I was shocked."

"Who wouldn't be to discover they had a child they never knew about? A grown adult? But she seemed… distant." He seemed to need verification from Jamie, the only other person who knew Reese, even if only minimally.

"Like she pushes off serious relationships, be they father-daughter or boyfriend-girlfriend?" Jamie said.

"Yeah. That's it. You noticed?" Then he angled his head. "Did the two of you cover a lot of ground that night you went to dinner?"

Was he fishing for information? He must have needed the last couple of days for it to sink in that Reese was truly his daughter.

"That's one way of putting it." Jamie wasn't comfortable talking about the type of ground he'd covered with Reese, not when Kadin was her father.

"Do you think she wants to have a father-daughter relationship with me?"

"She didn't tell me you were her father. I found out when you did. But Reese is an extremely independent woman." She thought she could walk away from her biological father and Jamie and not have that independence threatened. What she didn't take into account was that not everyone would try to take it away. "I think she has a hard time with change."

Kadin nodded in thought. "She grew up with adoptive parents and has her own life in that small mountain town."

"And she wants to be sheriff."

For a moment Kadin appeared discouraged, a rarity for a man like him. But then he brightened. "She could be a detective here."

He clearly wanted his daughter in his life, more so than she likely wanted him in hers. Would he use his agency as incentive? Would Reese change her goal of being sheriff to working as a detective at DAI? To Jamie, that was a no-brainer. This agency would be a much bigger advancement in her career than being sheriff in some unknown town in the middle of remote mountains. But Reese would view any coercive efforts to get her to leave that life very differently. She'd accuse them of asking her to follow someone else's life, not hers. Her vulnerability had given him the first sign. Racing off to the shower before he woke had been the second and last he needed.

He'd met women like her before. He'd sought them out in his previous life. Should he avoid them in his next? No. It was too early to make that judgment, and more than her independence made her interesting to him. He'd risk everything pursuing her, even with the remote possibility she'd surrender to him.

"It must have been quite a blow learning she was your daughter." It had come as a big shock to him. Kadin must have almost collapsed.

"It just about killed me, making the comparisons and dealing with never being able to see my daughter again. But then I realized what a gift this is. *I have another daughter.*" He sounded awe-stricken.

"How does your wife feel about it?"

"She was thrilled. She's the one who came up with the idea of taking a vacation to Never Summer."

"A…vacation?" He'd inject himself into her life and Reese would recoil.

"I won't crowd her. It's a way to get close without

suffocating her. I'm sure she needs time to get accustomed to meeting her real father."

"I doubt she'll throw you out of town, but you might drive her away if you push too hard."

"You seem to know her pretty well."

"Intuition." Kadin didn't need to know how Jamie had learned so much about Reese. Or when. "Why are you telling me all this?"

"I want you to go with us."

"You… With your family?" He felt his eyebrows rise and he leaned on his elbows.

"We'd meet there. And you'd have to stay at a hotel or something. I need you to be a sort of buffer, the guy offering to help with her case on behalf of DAI."

"I'm not a detective." And Jamie had planned on going to Never Summer, anyway. He didn't need an excuse. Reese was his excuse. He had to see her.

"No, but you'll keep her safe while she investigates a forty-year-old murder. The killer is still running free, remember, and he's avoided arrest all this time. He won't respond well to the prospect of going to prison now."

"If he's still alive."

"Might be better if he isn't."

Jamie curled his fingers near his mouth as he contemplated how much to tell Kadin about the status of his relationship with Reese. He'd find out soon enough, given how explosive Jamie and Reese were together, but he didn't need to know they'd already been intimate.

"As it happens, I was planning to ask you for some time away from the office to go see her," Jamie said.

Kadin seemed only marginally surprised. "She left without making plans to see you again?"

"Yes."

"She's a runner all right." Kadin laughed briefly.

Their parting kiss came back to haunt Jamie again. As potent as that had been, Reese still stuck to her resolve and had left. "That's putting it mildly. She's stubborn."

Kadin chuckled again. "I just find out she's my daughter and you're already making moves on her? I'm sure I don't have to tell you what will happen if you hurt her."

"No, sir." Why did he get the feeling if anyone would wind up hurt it would be Jamie?

"Go pack." Standing, Kadin moved away from the desk. "Bring your work with you. We can fly in candidates for interviews, if necessary. Penny and I are leaving this afternoon. Lucas Curran is in charge while I'm away. I would have asked Brycen Cage but he's busy recording a new show."

"Lucas is in town?" Lucas worked remotely most of the time and had an office next to Kadin's. Brycen had no local office.

"Yes. At my request."

He'd met a few of the investigators but not all of them.

Kadin stopped at the door. "Oh, and don't tell Reese. I'll make contact when I think the time is right."

As Reese reached the town center, she spotted Sawyer Bennington unlocking the front door of his new restaurant. She almost crossed the street to avoid him when he saw her and smiled. Darn.

With under five hundred residents in Never Summer, everyone knew everyone else and who they slept with. He'd been awfully chatty lately. And the way he looked at her made her uncomfortable. Not that he'd be a bad catch. He was rather nice-looking and in shape. He'd also just come back after completing a business and culinary degree, rented the commercial space right in town and opened a pub called The Ore House. But hooking up with a local didn't appeal to her. What if it didn't work out? Hooking up with anyone didn't appeal to her right now.

Not even Jamie?

He came to her mind a lot. In fact she didn't think he'd left since she'd met him. As crazy as it was, she missed him. No, yearned for him.

She stopped at the dark brown brick front with double-paned windows reflecting morning sunlight, giving only a glimpse of wood tables and a back-lit bar that made the bottles of booze look like lamps. He always started early preparing the restaurant for business.

"Morning, Reese," he drawled. He was much more country than his father. If he wasn't from Never Summer, she'd consider dating him.

Jamie wasn't from Never Summer...

"Hello, Sawyer."

"Good to see you." His eyes took a trip down her body in a way she disliked from most men. It was disrespectful and a cheap way to let a woman know he thought she was pretty. "Heard you cashed in on a windfall."

A lot of people had commented on her find. "How's business?"

His face beamed pride. "Very well. I can take real good care of my lady on the income I bring in." He winked at her. "Tourist season was generous."

Her cue to move on. Scratch the idea of dating him at all. His innuendo made her recoil. Besides, he paled in comparison to Jamie. She started to think Jamie may have ruined her for any other man. At least for a while.

She smiled to be polite and started walking again.

"I'll keep your secret if you have dinner with me."

The hidden money was no secret. She waved without stopping or looking back. Someday he'd get the hint she wasn't interested.

She spotted a man standing outside the local coffee shop, smartphone in one hand. He looked up as she passed. She didn't recognize him, and she knew every face in town. Must be a tourist.

Since she moved to her house in town, she could walk to work every day. On her way, she usually ran into residents. Betsy and Horace Milton approached on the sidewalk, Betsy giggling at something Horace said. With her short, spiky gray hair and dancing bright blue eyes, she exuded an abundance of energy. She and Horace led active lifestyles, as evidenced by their fit bodies—despite having lost muscle mass with age. At nearly seventy, they behaved like forty-year-olds.

"Reese, hello," Betsy said as she neared.

"What kind of trouble are you two causing this morning?" Reese teased.

Betsy laughed and Horace smiled white-crowned front teeth. He'd had a bridge done last year.

"Horace is threatening to take me down to the creek and have his way with me."

Betsy was a real Clairee Belcher from *Steel Magnolias*.

"Maybe you should just open the gas station late today." Reese winked.

"I tried to, but he's a hard worker, my Horace." She leaned against him with happy, love-filled eyes.

The two had met later in life, after each of them lost their first spouses, Horace's to death and Betsy's to unfaithfulness. Reese had only been five when they'd gotten together, but her adoptive mother had told her all about the scandals.

"Enough kidding about us," Horace said. "What's this we hear about you finding a treasure?"

And Sawyer had offered to keep a secret? Not in this town. "It may be part of a murder investigation. You remember Ella Neville?"

Horace's cheerful mood seemed to dim, as did Betsy's. "Why, yes," he said. "Terrible tragedy. Jeffrey was never himself after that."

"The two of you were friends?"

"Not close. He lived in town and we were close to the same age. Sheriff back then asked me all sorts of questions. But Ella didn't live here long before she and Jeffrey got together. I never had a chance to get to know her very well."

"Me, either," Betsy said. "Why do you think the money is related?"

"I don't know if it is. Seems awfully strange someone would hide it in my house, though."

"Yes, that is strange. Have you learned anything new?" Betsy asked. "It's been so long. We gave up hope the killer would ever be caught."

Everyone in town had. "No, nothing yet." She refrained from revealing she'd enlisted Kadin Tandy's agency to help. "I should let you be on your way. I'll be late to work."

"Good running in to you, Reese," Betsy said.

Her cell phone rang. Seeing it was Sheriff Robison, she answered.

"Lavinia Church called. Virgil is at it again. Would you go by there on your way in?"

She stopped walking. She needed a vehicle for that. "Sure."

Turning back, she headed up the street toward her house. As she neared the corner, she spotted a familiar truck parked in front of the hotel across the street. Her steps slowed. That couldn't be…

Reese stopped walking as a man opened the door. Two combat-booted feet met the pavement and then a tall man wearing a cowboy hat emerged. He looked right at her, but she was too far away to see his blue eyes. His muscled arms and chest bedazzled her next. In a tight, thin gray sweater and jeans, he took a jacket out of the cab and put it on, concealing all but part of his chest and stomach. She remembered that body.

Holy…

"Jamie?" Of all the things she anticipated today, this landed last on the list. It didn't even make the list.

He grinned, a sexy lopsided smile that contradicted his size and ruggedness. Striding toward her, he checked traffic and waited for a single car to pass. His distraction gave her a few seconds to devour the sight of him, which punched her most vulnerable senses. The last time she'd felt vulnerable… Had she ever felt vulnerable? The day her parents dropped her off at college. But that had been mild and fleeting. As soon as she realized she was on her own and could do whatever she wanted, the liberation had taken over and she'd soared. So that didn't count. There was also that second time she and Jamie had made love…

She would not go there.

Jamie reached her side of the street and stopped before her, the sun lighting his eyes. His hair had grown a little longer, though it was still short. She had to take deeper breaths. Doing so through parted lips that he noticed, she shut her mouth and swallowed.

"Good morning, Reese."

His deep voice transported her back to their night. As if she needed any more stimulation to do that, anyway.

"What are you doing here?"

"What do you think I'm doing here?"

He'd come for her. Did he mean to start up a relationship? What did he think would come of that? He lived in Wyoming and she lived in Colorado. She didn't want to move. Would he? Could he? She doubted that, and chided herself for even considering the possibility. What they'd had was one night. If he wanted more nights, would she give him that? Is that all he wanted? She began to worry he may be looking for more. Why else would he have come all this way?

"I plan to work while I'm here. I have a series of interviews I need to do and I can do those from anywhere since the candidates are from different states, anyway," he said. "Some we may fly in."

"But…" Should she come right out and say she wouldn't spend time with him? She had a deep, dark feeling she'd be lying if she did.

"We didn't get a chance to get to know each other.

I'm not here to lure you into bed again. I want to start from the beginning, rather than jump to home plate before the game even starts."

As they had done in Rock Springs? She didn't like his reference to baseball. Though he accurately summed up what had occurred, it made her feel indecent. They had jumped to home plate, but she'd rather not analyze why too much. And it was not because she was indecent.

"You should have called first," she said.

"So you could tell me not to come over the phone? I like this much better."

The element of surprise. So, he wouldn't leave, even if she asked him to. When his determination flattered and delighted her, she turned down her street. "I have to work."

"Isn't the sheriff's office that way?" He pointed up the street as he kept up with her.

"Yes, but I need my Jeep."

He took hold of her hand and stopped her from walking. "I can take you wherever you need to go."

Taking in his tall, gorgeous form, she felt her resistance slip. "That's okay. I'll manage."

"I'll take you. We can talk on the way."

Talk? She loved talking to him. "No, really." She started back down the street.

"Afraid?"

She stopped again and faced him. "Of what?"

He stepped close. "Me. What I make you feel." He leaned in as he said the last part, a playful light in his eyes, shadowed by the rim of his hat.

His heat radiated to her, or maybe he just heated

her. Oh, yes, she should be scared of that. Just his face close to hers triggered a hot reaction.

"My truck is right there. Your house is three blocks away."

He knew where she lived? And as if three blocks was such a long way. She found that sort of funny, that he'd try and use the marginally shorter distance to coerce her into his truck. She smiled, unable to help it. What harm would a ride do? If he wanted to talk, maybe he'd leave once they did.

"All right. I have to answer a call. It's a bit of a drive. Do you have time?"

"Of course."

He walked with her to the passenger side and opened the door for her. She saw a few people on the street take notice and got in.

"You're sexy in your uniform, by the way." He closed the door. When he climbed behind the wheel, he added, "I think I even like the ponytail."

Was he teasing her? She didn't think so. "You're one of those cavemen who prefer their women with their hair down?"

"Only when the mood is right."

Now he teased.

"You seem to like to let your hair down every once in a while," he said.

Reese recognized that for the leading comment it was. She'd let her hair down with him. "Why don't you just ask me what you want to know?"

"All right. What made you decide not to get involved in serious relationships?"

How had he come to that conclusion? She'd told

him what kind of relationships she'd had. Well, not everything about them.

"I guess I got tired of men latching on to me. I don't mean to sound crass. I just felt they expected more than I was ready to give. They got hurt. I didn't. Now I don't want anyone else to get hurt."

He drove in silence for a while. Was he looking for more than she could give? It wasn't the first time she'd wondered and it bothered her. How could his feelings escalate so quickly? And what about hers? A panicky flare mushroomed. What if she fell for him?

"I don't sleep with men like I did with you." She'd already told him that but felt the need to make sure he understood. "It's been a long time and you, we…"

"Yes—we. Reese, are you trying to say you want me to leave?" he asked.

She should say yes, but she couldn't. Instead, she turned toward the windshield. Relieved he didn't say anything more, she watched for the turn ahead.

"That's the road there." She pointed to a barely discernable one-lane gravel road.

He turned and drove slowly up the long, curving driveway. At the small cabin in a clearing of thick forest, he parked.

Reese got out and so did he. She stopped when he intercepted her.

"Just so we're clear." He put his hand on her lower back and slowly pulled her to him. She would have jumped away without the fire swirling to life on its own. "I won't stick around long enough to get hurt."

She liked the sound of that. Not that he'd leave eventually. That he possessed so much certainty. He knew his limits. His strength set off a chorus of delightful tingles. His confidence and hard determination rang true in his voice and shone bright in his eyes.

"And you should take into account that I'm not the one who could end up that way."

While she absorbed that enlightening piece of information, he kissed her. Hard at first, then the warmth permeated and took control. His mouth meshed with hers, moving and fitting in perfect harmony. She melted against him, just as she had in Rock Springs.

Shouting from inside reminded her of her purpose. He let her go and she walked hurriedly to the front door.

Reese knocked. "Deputy Harlow. Open up!"

Virgil Church swung open the door, his bushy eyebrows crowded low over hazel eyes. He kept his silver hair combed back. He and his wife must have been around when Ella was murdered. They fit the age bracket. Were they married back then?

"It's about time you got here." Lavinia pushed Virgil aside as she appeared in the doorway. Barely topping five feet, her short, curly, white-bleached hair looked frozen in place. "He broke my grandmother's vase. That vase has been in my family for three generations and he broke it!"

"Lavinia is suffering from dementia and it affects her mood," Virgil explained. "We had an argument and I smashed the vase on the floor." He looked at Lavinia. "I lost my temper. I'm sorry. But you're not an easy woman to live with, especially when you forget things."

Lavinia's blue eyes, which must have been strikingly beautiful in youth, flashed anger. "His temper is horrible. I want a divorce!"

"May we come in?" Reese asked. This would take some finesse to defuse the situation.

This wasn't the first time the sheriff's office had responded to one of Lavinia's calls and everyone in town knew she had dementia. On a few occasions, someone had to drive her back home when she got lost. She often lashed out at her poor husband, accusing him of flying into a temper, but Lavinia was always the one in a temper when the sheriff's office responded. It couldn't be easy living with someone with dementia and it couldn't be easy being the one *with* dementia. It was an all-around sad situation.

Reese stepped inside before Jamie. Lavinia and Virgil lived in a moderately sized cabin with a detached garage. The A-frame provided wonderful views from the front, and Lavinia had decorated in cottage style that passing time had worn and dated.

"Walk me through what happened," Reese said.

"I was looking for something to watch on TV when Virgil took the remote from me and told me to shut up." Lavinia's brow shaped her eyes into a beaten-puppy look, the passion coming from her outweighing the severity of the offense.

"I was already watching something when she changed the channel," Virgil said, sending his wife an irritated glance. "She started to yell at me and then I told her to shut up."

"We fought until he lifted my vase and threatened to break it if I didn't shut up."

"She didn't shut up."

Reese rubbed beneath her nose, trying not to laugh and to decide the best approach. Beside her, Jamie clasped his hands in front of him as though struggling with the same dilemma.

"I admit, I shouldn't have broken the vase," Virgil said. "I just couldn't take her badgering anymore."

"I badgered? You're the one who badgers!"

"Now, now," Reese said. "Calm down or I'll have to take you both to town." She would rather avoid taking the elderly to jail.

"She doesn't remember what she says," Virgil said. "I get so exhausted explaining things all the time. It can be anything from what we had for breakfast to a visit from our kids. I tell her we went out for breakfast and she had pancakes and she argues and says she hates pancakes. She did hate them before all this, but she eats them now. She wouldn't believe me. And then the kids come over and I have to tell her everything that happened and what we all talked about and she gets upset and argues that she would never forget her own kids coming to visit. That turns into an argument. Everything turns into an argument. Now this time it was the remote. We argued over whether I was watching TV or not. I should have just let her change the channel."

Lavinia's emotion appeared to have leveled off a bit. She looked at her husband as though finally beginning to believe him and realizing the torment she must put him through, arguing over anything she can't recall.

"Lavinia, did you ask Virgil if you could change the channel?" Reese asked.

Lavinia thought for a few seconds and then averted her gaze when she answered. "Of course I did."

"You didn't ask," Virgil said.

"I wouldn't have just changed it," she countered.

And this was exactly how the arguments started. Reese shared a glance with Jamie. He remained patiently silent. She looked at him a moment longer than necessary, too caught by his manly attractiveness.

Reese turned back to Lavinia. "Do you remember if Virgil was watching a TV program when you changed the channel, Lavinia?"

Again, she averted her gaze.

"She doesn't."

Reese held her hand up at Virgil. "Let her answer herself, please."

"No. I don't." Tears welled, one falling over.

"Lavinia." Virgil moved to her, pulling her into his arms. She laid her head on his shoulder and cried. "I'm sorry I broke your grandmother's vase. I'll make it up to you and you can watch whatever you want whenever you want."

And it always ended up like this. Lavinia declared she wanted a divorce at nearly seventy and then they made up with someone from the sheriff's office at their house.

Reese glanced again at Jamie, who turned his affectionate look from the couple to her. Then he leaned over where a box of tissues sat on an end table, picked one out and handed it to Lavinia.

The woman moved back from Virgil and took it with a teary look up at him. Virgil kept one arm around her. Dabbing her eyes and then blowing her nose, she lowered the soggy tissue and eyed Jamie some more.

"Who are you?"

"I'm visiting Reese. My apology if I've intruded."

Lavinia waved her hand, the tissue flapping. "Last

time the sheriff brought his daughter and her family, who were visiting from Denver. Things here don't go the way they do in the city."

"Evidently not." A breathy but short laugh came from him.

Lavinia looked at her husband as though forgiving him, but was still in a state of hurt over what had happened. He was old enough to have been around when Ella was murdered.

"How long have the two of you been married?" she asked as though just curious.

She felt Jamie glance at her.

Lavinia seemed confused with the question. The poor thing didn't remember.

"We celebrated our twenty-fifth last August," Virgil said with pride.

"Have you always lived in Never Summer?"

Lavinia smiled and put her hand on Reese's arm. "You're forgiven for not knowing. As young as you are, how could you know such a thing?"

"You have, then?"

"I have." Lavinia dropped her arm and looked fondly at Virgil, who rubbed her back. "He moved here in…what year was that, honey?"

Virgil tipped his head as he tried to recall the year. Clearly it had been a while.

"In the eighties," he said. "Eighty-five?" He looked uncertainly at Reese.

"Do you remember Ella Neville?" she asked Lavinia, not expecting anything to come of it.

"Oh, yes," Lavinia said. "The murdered girl."

"We've heard all the talk about it. Are you reopening her case?" Virgil asked, lowering his hand from Lavinia's back.

"It's never been closed. I'm taking another look at it."

"We knew Jeffrey," Virgil said. "Used to have barbecues at each other's houses."

Lavinia nodded, the key words triggering something in her. Murdered girl…barbecues…

"Caused quite a stir in town," Lavinia said. "Her death."

Reese thought she dramatized a little, saying it had caused a stir when she likely didn't know any details of what people had said or how anyone had reacted. Even if Lavinia could be a suspect, she wouldn't remember enough to be of any help. And Virgil hadn't even lived here at the time.

"Are you going to stay married to Virgil, Lavinia?" Reese asked to end this on a happy note.

She smiled, fine wrinkles fanning out from her eyes and mouth. "Yes."

The vase was unfortunate and Reese did have concerns over Virgil breaking things. "Virgil, do you think you can get your temper under control? I understand it can get difficult at times, but maybe you could find another outlet? Take some deep breaths? Step away and write down everything hateful you're feeling about your wife and then burn it afterward? Scream into a pillow…?"

Virgil nodded halfheartedly. Maybe he had little hope of making it through his wife's condition.

"I could send you some literature on how to manage this stressful time in your life," Reese said. "And hook you up with someone to talk to when you need that."

His hopelessness cheered a bit. "Thank you. I would appreciate that."

"So would I."

Reese turned admonishing eyes to Lavinia for her biting tone.

"Because I love my Virgil." She put her head on his shoulder and her hand on his chest. "At least, I think I do." She winked up at him.

This must be one of her clearer moments, Reese thought. Much different than when she'd called for help. But her lucidity roped in Virgil and he smiled lovingly.

"What you feel deep down is all that matters," Jamie said, turning sly, playfully mischievous eyes to Reese.

A shock wave gripped her. He meant love. Lavinia might instinctively know or feel love for Virgil. In her forgetful states, she may not be aware of that feeling, but it could still be there. While the passionate attraction Reese and Jamie had experienced when they'd first met may not be love or the initial signs leading to love, Jamie intended to point out the deep-down feeling had been there, undeniable and significant. Instinct. Animal drive. Something not thought out consciously.

She distracted herself with bidding farewell and leaving the cabin. Outside, they walked toward the truck.

"Other than that last comment, you were awfully quiet in there," she said.

"Letting you do your job."

"So says the man who Kadin hired." More likely he was biding his time, strategizing when he'd make his next move—trap her into a relationship she couldn't resist.

"Kadin did give me a list of residents living in Never Summer at the time of Ella Neville's murder."

She stopped at the side of his truck to gape at him. "Already?"

He faced her, getting closer than she felt comfortable with. That was the intent, she was sure. He put his hand on the door handle, arm stretched beside her. "Maybe he thinks it's important, you being his daughter and all."

Glancing warily at his arm, Reese asked, "Do you have the list with you?"

"It's on my laptop and my laptop is in my hotel room."

His eyes were entirely too captivating for her, with a smile in them even though his mouth remained flat. "Well…maybe you could bring it by the office tomorrow morning?" Certainly she would not go to his hotel room.

"Sure. It's a date."

"It is not a date." She turned to the door and he opened it for her.

"Then I'll take you on one after. Something non-threatening, like lunch."

Nothing would be nonthreatening with him. Even a walk in the park would set her on fire. She climbed up into the truck and reached for the handle. He still held the frame and didn't let her close it.

She should say no to lunch, which would be harmless to him but potentially dangerous to her. But that flirty light in his eyes kept tickling her senses.

"All right. Lunch. But you have to leave town after that."

He chuckled. "It'll take a lot more than that to get me to leave."

Closing the door, he kept his gaze on her as he moved around to the other side. She felt caught, hooked by his line of sensuality. How could a man rev her up with only a look like that? His long strides and muscular chest and arms also played havoc with her. Watching him climb into the truck, slide his strong legs onto the seat and reach for the ignition, she felt ignited herself. How would she ever make it through the inferno?

Chapter 5

Jamie still gave in to an occasional chuckle when he thought of how fast Reese got out of his truck and went into the sheriff's office yesterday. At the door she'd glanced back, wary and apprehensive and probably wishing he'd go away. Not a chance. When he'd asked her if she wanted him to leave, she hadn't answered. And when he'd kissed her, she'd responded. She gave the outward appearance of distance, but inside her warmth seemed boundless.

"You new in town?"

He gave his debit card to the florist, who was five-four and in her early forties with thick, round glasses and a brown shoulder-length bob.

"Just visiting for a while."

"Visiting who?" Her brown eyes flashed to him as she processed his payment.

"Reese Harlow."

She smiled. "Ah. Deputy Harlow. I've sold lots of flowers to men who've tried to capture her heart."

So, she had a reputation? Not a good sign. "All local?"

"Sawyer Bennington sends her flowers on her birthday and Valentine's Day. He owns The Ore House. If he can't win her over, no man can. He's successful and an honorable man."

"She never even dated him?"

"Nope."

"Why not?" Maybe he'd get the rumors going around.

"Her mother says she's focused on her career right now. But others think she's afraid to commit."

"Yeah, that's my assessment."

She handed back his card, angling her head as she studied him. "Where you from?"

"Wyoming. I work for her father—her biological father."

"Oh, yeah. She recently did track down her real parents." She studied him more, eyes taking in his upper body. "You came all the way here to see her?"

"Has to count for something, right?"

"It would for me."

Jamie signed the charge slip and took the vase of red roses. Going traditional never felt better. Well, he'd never gone traditional. It felt good to go traditional.

"Good luck," the clerk said as he walked toward the door. "You're going to need it."

Jamie got out of his truck with the flowers and headed for the sheriff's office. Reese may not have welcomed her physical reaction to him, but he intended to stay and find out why. Then he'd tear down whatever obstacles stood in his way. He felt good about this, despite Reese's words that kept repeating in his mind.

I got tired of men latching on to me, expecting more than I was ready to give.

Inside the small office, the old wood floor creaked as he walked into the open area with three desks and walls cluttered with pictures of the town, calendars and plaques. The sheriff's office took up one corner, the break room was straight ahead and a conference room took up the opposite corner. The sheriff had his back to the office door, facing the window, as he worked on the computer.

Reese sat at her desk, the only one occupied, staring at him. She had a stack of files to the side and held one open in front of her.

He walked to her. First the flowers, then the list of residents.

"What are you doing?" she asked.

Seeing her wide eyes he ignored her surprise and set down the full bouquet of flowers. "What does it look like?"

She looked at the flowers and then up at him, flustered. "Take them back."

"No." He grinned. She did not want him to take them back. She might feel threatened with what his gesture meant for them going forward, but she liked the flowers. He could tell. He'd thrown her. She hadn't expected him to do this.

"Take them back." Her eyes shifted nervously from the flowers to him.

The sheriff twisted on his chair to look through his

open office door. He studied Jamie for a bit and then saw the flowers. With a slight smile, he turned back to his computer.

"Calm down," Jamie said, stopping her jittery eyes and holding them with his. "I'm not proposing." Yet.

She looked like a caged animal shying away from a kid with a stick.

"Are you afraid of rejection or something?" He wasn't sure he completely bought her explanation of not wanting to hurt another man. What made her run from men?

"No." But she eyed the flowers, this time as though she'd like to lean in and take a sniff.

"Are you an only child?"

That question seemed to divert her apprehension in another direction. "Why would that matter?"

Because she was an only child. Maybe that contributed, maybe it didn't. It was worth looking deeper. "What were your adoptive parents like?"

She let out an incredulous grunt, mouth dropping open. "Why are you asking me that? They had nothing to do with why I chose to go after a career before I think about settling down with someone."

Why did he get the feeling she'd come up with that as an excuse? "Did you have your heart broken?"

"No." She closed her mouth and leaned back, folding her arms.

"That's right. You're the heartbreaker."

She turned her gaze away. And as she did, he noticed the file contained documents on Ella Neville's murder case.

The sheriff's office phone rang.

Jamie saw the sheriff answer. "Well, hello, Tad. I

haven't heard from you in over a week. Is everything all right over there in San Francisco?" He listened for a while, leaning back for what he must have decided would take longer than he'd thought. By the sound of his voice, Jamie would say his son had called. "Have you talked to him? If the two of you fought last night and he left upset, I'm sure he just went somewhere to cool off."

Reese glanced up at Jamie. "I was an only child."

He returned his attention to her, not expecting her to give out any personal information and glad she had.

"You say that as if you were cursed."

From the sheriff's office, he heard Sheriff Robison say, "Don't jump to conclusions. Eddy is probably just trying to make you suffer. It's called manipulation. Your mother does the same thing when we have fights like that."

"Not cursed. My parents were good to me," Reese said, oblivious to the conversation taking place behind her in her boss's office.

"Now you sound like you have to convince yourself of that," Jamie said. "Were your parents as good as you needed them to be?" She'd been adopted. Maybe she felt something had been missing.

"Wait until you can talk to him," Sheriff Robison said. "All right. Call if you need to. If it gets worse, then fly out and see your mother and me."

The sheriff told his son he loved him and hung up.

Reese glanced back into the sheriff's office with a soft smile and then faced Jamie again. "Maybe not as communicative as they could have been, but good and loving."

"Communicative?"

Her eyes moved up to look at him briefly before going back to the list, but she didn't seem to read. "My mother couldn't have children and that's why they adopted me, but I think they did it more out of a sense of duty. People graduated from high school and college and then got married and had kids. They made families together. I think they would have felt like outcasts if they hadn't done that." She looked up at the flowers. "My grandparents were born here. That's what brought my parents here." Then she tipped her head up to him. "They couldn't be a real family in New York, so far away. They saw this town as a place much more appropriate for that. But fitting in was always so important to them. Still is. They need to be respected by the community, and they are. I just think they might have chosen different paths if the pressure of doing what was expected of them had been removed."

"You aren't close to them?"

"No. I'm close. They're just, I don't know... They keep a lot bottled up."

She didn't seem completely truthful. "You fended for yourself growing up?"

"They took care of me, but I did do a lot on my own. Why are you picking me apart like this? Oh, wait. You're trying to get to the root of my decision not to get involved in a serious relationship, not yet, anyway. Someday I'm sure I'll be ready."

"You told me you were an only child. I think it might have something to do with your phobia."

"Phobia?" She blinked sarcastically and met his eyes.

"Are you really sure you'll be ready?"

With her blank look, he surmised she hadn't thought much on it.

Her parents' aloofness must have had something to do with her uncertainty. Did she even know how to recognize love? Real love. More than companionship.

Time for a test. Just a little one.

He slid out a single rose. Water dripped minimally. Putting one hand on the desk surface, he tipped the rose and touched the petals to her skin just beneath her nose. "Do you really see yourself ever doing that? The whole enchilada…marriage, kids?"

She inhaled the fresh scent of the flower, then took the stem from him, holding it there herself. "I guess I haven't pictured myself doing that, no."

She was still young. Maybe she just didn't realize she was getting to the age where she would be ready.

"Picture it now." He held her gaze while she thought.

"I don't want to make the wrong decision," she said. "To make the right decision I have to know I'm ready."

Fair enough. He admired her ability to communicate without offending. She had confidence and plans and wouldn't let anything derail her unless she was sure.

She smelled the rose some more. Then, after contemplating him, she put it back into the vase. "Why are you so determined to hook up with someone?"

"I'm ready for that." And he was sure that was what he wanted.

"Why weren't you before? Did the private company you worked for have something to do with that? You told me when we had dinner that it wasn't good for you."

Yes, and he still didn't want to talk about that. But now he had to.

"It was a private military company. Aesir International. The man who ran it wasn't on the straight and narrow."

She contemplated him again. "You were a mercenary?"

"Security contractor." He hated the term *mercenary*.

"There's a difference?"

He had to calm his irritation. "A big one."

"Just because you're a mercenary doesn't mean you're a bad one."

"I am not a mercenary, nor have I ever been a mercenary." He couldn't keep the sharpness out of his tone.

She stared at him, now understanding. "I'm sorry, I didn't…"

Valdemar Stankovich had made him a mercenary against his will. He would never get past his bitterness.

"What went wrong?" she asked.

Everything. Nothing she could imagine would be worse than the truth. "They did some questionable things. I got out as soon as I could."

"What do you mean as soon as you could? Didn't you just quit?"

He didn't like her wariness. She may not know, but she had nothing to fear from him. His time with Aesir made him look crooked. "I'd rather not talk about that."

"I'd rather not talk about why I don't want to settle down right now." She smiled slightly, tempering the sober topic.

"I already know why." Winning her would be a welcome challenge. He just had to be careful deciding when—or if—the time came to give up.

"Can I look at the list of residents again?" she asked.

"I emailed it to you." He gestured to the Neville murder case file. "What have you got that out for?"

She woke up her computer and navigated to the email. "Looking for anything that might tip us off to Jeffrey's involvement." Printing the page, she got up and went to the printer to retrieve it. Jamie took advantage of her turned back to admire her rear. As she headed back, she caught him. Whether involuntary or not, her gaze wandered down the front of him and back up.

Then she seemed to shake herself back to business, reaching her chair and putting down the page as she sat. "I don't think he had anything to do with it."

Jamie moved the wooden chair beside her desk next to her more comfortable one and sat beside her, liking their nearness.

"Jeffrey's friends were all interviewed," she said. "Ella didn't have many, since she was so new to the community. None of them had said anything unusual that stood out as suspicious." She looked over the names of residents. "One of them said Jeffrey took her to dinner a few nights before and heard him say he bought plane tickets to Tahiti. Who would do that if they were planning to kill their spouse?"

She jotted down the names of male residents who fit the age bracket. There weren't many and one had died.

"Someone planning to convince a jury of their innocence," Jamie said.

Reese lifted her eyes and he saw her concern. Would she be another deputy sheriff to fail at cracking this case?

When Reese arrived home later that night, she walked toward the white steps and railing that bordered her front porch, still floating from lunch with Jamie. She floated a lot with him. He hadn't talked about anything serious, just like their first dinner. He talked about fun things, like the time he bought his mother a cat for her birthday. He'd been sixteen. His mother didn't like cats and tried to hide her disappointment. Jamie had felt bad for days, until he noticed his mother taking a shine to the thing. The way he told the story made her laugh. It was so easy to talk to him. And he made her feel good. Happy.

She'd barely been able to concentrate all afternoon and into the evening. The walk home had only given her peace and quiet to think about him some more. That couldn't be good.

As she reached the first porch step, she saw the lower corner of the window of the top half of the door had been broken.

Stopping, she drew her pistol and searched the yard and sides of the house, then the street in both directions and behind her. Across the street, light illuminated windows but no one stirred.

She'd stayed late studying the Neville file. It was nearly ten and the street was dark and quiet. No cars passed. Nothing made a sound. It was a cool, still night with no moon.

Facing her house, she checked the yard again and looked closely at the dark windows. Creeping forward, she listened for any sounds coming from inside. Like the night, it was silent.

Stepping up to the door, she stood to the side, seeing it was open a crack. Should she call for backup? So far it didn't appear anyone was inside. They could be hiding. Waiting. Maybe they'd seen her drive up. Backup might take too long. She had a gun and she had training. She'd check it out first.

Taking her flashlight out, she pushed the door open. With her pistol ready in one hand, she flashed light into the entry, searching the stairway going up the right wall. She saw nothing and moved to the opening to the living room. Her couch had been knifed and tipped over. The bookshelf had been cleared of its holdings and also tipped over. Throw pillows, lamps and tables had all been toppled. Someone had ransacked her house.

Moving down the hall past the staircase, she reached the entry to the great room that opened to her kitchen and a nook area. The same had been done here, with her sectional knifed, bookshelf with all her movies tipped over and movies everywhere. Plates and glass lay broken on the new wood floor in the kitchen. The only thing left untouched was the kitchen table in the nook.

To her right, she inched to the doorway of her master bedroom. Her mattress had been ripped open. Bedding lay strewn on the floor. Her dresser drawers had been emptied and clothes mixed with bedding. At her walk-in closet door, she flashed her light inside. More mess but no intruder. Back out in the great room, she stayed at the edge of the hall, peering up to the small loft area at the top of the stairs.

A shadow moved.

Reese's heart slammed with her alarm. But she remained calm, calling on her training. The figure had ducked into one of three upstairs rooms—the office above her walk-in closet and bathroom. She clipped the flashlight to her duty belt.

Going to the stairs, she climbed quietly and slowly. At the top, she checked the landing area and looked over the great room. She hadn't finished renovating the second level yet. She aimed her weapon into the office, the only furnished room upstairs. This room had been partially searched and one of the two windows was open, the screen knifed and torn. She went there and glanced outside. A figure ran down the street.

Closing the window, she hurried down the hall and checked what would soon be the second master bedroom and then the room she planned to turn into a library. It had its own balcony and would make a lovely place to spend an afternoon reading, especially with the partial mountain views. But right now it felt violated. Unsafe.

After going back downstairs, she went out the front door and ran to the street. Whoever had broken into her house was gone.

Back inside, she closed and locked the door. Staring at the broken window, her unease didn't calm. She needed an alarm system.

Still holding her pistol, she flipped on lights as she went through the house to the back door next to the nook. She still had leftover construction material from the renovations. Finding a board that would fit the front window, she took hammer and nails to the front door and boarded the entire window.

Standing back, she still felt insecure. Who had broken into her house? And why?

It had to be the money. Word had spread like wildfire of her treasure find. But Candace must not have told anyone Reese had put the money in the safe-deposit box. She did have a reputation of confidentiality with her role at the bank.

If the money was connected to Ella's murder, could that mean the killer was local? And still alive?

She took out her phone and started to call Jamie. Then stopped. What had prompted that instinct? He was a security expert. He could keep her safe until she had an alarm system installed. Or was that an excuse to spend time with him? She battled with a deep and tempting urge to use the excuse. And then a familiar apprehension clenched within her. She felt it every time a man began to weave his way too far into her life.

When the sheriff told Jamie that Reese wasn't in the office yet and that the reason she hadn't shown up for work yet was because someone had broken into her house last night, Jamie was livid. She'd called the sheriff and a team had gone to her house. They'd just finished, the sheriff had told him. Now late afternoon, Jamie parked in front of her flax-yellow and white-trimmed Victorian and walked with long strides to her front door. Seeing the boarded window, he pounded the door below that and rang the bell.

After several seconds and more pounding, Reese opened the door.

"Why didn't you call me?" He stepped forward, forcing her to step back, and shut the door behind him.

"Call you?" She looked like a trapped animal.

Hadn't she even considered calling him? Was she that independent?

"You could have been hurt." Or worse.

"I'm a deputy sheriff." She turned and walked down the hall.

He followed. "Did you call anyone for help?"

"No. I didn't need to. The burglar ran away."

"You saw him?"

"I saw his shadow, and then his back as he ran down the street."

He must have been looking for the money. "How many people know about the money you found?"

"Just the locals." She faced him in the great room, which was missing a couch, as was the living room. Had they been damaged in the break-in? Looking for the money. The man probably had a knife. And a gun. Reese had been alone.

"Is anything missing?" he asked.

"Nothing that I've noticed. But I think Ella's killer is a local and the money must have something to do with why she was killed."

The killer had been here all along? How else would he or she know about the money? Unless they were in contact with someone who'd know. He checked her back door and all her windows.

"I'm having a security system installed."

Well, that was good to hear. He passed her and went to the front, checking the boarded-up window and the door lock and then the front windows in the living room.

"I already did that," she said from the living room entry.

Ignoring her, he went up the stairs. The front two rooms still had old flooring and walls and no furniture. The wallpaper was torn in places and the carpeting was partially pulled up.

"I delayed the construction workers a day so we could collect evidence," she said from the top of the stairs, back to the railing open to the lower level. "No prints."

"He wore gloves." Jamie walked into the office, temporarily set up on plywood flooring that had been replaced. The walls hadn't been done yet, covered in dark, fine-printed wallpaper.

Reese came into the office, which she began straightening out.

Seeing the wallpaper was pulled back in here, too, he began to wonder why. As he continued to study the torn wallpaper, he noticed one strip had been pulled back enough to reveal what appeared to be a break in the wall. He went there.

"Was this pulled back before?" he asked.

Reese absently glanced up from her work on the desk. "The construction workers probably did that."

"No, they'd have torn down the whole wall. Isn't that what you're doing? Gutting and restoring the place?" He pulled the wallpaper down farther than it had been.

Reese stopped stacking papers, dropping the sheet in her hand to look at him and the wall. "What is that?"

She walked over to him and began helping him tear the paper. It came off easily, unusual for wallpaper.

He looked up and saw finishing nails had held up this section of wallpaper up. Reese pulled off a big piece of it and he stood with her, staring at a door someone had covered. The trim and knob had been removed.

Glancing at her, he hooked his finger in the round hole where the knob would have been. The door remained shut. He felt inside the hole and found a latch. He pressed it and the door released.

"Whoever broke in here knew to look for something hidden," Jamie said.

"He must have found the door."

"And you interrupted him before he could see what was in here." He met her gaze while the significance of this sank in.

He opened the door to a small closet. On the floor sat one small trunk, full of dust and sealed shut with a padlock.

Had the man known there would be something else hidden in this house? The story about the way the money had been found had spread all through town. It had been hidden under the floorboards.

"Do you have any tools?" Jamie asked. "That lock is old and the trunk wasn't built with quality in mind."

It was more of a decorative trunk. She left the office and went down to the laundry room, where she kept a toolbox. After carrying it upstairs, she gave it to Jamie.

He took out a hammer and banged the lock. It broke off the trunk with the first hit.

"You don't know your own strength."

He looked at her with a raised brow.

Kneeling on the floor, Reese opened the trunk. Jamie crouched next to her.

Inside, someone had placed a variety of memorabilia. A few old *Life* magazines. Books. Maps. Records. A picture album and a few Polaroid photos.

"Wow." Then she lifted a Sperry & Hutchinson collector's book, half filled with green stamps. "Double wow." Putting the book aside, she took out the photo album.

"Definitely reflects the time." Jamie picked up the book filled with green stamps. "My grandmother talked about these things."

Reese opened the photo album.

Jamie expected to find pictures of Ella and Jeffrey. There were pictures of Ella. He recognized her from the photos in her murder case file. Most of the photos were individual, but Ella was captured in a few with a man he didn't recognize.

"Is that Jeffrey?" he asked.

"No. I don't think so. I wasn't born when he and Ella married and he was older when I first met him."

Several of the pages in the photo album were empty. Just three were filled with photos and it appeared to be a trip she'd taken with the man. Some were in a hotel room, others at Disneyland. And then dressed up in a restaurant for dinner. Another was taken outside the restaurant, a sign illuminated above their heads. Charlie's. The man must have been a boyfriend of Ella's before she came to Never Summer. There were a few other photos of the two of them with another couple. Friends they'd visited?

"Do you think Ella could have hidden this trunk?" she asked.

"Why would Jeffrey hide it if she kept pictures of her with another man?"

"Maybe she knew him before she met him."

"And forgot to take it out of the closet before coming up with the bright idea of wallpapering over the door?" He looked up at what was left of the finishing nails. "I kind of doubt she forgot."

Had she still loved the other man?

"I kind of doubt that, too. She must have hidden the trunk from Jeffrey. But why?"

"Maybe she still loved him and kept a secret from Jeffrey."

"All the stories I heard about her and Jeffrey were straight out of a fairy tale." Reese lifted a scarf from the bottom of the trunk.

Jamie thought it was the last item inside. But it wasn't. He looked down with her at bundles of hundred-dollar bills that lined the bottom of the trunk.

Chapter 6

"I feel like a bank robber."

Jamie looked over at Reese as she zipped up the duffel bag. They'd counted two hundred and fifty thousand. The stash under the bedroom floor had been considerably less.

"I think you should stay at my hotel until this is over." Convincing her wouldn't be easy, but Jamie had serious concerns over the break-in. Along with the money she found under her bedroom floor, she had close to three hundred thousand.

"I'll be fine."

"I know you can take care of yourself. But I'm an expert at security. Just let me make sure. Two pairs of eyes and ears are better than one."

"I—I appreciate your concern, but…"

"Reese. Please. I'll be considerate of your need for

space. The hotel is public. You'll be safer there. Just stay until your renovations are finished and your security alarm is installed." That should give him enough time to win her over, if winning a woman like her was even possible.

He waited while she thought it over.

Ella had somehow taken into her possession a large sum of money, hidden it and didn't have time to spend any of it. Now someone had learned Reese had discovered the nest egg and had tried to take it. What bothered Jamie most was that it seemed the intruder had known where to look. But that would imply he'd known where Ella had hidden the money. Why not try to steal it long before now? Why wait?

The intruder hadn't known where to look. Maybe the location of the first find had tipped him off to look in other unexpected places. He'd known there was more money than what Reese had found. Jamie imagined him looking for secret passages or closed spaces. He could have tapped walls. The floors had all been redone, so he wouldn't have looked there. The construction workers would have discovered more money.

"I'm not comfortable staying in a hotel room with you, but you can stay here," Reese finally said.

He'd take that. Her agreement felt like a milestone. He hoped her invitation to stay at her house wasn't just for safety reasons.

"Let's go put this money somewhere safe and get my things. Then we should start questioning the locals who lived here when Ella was killed."

"I'll have to get a bigger safe-deposit box." Reese yawned. "Or get more than one."

Jamie realized why. "Did you get any sleep last

night?" He stepped closer and brushed his hand along the side of her face, moving the strands of hair back. She had such a beautiful face.

Her eyes met his for a few seconds. "No."

"Why don't you go lie down for a while? We'll take care of the money later."

A look of sheer pleasure lightened her face. "I would love that."

"Why don't you take a bath first?" He started for the lower level bedroom. "I'll start it for you."

"That isn't necessary." She trailed him into her bedroom, as though lured by temptation.

No, not necessary to help her rest, but an opportunity to explore how much each of them had fallen for each other during that one night in Wyoming.

"When's the last time you let someone take care of you?" He entered her bedroom, careful to keep this casual.

"Let?" With childlike hesitance, she stood just inside the bedroom door.

He could see her struggle with letting go. "No wonder you covet your independence so much. You didn't learn any other way growing up." He went into the bathroom.

She came to the bathroom door. "You think you know me."

"Just let someone take care of you. Just once. Let me. Now. This moment."

Her eyes lowered, head angled slightly, and then she looked at his eyes. He could feel her respond and fight the reaction.

"Think of me as your brother," he said.

She snorted a cynical laugh. "That will be impossible."

As he reached down to start the bath, she leaned against the sink counter. Seeing her soft smile, he took heart that his instinct was on target. She may have plans that didn't include a steady boyfriend, but she wasn't immune to him as a man.

"I don't have a brother." Her eyes glinted with teasing.

"Use your imagination."

"That could be dangerous."

The tub began to fill.

"When's the last time you let someone take care of you? You didn't answer before." And he really wanted to know.

Eyes falling low, she drew a small line with her big toe in the bathroom rug. Then finally looked up. "My mother. When I was sick."

"No other times? She didn't pamper you for no reason?" She'd touched on the aloofness of her parents before.

"She told me where the medicine was."

And that had been her mother's way of taking care of her? What kind of childhood did she have?

"Did she love you?"

Her mouth opened as though the notion her mother didn't love her was absurd. "Of course. She just… She had a different way of parenting than some of my friends' parents did. She told me she loved me. Combed my hair. Braided it. Made me chocolate milk and threw me birthday parties."

"She did what she was supposed to do but the feeling was missing? What about your father?"

Reese started to walk out of the bathroom. Jamie stopped her with an arm across the doorway.

Slowly she looked over at him. "He gave me an allowance and took us to family outings. Camping. Movies. Town events."

"But he didn't talk to you? About the important things?"

"My mother did that."

"You weren't close to your father, then."

"They loved me," she insisted.

Jamie didn't want to be harsh, but he had to say the truth. She needed to hear it. He put his hand on her upper arm, making sure she met his eyes.

"I'm sure they wanted to."

He would never in his wildest dreams have imagined that the source of her extreme need for independence stemmed from being raised by parents who wanted children, but hadn't anticipated the difference between having their own and adopting or how that would affect them. He was sure they meant well and the desire to have a child had been real and they had thought they could love the same way. But they hadn't. Some people couldn't. He didn't hold it against them and he hoped Reese wouldn't, either.

"They loved me," she insisted again, weaker this time.

"Yes. In their own way, as you said." From a distance. Close but not as close as Reese seemed to have needed.

Maybe her parents had convinced themselves that the hole from being unable to conceive on their own was filled with Reese. But the brutal truth was it wasn't.

He didn't want to hurt Reese. But he understood—probably more than she did—why she'd reached out to find her real parents. Her dad.

Putting his hands on each side of her face, he brought his mouth close to hers, a deliberate distraction, a strategy, something he hoped would work in his favor. Her stubborn denial lost its strength. When her eyes drooped and she tipped her head back to accommodate his height, a surge of passion coursed through him.

He kissed her softly, just a touch and a brush of his lips. Her quickened breathing and flexing fingers on his shoulders told him she felt it as much as him. He kissed her awhile longer, until he couldn't hold back anymore. And neither could she.

Lifting his head, he watched her open her eyes and look up at him. "Your bath is ready."

She stepped back, eyeing him warily and maybe with a little confusion. Good. Confusion was good. She was growing past her old ideals, what she'd perceived as right for her.

A nagging feeling persisted in him that he could be wrong. She might be moved by him, his efforts, but would it be enough to change her mind?

He left her alone for her bath. When he heard the tub draining, he thought she'd stay in her room. He wouldn't push her more than he thought she could take all at once. When she appeared in her nightgown in the opening to the great room, a wave of satisfaction swept him. She wouldn't turn him away. What he'd shed light on had made a difference, softened her.

"I'd rather not be alone tonight," she said. "The break-in shook me up more than I thought."

Was she blaming her vulnerability on that? He stood from his reclined position on the couch and went to her.

"I don't want to…you know. Just…"

"I get it. You wouldn't have put on that nightgown if you had that intent."

He stripped to his underwear as she crawled into bed, watching him with the covers to her chin as he joined her.

"Come here." He opened his arms for her and she cuddled close.

Hearing her deep sigh and feeling her muscles relax so that her body molded to his, he fought a mighty urge to roll on top of her.

"I think you're right about my parents," she said quietly. "But they do love me."

"I know. Get some sleep. Tomorrow's going to be a long day."

Reese still felt out of sorts the next day. She felt stiff and as if she was operating on autopilot. Having Jamie nearby gave her a warm glow, stronger than when they'd had dinner and then lunch. A connection seemed to be growing, one that made her nervous.

She'd gotten up before Jamie and cleared out the office for the construction workers so they could work on the walls. Then she'd stayed with the construction workers while he'd gone to buy breakfast. That had taken some arguing. Just because she had a break-in didn't mean he had to guard her 24/7. Even though she secretly liked how much he cared.

Now they headed for the doors of the town grange, where the weekly bingo game took place. All day she'd been plagued with thoughts she wished she could expunge from her head.

The things Jamie had made her realize didn't settle well with her. She felt like she didn't know herself anymore. Who had that kid been who'd grown up in the Harlow residence? She had tons of good memories. Fun memories. There had been lots of laughter and support. Both her mom and dad had been there for her at all the big stages of her life. Getting her period. Boys. Challenging schoolwork. Graduating from high school and college.

Jamie had struck a chord when he'd called out their good intentions not measuring up to the reality of her adoption. Her parents had loved her. They'd loved having a child in their home. But nothing would change the fact that they'd lost their ability to have their own child, something they had deeply desired and must have felt immense disappointment to learn they couldn't do. Maybe they'd never gotten over it, even if they didn't realize it. They might have convinced themselves that having Reese was enough, and in all the ways that mattered, it was. Reese was the next best thing to a biological child. Her parents had never treated her that way, but the truth lay buried.

Is that why she'd sought out her real parents? Reese did not like admitting she hadn't been close to her adoptive father. She hadn't been. He'd always put on a smile for her and had always encouraged her and supported her. But she couldn't recall a single time when the two of them connected. Sure, they had been there at important stages of her growth, but it had felt almost mechanical, now that she thought of it. She remembered him as an optimist who liked his work and the people in town. Now that she analyzed it, he treated her the same as everyone else. If not for her mother's need to have a child, Reese doubted her father would have adopted anyone. He never expressed his feelings and she had never felt open to tell him hers. He never told her he loved her, either. Her mother had, and Reese believed she did love her. Her father cared for her and her mother loved her. But maybe that hadn't been enough. For Reese. As she'd told Jamie, they had loved her in their own way. But it had not been real. That was the part she had difficulty accepting.

"You're awfully quiet."

They reached the grange doors. She opened one and stepped inside.

"Are you all right?" he asked.

"Yes. Fine." She scanned the room of mostly older people sitting at long tables with a man behind a podium reading letters and numbers, glad to be back to work. Music played at a low volume through speakers where a DJ sat behind his kiosk. This was no ordinary bingo game. Never Summer treated this like a night out on the town. They took breaks to dance and some drank alcohol. Two men sat on stools around a tall, round table, clearly only there while their wives played bingo. The room next to this had been converted into a theater. She could hear a movie playing, deep bass rumbling at a low level.

"N, forty-one," the sixtysomething man behind the podium said into a microphone. Above his head on the wall, a big sign read Death Bingo Night. Losers Win All. The object of this game was not to win bingo. The player with the most spaces filled before getting a bingo won.

Reese jabbed Jamie with her elbow, not hard, just enough to get his attention. "That's Bert at the bar. He was married five times and met them all at bars in other cities. He met his latest wife while vacationing in Texas. She left him a few months ago and moved back to her hometown." She covertly indicated another man sitting at one of the middle tables with his wife. "That's Harold. He lost his first wife to cancer just before Ella's murder. He remarried almost twelve years later. That's her next to him."

"B, fourteen."

"Let's talk to Bert first." Jamie started toward the man.

"Don't you want to play bingo?"

"Do you?"

She elbowed him again, wishing she hadn't. "I was teasing." She felt like she was flirting. His big, fit body made it hard not to. When she'd first awakened, she got hot all over with just the realization she was in bed with him. Then the rest of the day, every time she encountered him, she had the same reaction, an automatic attraction she couldn't control. And then, of course, the way he looked at her sometimes may as well have been a physical caress. His eyes held so much masculine certainty, as though he saw through her to the woman who'd shared one firecracker of a night with him and the promise all that explosiveness held.

"Hey, Bert," she said, greeting the older man.

He turned on the stool and his smile didn't change his sad eyes. A man who had never found true love looked back at her.

"Reese. I didn't know you played bingo."

"I didn't know you did, either."

"I don't." He held up the glass of dark liquid, some kind of whiskey.

"O, seventy."

"You and Jeffrey were friends, weren't you?"

Bert studied her for a time. "This have anything to do with that money you found?"

"Maybe. I've reopened Ella's case." Actually, it had never been closed.

"Oh. Am I a suspect?" He laughed at what he must have intended to be a joke.

"No. We're just trying to pick up some new information."

"That was a long time ago."

"Did the sheriff or anyone else talk to you back then?"

"No. No need to. I knew Jeffrey, not his wife. I met her a couple of times and that's it. Jeffrey didn't go out much after he met her. Those two were smitten."

She had heard that from many people. "Do you know of any other of Jeffrey's and Ella's friends? Maybe someone Ella met when she first arrived in Never Summer?"

He thought a moment and then listed a few names, all of which she and Jamie already had on their list. "Most everyone knew him. Small town. From what I heard his neighbors were all questioned."

She asked him a few more questions before leaving him to his drink, then walked across the dance floor with Jamie.

"I'll ask Kadin to look into Ella's past," he said on

the way out of the grange. "Maybe someone close to her was overlooked and not questioned or not questioned enough."

"Kadin?"

"You asked him to look into the case." He seemed confused by her hesitation.

"Yes, but…" She endured an odd feeling, a torn, restricted feeling. Again, she wondered how much she wanted him in her life, if at all. Maybe what bothered her most was that she didn't fully understand why she'd found her biological parents, especially after her conversation with Jamie.

"He's here, you know."

She stopped in the middle of the dance floor to gape at him.

"I don't think I was supposed to tell you, but maybe you should know. He didn't want to pressure you. He brought his family here for a vacation, and to see you."

Reese looked down and then across the bingo hall.

"I, twenty-one."

"Bingo," a disappointed face called, a victim of the death bingo game.

"Hey." Jamie used his finger to guide her face so she had to look up at him. She loved his height. "Don't get upset. He won't descend upon your life if you aren't willing. But he would like to get to know the daughter he only recently discovered he had."

Jamie was either damn good at manipulating her or he understood way too much about her. She feared the latter more accurately pinned the answer. Right now, she didn't care. She appreciated how he made light of it.

"So, he's not doing what you're doing? Descending upon my life?"

"I'm descending upon what we started in Wyoming." With a sexy grin, he took her hand and slid the other around her waist as a snappy country Western song started.

She laughed, delighted, as he swept her around the dance floor. At first they were the only couple out there, but many noticed and a few others trickled onto the floor to join them. She recognized all of them and enjoyed the fond looks she began to receive from the women.

"Where did a city boy like you learn to two-step?" she asked to avoid paying attention to the others.

"My mother loved to dance when I was a kid and she loved this kind of music even more."

"Couldn't she dance with your father?"

He slowed as he swung her for another turn.

"I hail from Whitman Park in Camden, New Jersey."

Did he think that would explain everything? She waited, meeting his eyes and hoping her look would say all that was needed.

He stopped dancing with the end of the song, but still held her close. "My father went to prison for armed robbery. He got twenty years but was released on parole after about ten. He went back to New Jersey and never tried to contact me or my mother. He was only trying to feed us all, but he made a bad choice. Prison changed him."

"Oh...that's terrible."

"That happened not long after my older brother was shot to death in a gang-related incident."

Speechless, Reese had nothing to say.

"My mother succumbed to drugs after she lost him. My father was desperate to try to make things better for us. He only made things worse."

"You're not trying to win me over now, are you?" He didn't have to tell her all of this. "Jamie, that's awful." And he'd told her despite how it might taint her opinion of him.

"It was. Until I joined the military and took my mother away from that place and all the bad memories. She now has a respectable circle of friends who accompany her to movies and afternoon tea in Portsmouth, New Hampshire. It's a quiet, friendly, safe community. She thrives there. That's why I moved to New York after working for Aesir. I could be closer to her."

He looked off as he must be thinking how far he was from her now.

"And still in a big city." He had said he loved big cities. Maybe she'd have to cure him of that. And they could always travel to see his mother.

Or…not! Where had that idea come from?

"Big cities aren't everything, I'm beginning to learn," Jamie said. "And I can see my mother as often as I like. I talk to her on the phone almost every day."

How touching. He took good care of his mother and had been instrumental in making her life better. Where his father had failed, he'd succeeded.

Feeling herself falling for him, the warmth gathering in her center, the core of her, she resisted. He never liked talking about his job with Aesir. He hadn't told her anything about it, really. He'd only taken offense to being called a mercenary, so whatever had happened must not have been good.

"What questionable things did your boss at Aesir do?" she asked daringly.

He didn't seem affected. "Enough gloomy talk." He swung her into another dance. "I like this song."

The singer sang about tasting a woman like sweet wine.

She danced with him a few turns, having fun and not because of the song. She liked being with him like this. The light of happiness heated in his eyes as she shared a long, infatuated stare with him.

"Careful, you might start having feelings for me."

Maybe she already did. A familiar instinct reared up. She couldn't get too close to him!

"You can't run a bath for me and offer an arm in bed when I'm in a weak moment and expect me to melt into something I'm not," she said.

"I'm not trying to make something work that won't," he replied. "I'm just getting to know you. I have no expectations."

Reese cautiously believed him as her stomach did a light flip with one of his graceful turns. She had no doubt he planned to get to know her, or try, but he had to have some expectations. He wouldn't have come all this way if he didn't. That's what scared her. She didn't fear him. She feared herself. He would use the ammunition of her attraction to him in his favor and she just might wind up shot.

Just then she noticed a young man standing near the entrance. He leaned against the wall, no drink in hand. He seemed out of place in an older crowd. She recognized him.

"I saw him, too," Jamie said with his head next to hers. "Let's go and see what he does."

"I saw him in town," she said. "Outside the coffee shop before Lavinia called." She'd thought he was a tourist.

Chapter 7

Leaving the bingo hall, Jamie kept Reese to his right as they passed the man at the entrance. If he tried anything, which Jamie didn't expect in such a public place, and if he was a suspicious character, Jamie would be able to block Reese from any harm. After exiting the hall, he kept her slightly in front of him on the way to his truck. He'd had to park far down the street.

When he glanced back, he saw the man had followed.

Why would he so brazenly follow them? And stalk Reese? The instinct that a threat lurked rose up in Jamie. He'd often had this feeling working for Aesir and it had saved him many times.

Almost at his truck, he put his hand on Reese's back and stopped with her. Looking back, he saw the man had also stopped and was watching them.

"What's he doing?"

Jamie didn't know. Was he trying to intimidate them or did he have other plans he needed to see completed?

As he searched the street, Jamie didn't see anyone else or any other sign something was amiss.

"Wait here." Jamie started back up the street toward the man.

The stranger didn't seem alarmed that Jamie was about to confront him. But he started walking in the other direction, back toward the grange. The man tossed his cigarette and stuffed his hands into his pockets as he entered the building.

Jamie reached the building several seconds later, checking down the street to make sure Reese hadn't followed. She had, but stayed a few lengths behind.

Inside the grange, he weaved through the crowd, spotting the stranger as he disappeared down a hall. Jamie hurried after him. He went into the men's bathroom. A man washed his hands and another stood at a urinal. He looked under the stalls. No feet.

Back out in the hall, he saw a door at the end and pushed it open. A small area had been enclosed for trash and the gate was partially open. He pushed it wider and jogged out into the alley, looking both ways. A car squealed tires as it turned onto the street, too far away and too dark to see much detail.

Jamie went back into the grange, seeing Reese looking for him. She walked with him toward the exit.

"Did you get anything?"

"No." Why would the man park in the back, watch them all night and follow them to Jamie's truck?

They headed for the truck. The sense of unease remained.

At his truck, he unlocked the doors. Reese reached for the passenger door handle.

The truck.

Jamie stopped her from opening the door. "Hold on." He guided her to stand on someone's front lawn.

"What's wrong?"

"I'm not sure. Something doesn't seem right."

"Yeah, like that man watching us, following us."

The sound of a car turning onto the street captured his attention. It might be the same car. As it neared, he saw that it was. The car stopped, engine rumbling, exhaust clouding the air beneath a single streetlight.

Jamie pushed Reese back farther onto the grass just as an explosion cracked and boomed. Pressure from the detonation threw him against Reese and they fell to the lawn. Debris and glass rained down on them. Jamie protected her with his body, covering her head with his arms as best he could.

When the shower eased, he rolled off her and stared at his truck with an incredulous curse. That man had put a bomb on his truck, one with a remote control. He'd followed to detonate the bomb—when they got inside.

He'd tried to kill them both.

The car had sped away as soon as the bomb had gone off. The car was nowhere in sight.

He faced Reese, who sat propped up on her elbows. "Are you all right?"

"Yes. I might have a bruise or two, but I'm fine." She looked up at him. "How did you know that was going to happen?"

"I didn't. I got used to paying attention to a sixth sense while I worked for Aesir."

"And it told you something bad was going to happen now?"

"Yes." He stood and offered his hand. She took it and he helped her to her feet.

He put his arm around her, needing her close. To his satisfaction, she didn't try to move away.

The front door of the house opened and a woman rushed out. "Oh, my Lord! Are you all right?"

"Yes. We're fine."

"I called 911."

A man from the neighboring house emerged and people from the grange began to pour outside.

Sirens approached and an older Jeep Grand Cherokee with Ute County Sheriff printed on the sides sped toward them.

The night just got longer. And he had lost his vehicle.

"Well, so much for driving back to Wyoming."

"As if you would have."

He looked down at her standing flush to his side and a warmth that was becoming more and more familiar began to chase away the adrenaline. But the gathering crowd and sheriff's vehicle coming to a stop had to take priority for the time being.

After the sheriff had driven them to Reese's house late that night, Reese saw the window had been broken again.

"He's not short on persistence, is he?" she quipped.

"I'd tell you to wait here, but…" He looked down at her hands, where she'd already drawn her gun, the holster hidden by the hem of her sweater.

"Are you one of those men who prefer his woman at home?"

"Only when I'm there." His crooked grin and witty response had her fighting a smile.

She'd baited him with control questions before and he always came back with something like what he'd just said. He tickled her cerebrally. His objective was to keep her safe. He didn't mind she had expertise in law enforcement.

She approached the front door cautiously, gun raised. The sheriff had already driven away.

Jamie entered first, having taken his own gun from the back of his pants. Reese covered his back, checking the stairs before they moved to the great room. He checked her bedroom. Unlike the first time, nothing had been disturbed on the lower level.

"Clear." He climbed the stairs before she did. The carpenters had started the loft and hallway.

Jamie lowered his gun as he entered the office. Nothing had been disturbed in here, either, but the closet door was open.

This was bizarre. Had the man who'd tried to kill them broken in yet again and tried to take the money? He wouldn't have known they'd found the trunk. But he'd seen the closet. He knew they'd found it now. She put her gun away.

"There's wood in the garage to cover the front window," she said.

"I'll take care of that. You go get comfortable."

Reese had to admit, more than her attraction to Jamie made her glad he stayed with her. That explosion and now another break-in had her rattled. The two had to be related, and if so, Ella's killer had to be at work. Did he really think killing them would stop the investigation? And if he really wanted the money, he wouldn't get it with both of them dead. Of course, he hadn't anticipated they'd find it in the hidden closet. He should have at least considered the possibility she'd notice the torn wallpaper. Maybe he thought he had time.

She went into her bedroom and changed into a long, soft nightgown, wondering if she should be concerned that she wasn't afraid with Jamie. After washing her face and brushing her teeth, she left her room and went to the kitchen to start some water for tea. Jamie's hammering stopped and he appeared in the great room. No one would have guessed that he'd just come from an explosion and tackled her on the ground. His jeans looked fresh and clean and fit him perfectly, and his gray Henley was free of dirt or soot. She wanted to run her hands over his short black hair, which never had to be combed.

He bent for his laptop case and removed the machine. Sitting at her kitchen island, he booted it up.

The teakettle began to whistle. She took out a cup and held it up in question as he looked at her.

"Sure."

She grabbed another cup out and put bags of a relaxing tea blend in each. After pouring hot water into them, she set his in front of him, amazed at how domestic and natural this felt.

"What are you doing?" she asked.

"Kadin sent me access to some criminal databases. Checking for similar cases to Ella's."

That seemed like a daunting task. Like looking for an earring stud in a swimming pool.

"That man was so young," she said. "How can he be involved in her murder?" He couldn't have, but how was he involved?

"He might know the killer. Or the killer could have hired someone," Jamie said.

An older man wouldn't be in as good shape as he'd been when Ella was killed. "It still seems odd that he'd go to such extremes after all this time. I only just started looking into the case. I couldn't have posed much of a threat. Not yet, anyway." She sipped her tea.

Jamie leaned back with his cup and looked at her, pausing in his work. "Money can bring out the worst in people. He probably didn't know where to look until you found the money under the floorboards. You finished the lower level so he must have assumed if there was any more you'd have found it."

"But he must have known how much was here."

"Yes. That, for sure."

She held the teacup between both hands. "And Ella must have convinced him she didn't have it, or lied about where she hid it before he killed her."

"I agree." He put his cup down and leaned forward, sliding the laptop aside as he took a much closer interest in her. "You'd make a good detective."

Was he making an innuendo that she'd make a good detective working for Kadin? His way of luring her to move to Wyoming? His sureness about her was unnerving. "There isn't much need for that sort of thing in Never Summer. For the most part, people behave."

"Just the occasional Lavinia call?"

"Yes, or teenagers stealing candy from the market."

"And a forty-year-old murder."

"Yes." That definitely mixed things up. Broke the monotony.

She could see why others before her hadn't been able to solve the Neville case. Aside from the lack of evidence, they didn't have the resources or experience bigger cities could afford.

The person who'd killed Ella had gotten away with murder for four decades. He'd lived his life, a full life. Even if he died today, he would have had the luxury of living for all this time. He'd stolen that from Ella. Against everything she aspired to in her life, some sicko had snuffed her out, taken every chance she had to do and see all she dreamed. Ella had found love with Jeffrey. Everything Reese had heard about their relationship had the markings of the real deal. At least she'd had that before her life had been cut so short.

"Hey." Jamie put his hand on hers.

She returned to the present. "Sorry. Drifting."

He moved his hand up her arm, tickling her skin along the way. At her shoulder, he curled his fingers and brushed them along her jawline. "Why don't you stop being a detective for tonight?"

The beginning of resistance faded with the fresh wave of desire he initiated. He ran his thumb over her lower lip. The passion felt different than their first night. Less impulsive. In fact, he didn't seem to act on any impulse now. And since she hadn't anticipated him touching her this way, neither did she. No, this felt deliberate. Like a thought-out choice.

While part of her warned her choice should be to stop, the more sensual one wasn't listening.

He slid his hand behind her head and coaxed her forward. As she leaned toward him, he stood and closed the distance. Maybe it was the long day. Maybe it was the explosion. She might be overtired and susceptible. But she wanted this. Him.

He kissed her firmly and moved his mouth over hers.

When he broke away, she asked, "Are you doing this on purpose?"

"Yes. And no." He kissed her again, caressing as before.

He intended to woo her, to seduce her into a steamy relationship with him. She wouldn't think about that now, not when he strummed such magic with his mouth.

Putting her hands on his shoulders, she pulled herself up onto the counter, glad he took the hint and hooked an arm under hers and helped her. With an effortless, smooth lift, he had her hips on the counter. She swung her legs to his side, parting them on each side of him. His height put his head just slightly lower than hers. She ran her fingers over his short hair, sliding her other hand over his right chest muscle. He put his hands on each cheek of her rear, pulling her to the edge of the counter.

Now the heat really simmered.

She kissed him, angling her head and loving that she was a little higher than him and that he let her have control.

He reached up with one hand and slid the tie from her blond hair, releasing the thick waves to tumble down over her shoulders. With his fingers gripping strands, he intensified the kiss. She gave in, kissing him back with more. She lost her breath. Only he existed.

Her nightgown buttoned up in the front, the neckline scooping in a modest curve above her breast. He turned the functional garment into something sexy when he began to unbutton the top buttons. The touch of his fingers aroused her, brushing lightly, parting material as he progressed. He exposed her breasts and admired them while he finished unbuttoning the nightgown to her waist. The sleeves fell off her shoulders and she sat in the pooled material, a flower blossoming for the sun, and in this case, that sun was Jamie. He heated her with the light of his passion.

At last he stopped torturing her with just his eyes, feasting on the sight of her. He didn't have to bend his head much to put his mouth on her. His tongue caressed. Fiery sensations had her closing her eyes to ecstasy. And then she had to have him as exposed. She took his shirt and pulled the hem up. He moved back to finish lifting it over his head and drop it to the floor.

Lost to the allure of his bare chest, Reese reveled in the feel of her hands on him, running over smooth skin with hard muscle underneath. Their kissing increased in urgency.

Cradling her rear, he lifted her off the counter and carried her across the great room. In her bedroom, he laid her down on the bed and crawled on top of her, kissing her the whole time. Reese couldn't believe how amazing he felt, how she felt with him. The magnitude of their chemistry faded to the background as he removed the rest of her nightgown.

* * *

Knocking woke Jamie the next morning. Reese began to rouse, one lovely leg bent and sticking out from the covers, arms above her head and covers over her breasts. He couldn't stop an affectionate smile as her honey-colored eyes opened drowsily.

"Someone is at the door." He flung off the covers and stood, putting on his jeans.

"What time is it?"

He checked the clock on the nightstand beside the bed. "After ten."

"Crap!" She threw the covers off her. "I have to work today."

"No, you don't. Sheriff said you should take the day off, with everything going on. Sorry. I meant to tell you last night." But things had gone a different way.

He left the room with her looking at him in mock accusation.

He made it to the door and opened it, seeing Kadin walking away. Kadin stopped with the sound of the opening door and turned. After pausing while he took in Jamie's form, apparently recovering from the significance of him staying with Reese, he walked back.

"Jamie. I tried calling."

"Sorry. We had a late night and I didn't hear my phone ring." He stepped aside to let the man in.

As Kadin entered, Reese appeared in the hall in her bathrobe. She sort of froze there, silhouetted by light streaming in from the great room, rumpled hair and all.

Kadin looked from Jamie to Reese and back at Jamie, clearly questioning. But he walked into the house, down the hall toward Reese, and removed his hat.

"Sheriff said you've had some excitement." Kadin stopped before Reese and looked into her bedroom. Not all of the bed could be seen from there, but enough could. He pinned a look on Jamie.

"I had her consent."

"What brings you by?" Reese walked rather briskly to the kitchen, going behind the kitchen island.

Uh-oh. She didn't welcome Kadin here. That wild spirit of hers kicked back against an imagined fence closing in.

"The test results from the Neville case are in. The clothes?" Kadin walked through the great room.

Reese stopped her reach for the coffeepot.

"They found a well-preserved hair follicle." Kadin put his hand on the back of one of the island counter chairs, opposite Reese.

Stunned by that good and unexpected news, Jamie stood beside him. "The clothes were stored correctly." Incredible. After all this time…

"Yes. We got lucky, I'd say." To Reese, Kadin said, "You got lucky. It takes the right humidity to preserve this kind of evidence, among other things."

It was her case.

"Did you run DNA?" Reese asked, excitement in her tone.

"Yes. And ran it through CODIS. Unfortunately, there was no match."

Reese visibly drooped with that news.

"Did Jeffrey ever give a DNA sample?" Kadin asked.

More disappointment came through in Reese's slow blink. "No."

There was no DNA testing in the seventies, and no

one had thought to get a sample from Jeffrey when they'd begun to be used. Everyone had assumed he was innocent.

"Is there a body to exhume?" Jamie asked. "Was he cremated?"

That lightened Reese's demeanor. "He was buried. I'll get the process going."

No DNA match put them at a distinct disadvantage. And the follicle alone may not be enough to convict someone of the crime. The hair may be from Jeffrey and could have gotten on Ella's clothes just by her living with him.

"The test came up with something else," Kadin said, holding his hat and giving it a tap against his hand. "Something pretty significant."

Jamie waited a tense second along with Reese.

"Another fiber was found on the victim's dress and it contains a small trace of blood that doesn't belong to the victim."

That, indeed, represented a huge break in the case. The ability to analyze a microscopic stain didn't become possible until around 2000, and the last time Ella's case had been revisited had been before that.

"Is it the killer's?" Reese asked. "She must have fought him."

Kadin nodded. "During the struggle, she may have injured him somehow, probably not much, or you'd see more evidence, more blood. The location of the fiber indicates she could have hit his nose and caused it to bleed. It was found on the shoulder of her dress."

"A drop of blood landed somewhere on the killer

and then a stained fiber transferred to her clothes," Reese said.

"Yes. She was strangled, so it's possible she hit him with the back of her hand. The killer's nose bled. A drop landed on his clothes. The victim's violent struggle for life dislodged the fiber. Two other fibers found match the stained fiber.

"We're going to have to find the killer to match DNA," Kadin said.

"We?" Reese said, and then seemed to catch herself being rude. "I mean…I mean…I didn't expect you to work this extensively on the case."

"I'll help as much as I can. You're my daughter, after all. Long lost or not." He wasn't going to back down. He must have picked up on Reese's weak comment that might be construed as leading him not to help her. Halfhearted, though. They could use Kadin's expertise.

Jamie watched Reese register Kadin's unyielding tone. He spoke calmly, but also asserted his position as her father.

Seeing her internal struggle to maintain control and independence, Jamie decided to spare her further torment and redirect. "If the DNA belongs to the killer, it says something about the nature of the crime if he's never been arrested for anything else."

Kadin turned to him. "It sure does." He tapped his hat against his hand again.

"Like what? He isn't a typical killer?" Reese said.

"He could have been an ordinary guy up until something drove him to kill Ella Neville," Jamie said.

"Or had never been caught," Reese said. "He could be a serial killer and meticulous at avoiding detection."

"Exactly," Kadin said, pride for his daughter showing. "Given the money involved, I lean more toward ordinary guy driven to kill over greed."

"And resentment," Reese said. "He hated her for leaving him, marrying Jeffrey. Maybe that's why he killed her before he got the money. Speaking of money." Reese looked at Jamie, silently asking him if he'd told Kadin yet.

"We found more," Jamie said to Kadin, then explained all about the other items. He led them upstairs and Reese opened a desk drawer to hand Kadin a photo of the man.

Kadin studied it for a while. "Too bad photos can't provide DNA. Peculiar that Ella would have kept these."

"And hidden them with the money," Reese said.

"She obviously hid the photos from Jeffrey."

"She must have still loved this man," Jamie said. "Couldn't quite let go."

Reese folded her arms, rubbing as though chilled in her robe. "She left him for a reason. If she stole the money that explains why she never told anyone here in Never Summer about him."

"There's nothing in her file about an ex-boyfriend," Kadin said.

"Maybe he wasn't her boyfriend," Reese said. "We'll show the photo around town—on the off chance anyone remembers seeing him."

"Good." Kadin tucked the photo into a pocket on the inside of his jacket with his free hand. "I'll let you both get ready for the day, then. Why don't you both come over for dinner tonight? Penny and I rented a cabin just outside of town."

"Oh, you don't have to go to that trouble. We don't want to interfere with your vacation."

Kadin glanced at Jamie, figuring out he'd already told Reese. He didn't seem to mind. And Jamie thought Reese's attempt to avoid facing her biological father was lame and obvious.

"I insist."

Apparently, Kadin had seen through Reese's evasion tactics, as well.

"You're the reason I came here, Reese," Kadin said when Reese didn't respond. "You and your case."

He cleverly disguised that Reese had been his only reason for coming here. The case was an excuse. He could have helped her from Wyoming. He didn't have to be here to do that. But Jamie kept his thoughts to himself as he followed the man downstairs to the front door. There, he pointed to the boarded-up window.

"If you weren't here, I'd also insist she stay with me."

"Now wait a minute." Reese folded her arms again. "I haven't needed you before now, what makes you think I need you now?"

"It's not only about what you need, my dear." Kadin put his hat on and met Reese's defiance head-on.

She didn't challenge him further.

"Six o'clock. The Pinecliff cabins. We're in number four."

When Kadin left and Jamie shut the door, he faced

Reese and her threatened control and individualism. "I couldn't say no to him, either."

Her beautiful eyes shifted from the closed door to him. Then she raised her brow with a little cock of her head.

"Neither could Brycen Cage," he said.

"I'm not one of his detectives."

"No, you're worse. You're his daughter." He put his hand on her back and guided her toward the bedroom. They weren't finished in there.

"That's not funny."

She didn't resist his guidance. "He's dealing with his own difficulty in this, Reese. He lost his young daughter. How do you think he feels about learning he's had another all this time and never knew?"

In her bedroom, she seemed to face him with growing uncertainty. Her resolve had lost its verve as a result of his reasoning. She had to have sympathy for a man who suffered as much as Kadin had.

"His losses are what made him a great man. Why not get to know him a little? No harm in that. He won't force you to live with him." He unfastened his belt.

While his talking calmed her, she also noticed what he was doing. Good. Time to get her mind off pushing family away. He removed his jeans and stood naked before her.

"Jamie?" She took a step back, but he saw the flare of her eyes and how her mouth stayed parted to allow freer airflow.

"Shower. Let's go."

"I'm not taking a shower with you."

He stepped close to her. "No?" Before she could

dodge him, he pressed a soft, warm kiss to her parted mouth. Hearing her sharply indrawn breath, he kissed her again.

"Jamie." His name came out on a whisper.

He untied her robe and pushed it off her shoulders. It slid to the floor and she was as naked as him.

Chapter 8

Reese got out of Jamie's new rental truck and walked with him toward the cabin, a bundle of nerves—and not just over spending time with her biological father. She'd thought all the way here and had to ease her mind somehow. She couldn't make it through this evening with two people vying for a close and personal place in her life. That level of commitment loomed over her, ensnared her with potential obligations she wasn't sure she could meet. At the door, Jamie reached for the bell and she stopped him with her hand.

"I need to talk to you."

He surveyed her face as though reading her angst. "Now?"

She nodded. "I need to clear the air before—before I go in there a-a-and spend time with...my father." Realizing she was talking with her hands and Jamie saw it, she said, "We have to stop. You and me. Have to...stop."

Gradually his expression went from absorbing her restlessness to complete understanding, almost smug understanding.

"I'm not asking you to settle down with me in a long-term relationship, Reese. We're just testing the waters. Hot spring waters, but waters nonetheless."

"Stop making light of this. You made me make love with you. *Twice!* In less than twenty-four hours!"

"*I* made you?" His eyebrows rose slightly. "You climbed onto the kitchen counter."

She couldn't tell if he was teasing. "You kissed me to get me into the shower."

"Yes, and you didn't stop me."

She couldn't and that's what troubled her. "Please, Jamie."

With her sincere tone and genuine plea, he blinked and then relented. "All right. Calm down. Don't work yourself up into a frenzy. I'll wait for you to make the next move."

That should have comforted her. Instead, she wasn't any more relaxed than before. She could talk herself into making the next move. Isn't that what happened when she climbed onto the kitchen counter?

"Hey." He put his hands on her upper arms. "We'll slow it down."

That statement relaxed her as much as anything. But his care for her only melted her more.

Lowering his hands, he held his finger over the doorbell with a silent questioning look at her, seeming to ask if she was ready. She nodded. He rang the bell.

A vibrant, smiling face with sea-green eyes and

wavy auburn hair opened the door. "Hi. You must be Reese." The tall woman gave her a delighted once-over. "You're so beautiful!" She stepped aside to allow them to enter.

Reese led Jamie in and she may as well have been standing on thin ice. Any moment the ground would collapse underneath her feet.

"Jamie Knox." Jamie held out his hand.

"Penny Tandy."

The cabin was a decent size, with an open and rustic kitchen and living room. A gold-colored couch and a wood-and-metal coffee table faced a massive moss rock fireplace flanked by two gold leather high-back chairs. Two tall stools served as side tables to the chairs.

Kadin appeared from the stairs running down from a loft, more moss rock making up the wall underneath the staircase and wood railing.

"It smells good," Reese said. Would she talk about the weather next?

"The sheriff said you liked the chicken enchiladas at Marissa's. I attempted to emulate the recipe." Penny leaned toward her with her hand to the side of her mouth as though sharing a secret. "Don't be too hard on me if I missed the mark."

Reese was too taken aback to acknowledge the lighthearted banter. "You called him?"

"Kadin did." She turned to her husband and Reese saw her eyes go soft with adoration.

"I hope you don't mind." He indicated for them to go into the living room.

Reese took one of the chairs by the fireplace. No

one could sit next to her that way. Jamie eyed her in a way that said he was on to her and took the other chair.

"Something to drink?" Kadin offered.

"Just water," Reese said.

"I made iced tea," Penny said.

Did the sheriff tell Kadin that, too? "Tea would be wonderful."

"Same for me," Jamie said.

Kadin went to get the glasses and pitcher, already iced and on a tray. He set everything down on the big rectangular coffee table and sat beside his wife on the couch.

"The background came back on Ella today. The police report said Ella had no family. That's what Jeffrey told them, and it matches the background report. At first glance everything looks ordinary, but I ran her name in some different databases and her name came up as a deceased woman from San Diego, California."

Reese sat at the edge of her seat. Was he about to say Ella had assumed another person's identity?

"I checked into it some more. Her social security number is the same as the deceased woman, but the photographs don't match."

"She did assume a false identity."

"Who is Ella?" Jamie asked.

"That may not be easy to find out. We know nothing about her except what we know about her life in Never Summer."

"This explains why she hid those photos," Reese said, thinking back on what they might reveal.

"She had a secret past," Jamie added.

"One of the photos showed her with a man outside a restaurant called Charlie's," Reese said.

Penny got up and went to a computer case on the floor beside the couch. She removed a laptop and handed it to Kadin. He thanked her with another one of those intimate looks and then booted up the machine. Moments later he finished searching the internet and turned the screen to show the results of the images he'd found.

Reese moved closer, crouching before the screen and scrolling through several pictures. There were a lot of retail places called Charlie's. But she came to one that made her stop short. It was the same sign she'd seen in the photo. She remembered the front window, with its white trim and the small fenced-in patio.

"This is it."

Kadin leaned to see where she pointed then turned the laptop to face him. "It's in San Diego."

Ella was likely from San Diego, then. She'd stolen the identity of a woman also from San Diego. Had she kept those photos to tie the killer to her?

"I'll get searching for a woman who was either reported missing or wanted for a crime," Kadin said.

Ella had a reason to flee her hometown. Had she stolen the money?

"Which means he'll make flight reservations for tomorrow," Penny said. "And I'll have to wait here for him." She didn't seem happy about that but complained without acrimony. She supported his decision because she loved him.

Reese didn't think she'd ever met a couple like this before, where their love was so obvious.

"How did you meet Kadin?" The question tumbled from her before she had a chance to think first. She just had to know.

Penny glanced at Kadin with a smile. "That's a long story."

He put his arm over the back of the sofa as Penny leaned against him with her hand on his chest.

"She came to me with a case," Kadin said.

Penny sobered. "If it weren't for Kadin, a serial killer of young girls would have continued his demented ways."

"Penny never takes enough credit for her part. She's the one who came to me with her suspicions."

"We did work together. In the process, he showed me how wrong I was about my view of family compared to my career."

"And she taught me how to believe in love again. She changed my life."

"Not that much. We got lucky when we found each other." Penny looked at Reese and then Jamie.

"I felt the same way when I met Reese," Jamie said. "Finding love isn't so rare. It's having the ability to recognize it when it's presented to you." He looked at Reese pointedly.

Dang, he sure wasn't afraid to say it the way he saw it. Reese, uncomfortable and out of sorts, averted her gaze. He intensified the uneasiness that hadn't left her since they arrived.

A baby began to cry, a soft, sweet sound that carried from a back bedroom.

"That's what really brought us together," Kadin said, starting to rise.

"I'll go." Penny stood. Then she turned to Reese. "Would you like to meet your half brother?"

"Oh." Flustered, Reese sat stiffer. She hadn't anticipated this. She had known Kadin had a son, but she hadn't thought of the infant in terms of family.

"It's okay, Reese," Jamie said. "Go and meet him."

His encouragement oddly soothed her frayed nerves. Why was she so fish-out-of-water with this?

"If you're not comfortable…" Penny hedged. But her hope that Reese would join her was clear.

Kadin remained silent, although he studied Reese without giving away what he was thinking. If he had the same hope as his wife, Reese couldn't see it. But he likely possessed practiced stoicism when necessary. Criminals would never know what really went on in his mind as they were being questioned.

Reese got up from the chair and Penny smiled before leading her down the hall to the first bedroom. A portable crib had been set up in the bedroom, the queen-size bed undisturbed next to it.

Reese stepped slowly forward, both dread and amplified curiosity coursing through her. Bending over the crib, Penny lifted up the crying baby and brought him to her.

"What's the matter, my brave little one," Penny cooed, taking the baby to the changing table next to a small dresser.

The baby made soft mewling sounds in the arms of his mother, and then started up a new wail when she put him down and began to change him.

Fascination kept Reese riveted. She spent most of the time it took to change him staring at his face. She'd seen lots of babies and held a few of them, but all had been distant from her. Her family had been small growing up. Her parents didn't have a large extended family. She didn't know her cousins. Her aunt and uncle—her adoptive father's brother—lived in Texas and rarely visited. Her grandparents were getting up in age. She visited them every so often and they were together on holidays, but she had never felt a close bond with them. In a way, she thought they might have withheld the full extent of their love. Not intentionally. They just hadn't expressed themselves deeply.

The baby's crying stopped and he stared up at his mother.

"There we go." Penny lifted the child and kissed his pudgy cheek. She held the baby in front of her face, love melting in her eyes and curve of her mouth. The boy's mouth expanded into a joyously innocent, bunny smile, toothless except for the two front uppers and lowers. "There's someone I want you to meet." Adjusting the baby in her arms, she brought the boy over to Reese. "Reese, meet Clayton Tandy. Clayton, meet your half sister, Reese."

Clayton looked up at Reese, the exuberant smile fading, changing to a look of rapt fascination. The way babies registered their environment and the people in them amazed Reese, the mystery of it. What went on inside the new minds of infants?

"Hi, Clayton." Reese put her pinkie in the tiny child's hand. Clayton curled his small fingers around her in a surprisingly tight grip for one so young.

A sound of delight burst out of Clayton and he batted his hands and feet, then stretched as though wanting to be free of the confines of his mother's arms and fly into Reese's, giving Penny the challenge of hanging on to such a wiggle worm. Reese's adoptive mother said she had done that when she was a baby. She could never stay still for long.

"Kadin's mother said he did that when he was a baby," Penny said. "Always in a fight to defy gravity. She used to call him superbaby."

"My mother didn't call me that, but I was the same way."

Penny shot a startled glance her way. "Really? How funny. It runs in the family." She laughed softly and lightly, capturing the attention of her son again.

Clayton went still in trancelike wonder over the sight of his mother, his tiny brain processing every sound she made.

"Would you like to hold him?" Penny handed her the baby.

"Oh, I…"

Penny placed Clayton in her arms.

The warm, small bundle captivated Reese in an instant. Clayton stared up at the new face, focused and gathering information.

"He's taken to you quickly," Penny said. "I've never seen that. Usually he fusses when he's first out of my arms."

Reese couldn't attribute that to kinship, but holding this baby did feel different than others. The baby must be able to pick up on senses like that.

Clayton began making sounds as though trying to mimic talk. He said something that sounded like *Dada*.

Penny laughed. "His first word. Kadin was holding him when he said it. We cried for an hour, it was so touching. Don't ever tell Kadin I told you. This little baby can take him down with a word."

"I heard you."

Laughing, Reese saw Kadin and Jamie standing in

the doorway. Then she looked down at the baby again. "You must be in awe every day."

Kadin walked into the room. "Life couldn't be any better than it is right now."

"If he's as protective of Clayton when he grows up, the poor kid will have trouble making his own way," Penny said.

Reese handed him Clayton, who burst into another show of pure delight. "That's what we argue about now." He kissed Clayton's nose, speaking in baby talk that didn't match such a big and powerful man. "When we first met it was a battle over losing our hearts to each other." Kadin looked down at his son again, a look filled with the miracle and object of infinite and incomprehensible love. "If we would have only known."

The baby had most assuredly changed this man's life. Reese had a sneaking feeling that he was about to do the same to hers. She looked over at Jamie, who'd stepped into the room with them. And him, too.

"Come on, Jamie. Help me get dinner on the table." Penny put her arm on Jamie's and guided him toward the door.

He looked back at Reese with what she could only call glad hope. He was banking on what Kadin would do to her, or specifically, how he'd change her way of thinking.

But Reese didn't see it like that. She had clear goals. She had a plan for her immediate future. She wasn't ready to settle down. Jamie needed to believe her. She didn't want to go through another messy breakup. But she would break it off with him if she felt their relationship was taking her down a path she hadn't planned ahead.

"You have some of his features," Kadin said.

Reese looked down and had to agree the shape of his nose and mouth might resemble hers, but on such a young one it was hard to tell.

"What was your daughter like?" she asked, before thinking.

The question stunned him. She caught the brief cessation of joy in looking at his son, replaced by a haunting memory.

But he recovered and said, "Energetic. Strong. She had her mother's eyes and hair, but she had my build and adventurous spirit."

"She was muscular?"

He grunted a laugh. Clayton reached up to put his hand on Kadin's chest, unable to touch his face, which apparently had been his intent. "Not like a boy. She had long limbs and her arms weren't weak like some girls. Not to be insulting. If she'd have grown to be an adult, she might have cursed me for her muscles, but she'd have been beautiful."

"I've always had broad shoulders." She had great muscle tone. "No bony arms on me."

"Do you curse me?"

"No. It helps in my profession." That triggered a memory. "There was this girl in grade school that other kids picked on. She wore glasses and had thick red hair and freckles. She wasn't attractive. Her teeth were crooked and she had a big nose. One day some boys were giving her a hard time. She was trying to get on her bike to go home after school but they weren't letting her. They called her names, pulled her ponytail and tossed her glasses from one to the other.

"I was sick of watching them torment her. So I went

over there and yelled at the boy holding her glasses and calling her Raggedy Ann. I told him to give the glasses back or I'd give him a bloody nose." She smiled with what came next. "All four of them stared at me. But the boy with the glasses didn't do what I wanted, so I let my bike drop and marched over there and slugged him good. He fell to the ground and dropped the girl's glasses. I faced off the other three." She put her hands on her hips and moved her feet wider apart. "I stood like this and asked them if they wanted a piece of me. The girl picked up her glasses and pedaled fast down the street. One of the three boys said he didn't hit girls and the boy I slugged stood up and said neither did he. They left and the next day I had a new reputation in school."

"Nobody bullied that girl again, did they?" Kadin slipped his finger in Clayton's hand and the baby curled his fingers.

"Nope. She and I became close friends. I still talk to her to this day."

He looked up from Clayton, whose eyes had begun to droop closed. "I think Annabelle would have turned out the same way. She had a feisty streak in her. Her mother had trouble keeping her in check. I often had to have talks with her. She'd always listen, too. She was my little girl."

Reese wondered if he'd ever spoken of his daughter in such a happy way since her murder. Maybe he had, but she didn't think he had many moments like that, especially not before meeting Penny.

"You do her justice every day you work for your company."

"Annabelle is in a peaceful place now. Everything

I do is in the name of her memory, but if I was completely honest, it's more for me." He watched his son fall asleep in his arms. Lowering the baby into the crib, he tucked him in with the soft blanket and stood there a moment longer. "What made you decide to get into law enforcement?"

Reese couldn't single out one defining reason. "I don't know. I guess it just always interested me. Playing the game Clue. Watching crime stories. The news. Bullies…"

He nodded. "The depraved and heartless hurting the innocent. That always got me, too."

"I wanted to do something about it." She felt passionately about that. And in that moment, she realized that's what kept her from finding a man to marry and having kids.

"Maybe you should think about joining DAI. You'd be surrounded by like-minded people."

At first the suggestion lightened her, a spark of agreement showering. Then she thought of what it would take to make that happen. Leave Never Summer. Abandon her dream of becoming sheriff…

Two days later, Reese still felt melancholic after that evening with Kadin. He seemed less of a detective to her and more of a father. She would be more comfortable thinking of him only as a detective. She didn't even notice Jamie follow her into her room, preparing for bed as though they'd done it every night for years. He'd been her rock that night and had given her the space she needed to think over everything. She couldn't help feeling grateful. More. He made himself important to her. He meant something.

Before she could analyze the situation too much, he stripped to his underwear and crawled into bed, turning on the TV with the remote.

"You're making yourself awfully comfortable." Every night he did that.

"Come to bed, Reese."

He dismissed her complaint. She was too tired to argue. With her back to him, she undressed to her underwear and reached for her nightgown. Donning that, she went to her side of the bed, lying stiff and clutching the covers to her chin, hyperaware of him next to her, just a foot or so from her skin. His hard body. She wanted to feel his weight on her again. The longer she spent with him not touching, the more she craved him.

Would she create a problem for herself if she viewed this as a hot, sexual fling? Isn't that what she'd had with him in Wyoming?

She listened to him put down the remote as he seemed to content himself with watching TV.

She turned her head.

He turned his.

She saw the leashed passion in his eyes. She felt the same. He kept his word, though. He didn't move.

His hand rested on his stomach, a hard flat stomach. The covers came to just above his groin.

She burned for him. Lying in the same bed, looking at him. It was too much. She should have made him sleep on the couch. Why hadn't she? This was why. Melting for him. Itching to touch him and never stop falling into his eyes. He remained still.

She began by rolling onto her side with her head on her hand. Still, he didn't move. She smiled, unable to stop.

"Are you going to tease me now?" he asked.

She reached over and put her finger over his lips. "Shh." Right now she just wanted to look at him.

"Reese…?"

Realizing it wasn't fair to let him think she was teasing, she withdrew her finger. "Be quiet. You're going to ruin this if you keep talking. I'm not teasing. Just let me look at you."

His eyes took on a darker, smoldering heat, which only served to tempt her further. He swept her back into a soft float, sailing on this mysterious enticement. He wore no shirt and his hand rested on his rippling abdomen. She took her time taking him in, drinking the sight of him, letting the sensations build.

At last, she couldn't endure any more. She felt flushed and breathless by the time she reached over again and this time pushed the covers down, past his groin. Rewarded with the confirmation she'd see what she hoped she would, she put her hand over his erection beneath his underwear. His stomach rose and fell faster.

He moved his hands, folding them behind his head, causing his stomach muscles to contract and give her a jolt of desire.

She moved closer to him and had to put her mouth there, on the hard muscles. She kissed him. He tasted salty and smelled of spicy bath soap. She'd never experienced anything like this before. The men she'd dated hadn't fascinated her this much, or interested her to this degree.

She crawled on top of him, seeing him close his eyes to restrained passion. She loved that he let her do this. She enjoyed the feel and taste and texture of him, his ribs, his chest, one nipple, then the other. His pulse ticked through the veins in his neck and she pressed her lips to the evidence of his desire. Up his jawline to his chin and, finally, her destination. She arrived at his mouth, smelling his sweet breath just before he put his hand on the back of her head and kissed her. His other hand came down from behind his head to lift the hem of her nightgown. She rose up to get it off, on her knees to give him room to remove his underwear. Going back down on him, she felt his erection through her underwear and everywhere else her body came in contact with him. Meeting his gaze, she savored the sensation the connection caused before kissing him. The slow, soft, reverent movements of their mouths joining as one sent currents of electric desire through her. She quaked with need. She didn't care about consequences. She only cared about this. Him. How he made her feel. How *this* made her feel.

He seemed to be caught under the same potent spell. When they paused in the kiss and once again connected deeply with their eyes, he moved to put her on her back and then took over the position on top. He'd restrained all he could, she realized, as he pushed her legs wider and probed for her. Guiding himself, he slowly entered her. The magical sensations erupted and she knew she would not take long. He would bring her to orgasm faster than any man had before him. She tipped her head back into the mattress, consumed by unbearable pleasure, and cried out as he began to thrust harder.

When he collapsed on her and caught his breath along with her, long moments passed. She needed time to return to reality, too. Like her, he hadn't seemed to have planned to make love this way, with such gripping emotion and need. He might use their chemistry in his favor, but he was just as susceptible to the backlash. Knowing he was as vulnerable as her kept her from being frightened.

He lifted his head and looked down at her, confirming what she suspected. In his eyes she saw uncertainty, a rarity in a man like him. He pursued her and made no attempt to hide that from her. He charged forward with all he held in importance. Right now she was the most important thing to him. But he couldn't control his feelings for her, and having these intense relations with her came with risk. Would he ease up on her out of concern for the security of his heart? And did she really want him to?

Chapter 9

The next day, Jamie sat with Reese at a round table crammed in the small space of the Never Summer Hotel office, going through boxes of old guest records. Three desks lined the walls, surrounding the table and piled with binders. They'd checked the bed-and-breakfasts and motel in town—two had gone out of business and the motel hadn't kept records. A lodge and a cabin-rental resort had produced two possible names. They'd already shown the photo of Ella's mystery man around town and no one recognized him. Too much time had gone by. If the man had come to town or passed through, no one remembered seeing him.

Putting one binder aside, Jamie stood up to retrieve the next from a desk, bringing it back to the table but not sitting again. At the time of the murder the hotel had no computers. All the records were stored in binders. As luck would have it, the hotel hadn't purged any. The manager told them the records had been all but forgotten until they'd shown up.

He noticed Reese having a hard time concentrating again, as she read the list of entries in one of the binders and then lifted her head to stare off. Did her mind wander back to her conversation with Kadin? Had the things they'd said as father and daughter changed the way she thought of him? Or did her distraction come from Jamie? He'd avoided thinking too much about last night. She'd initiated the lovemaking and hadn't withdrawn afterward, but was she now? The closer they grew together, the more she might feel caught. While he secretly cheered that she hadn't been able to resist him, had come to him by choice and met him with equal fervor that had all the indications of budding love, he had to remain cautious. Reese's fiercely guarded independence would have its say eventually. There would come a time when she would no longer be able to deny what this was and where it would lead if they continued. When that occurred, she'd either decide to run from it, or his efforts would come to fruition.

"You and Kadin seemed to have a nice talk," he said.

Jarred from thought, she turned to him. "Yeah." She looked down at the binder.

"Are you okay with that?"

"Of course." Then she seemed to think again. "I think so." She put her fingers to her upper chest. "I've got this feeling, not bad, but I actually imagined more than once what it would be like to work with him in Wyoming."

"Sounds nothing but good to me." He didn't think she told him all she thought.

She looked up at him again, eyes guarded. "It gives me anxiety."

"Did last night give you anxiety?"

Her eyes lowered. "Not last night."

But today she'd had a different reaction. He didn't say he'd back off or promise to let her take the initiative in starting when the next opportunity came to make love. If the next time was anywhere close to as powerful as last night, it would work in his favor. He didn't press her for more on how she felt about them as a couple. No, with her, a man had to hold fast to his strategy and never falter in the face of possible failure.

He retrieved another guest book. "Here's another one dated the month of Ella's murder."

Abandoning her binder, she stood and moved closer to Jamie at the round table.

He flipped through to the end. "Looks like it spans almost four weeks. Last few pages are blank. Somebody must have tried to get organized and keep books by month."

Reese leaned over the table and slid the pen and paper toward herself. "I'll add the names to our list."

A few minutes later, she folded the paper and handed it to Jamie, facing him fully. He folded it some more and tucked it into his back pocket. He smiled ever so slightly when their fingers touched in the transfer, seeing how she responded with a similar one. He loved her involuntary reactions.

Now, in the quiet hotel office, with a calm ebb and flow of guests checking in or crossing the lobby in the distant background, she continued to stare at him.

"Were you always such a nice guy?" she asked.

As always with Reese, her questions seemed to tumble out without much thought. Curiosity made her ask, but he could see by her suddenly skittish gaze that she might wish she hadn't. Getting to know him well distressed her, as though she was headed for a dastardly serious relationship. Although at times she appeared stiff and standoffish, he saw through that exterior wall to the softer part of her, the part he doubted she even knew very well.

She should get to know her deepest self better. She was a pretty amazing woman, with all of that untapped capacity for love.

On to her question… He wasn't sure how to answer. He'd never been this open to embarking on a long-term commitment with any woman. And his previous profession made him a hard man. And then there was the potential to scare her off. Remember the strategy…

"No," he finally said. "I used to be a lot like you."

She moved her head back in surprise. "You don't think I'm nice?"

"Nice in this context is between a man and a woman who are extremely attracted to each other," he said. "You don't welcome men into your heart." He paused for emphasis. "You don't want to, anyway." He thought she did welcome him, but her mind kept pushing him away. "I think that's what you mean when you ask if I was always this nice. Am I wrong?"

Her eyes lowered and she rested her hand on the back of a chair. Then she looked into his eyes, head angled, that sultry heat sending messages she probably didn't realize.

"No." She straightened her head. "You didn't pursue women?"

"Only the ones who didn't mind casual. I was always gone, and overseas. I had no plans to settle down."

"And now you do."

He studied her face to see if she dreaded his answer. He couldn't tell. "Yes."

Now she studied him, as though uncertain how she felt about that. "You never did tell me why you quit that security company."

Did she ask to change the subject or was she checking to see if he was, indeed, a viable partner for her? He didn't really want to talk about this, but he suspected he wasn't going to get around telling her this time. And if she was genuinely curious, then hiding it from her might not be in his best interest. If he wanted a real relationship with her, he had to be honest.

"The man who ran Aesir International was a mercenary. I didn't check him out the way I should have. He sent me and my team on some questionable assignments. I saw his men do unethical things and told him I quit. He didn't like that very much. Apparently, he saw something in me he thought would be easy to mold into whatever he wanted, a gun for hire. Thug. In order to force me to keep working for him—and do the things he ordered—he…"

Admitting the next part didn't come easy. "He made it look like I committed some crimes."

"What crimes?"

Would he lose her if he told her? Either way, he had to be truthful.

"He presented me with evidence he manufactured to prove I committed…random murders in Iraq."

Reese all but blanched. He'd shocked her. She hadn't expected a story this dark. He was a security officer for her father who pursued her romantically. She had no concept of the man he had once been, or the man Stankovich had turned him into.

He went on regardless. She had to hear it all.

"It was a real Blackwater news story. Stankovich even produced a witness. What he had on me made me look like a mercenary, a dirty one. Discount soldier in constant conflict. Killer of the innocent." All the bitterness he'd felt back then returned now. "He threatened to turn all of it over to the US government if I left."

"A witness claimed he saw you kill people in Iraq?"

"Another mercenary, one Stankovich handpicked."

"Stankovich? He didn't handpick you?"

"Valdemar Stankovich. Yes, I'm sure he thought he did handpick me. I left the Army honorably, but he must have seen it as rebellion." In some senses, maybe he had rebelled, but not against his country, not against humanity. Just rules.

"He sounds like a gangster."

He smiled. "He might as well have added that to his sleazy résumé."

"How did you clear your name?"

"I had to work for him for a while. He forced me to work with a human trafficker based out of Alaska. I did my best to fake the job while I hacked the trafficker and Stankovich's computers. I broke into their houses. I helped another one of DAI's detectives take down the trafficker and his organization. I destroyed everything Stankovich falsified against me. Without a so-called witness, he couldn't do anything to stop me from leaving."

"Without a witness? What happened to him?"

He hesitated. How would she react to what he'd done? "I killed him."

"You." Her mouth dropped open.

"I had no choice. The man was a ruthless killer. I was blamed for crimes he committed. He got off on raping and killing women. He killed children, too, if they got in the way."

"So you took it upon yourself to execute him?"

"It didn't exactly go that way. I demanded all of the records he had that implicated me. He had sophisticated fingerprint falsification and videos. All things that might be disproved with the right investigation, but I wasn't about to take any chances. He refused to hand over what he had and pulled a gun on me. I was ready for him and shot him first. Wasn't my plan but I was prepared to do what I had to do to preserve my reputation and get away from a bad situation." He may have sounded a little flippant telling her, but the whole ordeal hadn't been easy and had caused him to grow in ways he would have never anticipated had he not experienced it. "Killing him made me realize the Army would have been better for me and I should have stuck with it. It made me realize I had a problem sticking with anything long-term." In particular, women, but he didn't say that out loud. He didn't need to. He saw Reese ascertain his meaning.

She had closed her mouth and now regarded him without expression. He couldn't tell what she thought.

"I'm not a mercenary," he said just in case she still thought of him that way. "I never was."

"Leaving the military lends you something of a rebel character," she said. "You may not be the kind of man who framed you, or who committed all the crimes, but you like adrenaline rushes. I'd have never thought that about you if you hadn't told me this story."

"I am not that kind of man. A rebel. And I used to like rushes, but not anymore. Excitement and adventure can come from different sources. It doesn't have to be controversial or on the edge. I can apply my knowledge and expertise much more productively than I have in the past. I learned that lesson working for Stankovich."

She seemed to be contemplating everything. He sensed her icing up again, an attempt to avoid agreeing that what he'd said was spot-on and she liked it. He suspected he intrigued her, fascinated her, attracted her, and she was still at odds as to what to do. He'd settle for that. Her desire kept her from shutting him out. He wouldn't push her.

"Let's get out of here." He put his hand on her lower back and guided her out of the office. The hotel lobby wasn't as large as some big chain hotels, but offered a seating area and plenty of room for people traffic.

The clerk saw them from her post behind the reception counter. "All set?"

"Ye—"

Reese's affirmative reply was cut short by an abrupt explosion. Gunfire. Jamie dove for her, taking her down to the floor as a rain of bullets sprayed the wall and the front of the counter. Glass from the front windows shattered and people screamed from the hotel restaurant off the lobby. He crushed Reese in her deputy uniform and felt her gear poke him. The clerk had taken refuge behind the counter. Jamie searched the lobby and the through the broken windows and saw no gunman.

Taking out his gun as he moved off Reese, he noticed her take out her own gun. "I'll cover you." He fired in the direction of the gunshots and Reese remaining crouched as she hurried to the front counter. Then she rose up over the top just enough to fire as he had, covering him.

The clerk, who was taking deep breaths, cowered in the corner. From the restaurant, pandemonium had broken loose as people rushed to escape through the kitchen. Luckily there had been no one sitting in the two or three seating areas in the lobby.

"Where is he?" Jamie whispered harshly.

"Right in front. Behind the brick next to the front entrance." She reloaded her weapon. "We have to draw him out."

"Cover me again." Before she could argue, he moved to the edge of the counter. Reese began firing and he ran for one of two support pillars trimmed in an ornate pattern and painted white. Peering around the far side, he ducked back when he saw the shooter stick his gun out from behind the brick. Paint and cement splintered on the side where his head had just been.

Reese fired again and forced the shooter back. Jamie ran for the corner wall at the entrance. Bullets tore through the material of a chair and broke a lamp on a table next to it as Jamie ran past them. He took cover against the wall leading to the restaurant and adjacent to the front entry. He had a clear sight of the shooter, dressed all in black with a masked hat. He fired just as the shooter spotted him and ran.

Reese fired, breaking more windows as the man ran away.

Jamie chased him, pushing through the front doors and running down the sidewalk. The gunman shoved a man out of his way. The man fell onto his hip with a cry. Jamie held his gun upright as he jumped over the fallen man.

The gunman glanced back at a full run and then went behind a car to shoot. Jamie crouched in front of a truck and then moved out to fire back. As a bullet struck the car, the gunman lowered.

He stayed crouched and ran on the street side of parked cars. When a line of cars passed, he ran between them, causing drivers to squeal to a stop. Jamie had no clear shot.

The gunman ran across the street to a used bookstore. As Jamie followed, he shot out the door window. Having anticipated he'd try something like that, Jamie kept himself behind a parked car.

He ran into the bookstore. The cashier bent low behind the counter. A tiny thing with dark-rimmed glasses and hair up in a messy bun, she pointed to the back rows of bookshelves.

Jamie moved along the side of the store, aiming down the aisles of books. At the third one down, the gunman appeared from the far aisle and fired. Jamie flattened his back against the wood shelving, hearing books take bullets and come crashing to the floor.

He reloaded.

The gunman ran to the rear of the store.

Jamie ran to the center aisle and shot the man's

lower leg. He yelped with the hit and went down, rolling to get onto his rear and no doubt take another shot at him.

Jamie knocked his gun arm as he shot and blocked a kick from the man's uninjured leg. He leaned over and punched first the man's face and then his sternum. With the gunman momentarily subdued, he took hold of his gun hand and slammed it against an adjacent shelf, blocking the man's attempts to grab Jamie's throat with his other arm. When the gunman didn't let go of his gun, Jamie pressed his pistol to the gunman's forehead.

The man went still, blue eyes staring at him through the mask.

Jamie pulled the gun back to yank off the hat and toss it aside.

The gunman was probably around thirty, had a scar on his upper left forehead and gritted big white teeth. Though his blue eyes were bright in color, they were empty of feeling.

"Who are you?" Jamie demanded.

"You shouldn't have done that." The gunman knocked the pistol away from his forehead and head-butted Jamie hard enough to make him jerk back.

Jamie kicked the man's gun arm, sending the gun falling as he struck the man's temple with his pistol.

Picking up the other pistol, Jamie stood with both weapons aimed. "Get up."

Showing no fear, only frustration over losing control of the fight, the gunman did as asked. Sirens sounded outside.

"I suggest you start talking."

"I'll take my chances with a lawyer."

"Who do you work for?" Jamie asked.

The door burst open and Reese entered with her gun raised. The sheriff and another deputy followed.

While Jamie held the man immobile at gunpoint, Reese took the man's hands and cuffed him, reading him his rights.

The following afternoon, Reese stood with Jamie at her desk. Christopher Bishop still hadn't talked, but he had a criminal record that included numerous assault charges, an attempted murder and theft. He'd been in and out of jail since he was fifteen.

"Why don't they lock people like this up and throw away the key?" Reese asked, the report in her hands. She stood beside Jamie behind her desk. Deputy Miller worked at his desk, facing the wall across from the conference room entrance. He had a bag of cheese-flavored crunchy snacks on top of a pile of files. He stuck his hand inside the bag before he finished chewing the last mouthful, his eyes on the computer screen and his other hand on the mouse.

Reese's desk was in the middle of the room, the break room behind her. The third desk sat empty across from the entrance to the sheriff's office. The sheriff must have gone for a late lunch.

"Do you think he's involved in Ella's murder somehow?" Jamie asked, and then added quickly, "I know he couldn't have done it, but the killer-for-hire angle bothers me."

"Why?"

He hesitated as though busy analyzing. "It's too professional. If Ella's murderer is still alive, why hire someone to kill those getting too close to finding him?

Sure, he is a lot older, but why not do the job himself? Beside, we have to assume he has no money since he never found it. How could he afford a professional?"

"You think Bishop is a professional?"

He ran his hand over his hair in agitation. "I don't know."

Jamie had a good point. If Bishop wasn't a gun for hire in relation to Ella's murder, then why was he trying to kill them?

"He started to come after us when we found the money." She dropped the report.

"Yeah. There's missing pieces."

"You found the money in your new house, right?" Deputy Miller asked, wiping his hands on a crumpled-up paper towel.

"Yes." Hadn't he heard the rumors?

"Jeffrey had some break-ins after his wife's murder. I came across the reports when I was filing some others yesterday. They were misfiled." He fished on his desk, looking for something.

"What?" She moved around her desk as Miller found what he searched for and handed her a file folder.

Reese took it and eagerly flipped open the file. Walking slowly back to her desk as she read, she stood next to Jamie again, allowing him to read with her.

"A month after the murder, and again five months after that," she said.

"Something tells me it's not the house," Deputy Miller said.

No, the burglar had reason to suspect the money was there back then. And now he'd learned the money had always been there.

The sound of the front door opening brought both Reese's and Jamie's heads up. Kadin stepped inside. The office manager, Margaret, greeted him from behind the reception counter.

In his cowboy hat, boots thudding on the floor, he passed the front counter and approached Reese's desk. The other deputy glanced back as he chewed his crunchy cheese snacks.

"Daughter."

She faltered a little. He said it so playfully she couldn't feel threatened, and thought she might be crazy for even associating her reaction to that. Why should she be threatened with the prospect of having her real father in her life? The strangeness? She had parents. Or the newness? The unknown factor. How would this change her life? Her plans. Those were safe. Predictable.

She saw Jamie notice and teasingly chided him with her eyes for always staying in tune with her.

"Ella's real name was Eva Sinclair," Kadin said. "I tracked her down going through massive paper files in San Diego. She has a mother, three siblings and an estranged father."

Reese looked at Kadin with new eyes. The investigation channeled her, kept her on target.

"The siblings basically slammed their doors on me, but the mother broke down when I told her why I was there." He bent his head, clearly not liking the recollection of having informed the woman—who must be advanced in age by now—that her missing daughter was Ella Neville and had been murdered four decades ago. "She suspected as much, of course, but…"

"Why did the siblings shut you out?" Weren't they concerned about what had become of their sister?

Deputy Miller noisily rolled the bag of snacks closed.

"Eva, aka Ella, was a bit of a rebel in her young adulthood," Kadin said, taking notice of the deputy. "Her mother said she was never the same after her father ran out on them when she was fourteen. He doted on Eva, or gave the impression he did. Eva believed he loved her, but it must have only been the idea of having a daddy's little girl that made him act charming with her. In any event, Eva started hanging around a rough crowd. Her grades slipped from top of her class to flunking. She dropped out of high school and took up with a boy who sold drugs, got arrested a few times and stole money from her siblings. Eventually she drifted away from her family. Her mother never stopped trying to stay in touch. One day she stopped by an apartment Eva had rented and the landlord said he had evicted her. After a week of no contact, she reported her missing."

"Who was the boy?" Jamie asked.

Kadin took out a photo from his inner jacket pocket. "Not our man."

Reese leaned in to see a picture that clearly didn't match any they had of the man Ella—Eva—had been with.

"So we have a woman who falsified her name and fled California." Nothing more.

"She was arrested for aiding in an armed robbery. Out on bail when she left the state. What's interesting about that is the money in the robbery was never recovered and more than a quarter of a million was taken."

The same amount as what Reese and Jamie had found. "The other robbers weren't caught? How many of them were there?"

Deputy Miller glanced back as he sipped from a green can of soda, obviously more interested in what they talked about than his own work.

"Only one. And no, he was never caught or identified. Eva used her own car in the heist. A witness got her plate number. That's how she was caught. She never gave away the name of her partner."

And she'd fled before her trial.

"She wouldn't have given away the name of her partner," Jamie said. "She must have planned to take the money and run. Telling the police would have led them straight to it and she might not ever have gotten it."

"Exactly," Kadin said, his cowboy hat dipping with his nod. "How's the search for tourists going?"

"We have a list of everyone who stayed on or through the night of Ella's murder." Reese picked up the handwritten list and showed it to Kadin. "Most of them were families. The others were four couples and two men travelling together. Two of the families checked out the day of the murder, the rest checked out each day after that through the weekend. One of the couples stayed the whole week. Two stayed one night—the night before the murder, and the other two stayed two and three nights, checking out the day after the murder. The men rented all-terrain vehicles from Shadow Mountain Ranch. They were riding the day of the murder, but could have made it back in time."

"How did you find that out?" Kadin asked.

"This morning we checked all the ranches and activities offered during that time. Shadow Mountain kept records." She pointed to the first name they'd highlighted. "We narrowed down our search to those who stayed the night before the murder but not the night of the murder. One is a couple who stayed in a rental cabin. The two families and the two couples who left the day of the murder, and the men who rented ATVs." She sat down on her desk chair. "The two families were from Missouri and Oregon. The couples were from California and Colorado. The men were from California. Only one was from San Diego." She awakened her computer. "We were just about to look up the couple from California when the report on Bishop came in."

"Bishop?"

Jamie explained what happened.

"Great. So I almost lost another daughter."

"No. I had Jamie with me." She knew that would be the best way to assure him she was fine.

Jamie sat on the chair he'd scooted close to hers when they'd arrived back from the lodge. Reese navigated to a DMV database and then moved a piece of paper aside to see the license numbers she'd listed. "The couple from San Diego registered under the man's name. Darius Richardson." She clicked her way through the pages on the site and found nothing current. "That's odd." She searched again. "There are no current records for him. His last registered address is in San Diego." She opened a photo of the man. Darius Richardson looked close to forty. "This is thirty years old." Darius would be almost seventy now, the perfect age for someone who could have murdered Eva. She printed copies of the information.

"Maybe he died," Deputy Miller said.

Reese looked over at him along with Jamie and Kadin. Then she searched another database for a death record and found none. "Nope. It's like he disappeared."

Kadin took a seat across from them on a wooden chair. "He stayed at the Never Summer Hotel the night before Eva's murder."

"And now he's nowhere to be found," Kadin said. "He's looking like he could be your killer."

Reese studied the photo. If this was the man in Eva's photographs, he'd gained weight and lost a lot of hair. It was hard to tell if he was the same person. She could see some similarities but they would need more proof.

"May I?" Kadin indicated her computer.

Reese turned the monitor so he could see the screen and put her keyboard and mouse in front of him on top of some papers. He navigated to a site he knew of and likely had special access to. The idea intrigued her. What would it be like to have such sophisticated resources a fingertip touch away?

Kadin must have found what he was looking for. He next took out his phone and called someone.

"Mallory. Kadin Tandy." He smiled slightly as the man on the other end spoke. "How are the kids?" He paused longer this time as the man likely rambled on and raved about his kids. "Penny and I are doing well. Clayton is growing like a weed and already feisty like his mother." He chuckled. "I called for a favor. I need you to check the nonpublic records on someone."

He'd called a law enforcement officer in San Diego.

"Darius Richardson."

Reese glanced at Jamie, who seemed as rapt as her. Meeting his eyes, she melted as always into their blue allure. The way he looked at her felt like a physical touch. He reached over and put his hand on her knee, heating up the moment. On purpose? Trepidation drowned in the wake of desire. He made her feel so good.

"Can you email me something over on that?"

Kadin's question pulled her from Jamie's gaze and they both looked at Kadin.

He ended the call. "Darius Richardson was wanted for questioning in relation to another missing person case. The woman's mother reported her daughter went out with him a few days before she disappeared. He was believed to be the last person to see her alive." He used his phone to type, then looked up at Reese. "Check your email."

Reese opened the email, Jamie leaning close, his body heat doing delicious things to her concentration. She read the email with him and quickly became stunned.

"Paula Kowalski went missing the week before Ella's murder." Darius hadn't been found. The woman hadn't been found. Could it be they were together?

The couple who had stayed the night before Eva was killed...

"This case is getting very bizarre," Jamie said. "Why disappear without the money?"

"If he murdered this missing woman, he'd have plenty of reason." Kadin pointed to her computer. "There's an address in the email. Darius's sister lives in Durango."

Reese gaped at him. "Eva's body was found on Highway 149."

"That's on the way to Durango," Deputy Miller said, now facing them on his chair.

"He might have been on his way to see her," Jamie said.

Reese looked at him as they added up all the clues. "With the missing woman."

"That's what you need to go find out." Kadin stood. "I'd go with you but I have a wife who's going to require copious amounts of attention."

Reese smiled, charmed with the love the two of them had for each other. "We can handle it." How easily she said *we*.

Chapter 10

Darius Richardson's sister lived in an old two-story colonial in downtown Durango. Reese didn't have much to say the entire trip. She kept going over what Jamie had told her. He'd literally been a mercenary and thought he'd gone to work for a reputable private military company. The things he'd done to escape such a dangerous man should trouble her, but discovering his brutal capability, learning the greater depth of a man she perceived as someone much softer, only made him more fascinating. That troubled her. She liked his ability to fight for his freedom and to remain on the right side of the law.

He was like no one she'd ever met. She couldn't get past that, its effect on her. She didn't know why he was so different. Mercenary, yes, but as a man after her heart. What was it about him that made him different?

She looked over at him as they walked toward the front door of the house. He looked back at her. He always had a way of dissecting her. He never said anything, she just knew he could see things in her that guided him in how he treated her. Would he use a touch or a kiss to manipulate her or would he use words? Turned out this time he used neither.

He must have known the night before last had shaken her foundation. She still wasn't sure how to handle her inner chaos. Doing nothing gave her the least discomfort. She could not pretend that night had been no different than the other times, a casual fling. But she couldn't face what it had really been.

A woman in her midsixties with light blue eyes, no glasses and white hair in a bob opened the door. Jamie had called ahead, so she was expecting them.

"Deputy Harlow?" she said to Reese.

"Yes, and this is Jamie Knox. He spoke to you on the phone."

"Yes, yes, of course. Come on in." She opened the door wider and stepped aside. "I called your office to make sure you were who you said you were." When Jamie and Reese entered she closed the door with a raised brow. "You never can be too sure these days."

"We wouldn't expect you not to call and check," Reese said, finding the woman endearing. She used honesty well.

The woman invited them into the small front living room. An archway to the right of the door led to a dining room with an antique table and hutch. Victorian furniture in the living room took Reese back in time. Red accents in throw pillows, flowers and a mosaic area rug drew the eye from a clutter of antique collectibles. Narrow windows kept the lighting dim.

Reese sat on the sofa next to Jamie. Darius's sister sat across from them on a wing-backed gold-and-red chair.

"When you said you needed to talk to me about Darius, you really got my attention. I haven't seen or heard from my brother in almost thirty years."

Reese shared a glance with Jamie. That news wasn't going to help them.

"We discovered he may have dated a woman who went missing before he took a trip to Never Summer forty years ago," Jamie said. "Another woman was reported missing shortly after he left California. We we're hoping you could tell us if he came to see you. I realize it was a long time ago."

"Oh, yes. I remember. Yes, it was a long time ago, but I remember it because he didn't come to see me very often. He was with a girl. Paula was her name. She had a Polish last name."

"Kowalski," Jamie said.

"Yes, that was it. Quiet as a mouse, that thing. I did all the talking." She leaned forward as though sharing a secret. "I do most of the talking, anyway, but most people at least interrupt me." She leaned back and gazed off in memory. "Not her."

Jamie took out the photo of Paula they'd obtained before traveling here and showed it to the woman. "Is this her?"

"Yes, that's her."

Next, Jamie took out the photo of the man with Eva and handed it to the woman. "Is this your brother?"

She took the photo and nodded almost immediately.

"Yes, that's him. Who is the girl he's with? She isn't the one he brought here."

Reese had to take time to recover from confirming the identity of the man in Ella's mysterious photos, and confirming he was with Paula. This was a huge break in the case. No one before her had uncovered this much in the investigation. She met Jamie's glance and more than the revelation passed between them. Every time she looked at him he gave her flutters of arousal. Maybe if she let herself stare into his eyes for however long it took not to be aroused she'd be cured of this strange spell. Maybe it wasn't possible to look at him and *not* be aroused.

"Did he mention anything about going to Never Summer while he was here?"

The woman had to think for a moment. "He talked about some of the things they did. Horseback riding, river rafting. He called before he left San Diego to tell me he was driving here. He didn't tell me he was bringing a girl."

"Did he talk about the women he was involved with in San Diego?"

She shook her head. "Darius never talked about his girlfriends. He and I grew up in a broken home. Our mother was an alcoholic. Darius coped far worse than me. He could never hold a steady job. He did drugs. He kept his emotions to himself. When we were kids he protected me and he took care of me at home. I think that early responsibility took its toll on him. He always struggled."

"But he was never arrested," Reese said.

"No." The woman smiled. "Darius was careful in his illegal activities. His reputation was very important to him. Nobody told him he had no reputation to protect." She laughed lightly. "Bless his heart, he saw himself an equal to everyone, rich or poor. He did illegal things but he thought of himself as an honorable and respectable citizen of this country. He was a proud man."

"Did he ever talk to you about money?" Jamie asked.

The woman shook her head again. "Another personal thing he didn't discuss. He was sensitive to how people perceived him. He didn't make a lot of money and had no special trade, but he coveted his image. Like I said, proud. Don't ever say to his face that he didn't amount to much. In his mind, he was a great man."

"You loved your brother," Reese said.

"Yes. It breaks my heart to speculate what must have become of him. He must be dead, or he'd have contacted me."

"Even if he was suspected in a murder?" Jamie asked.

The woman flinched and her pleasant, thoughtful look turned to one of dismay. "Murder? Darius would never murder anyone. Is that why you're here? Who was murdered?"

"The woman in the second photo I showed you," Jamie said. "She was the first to go missing. We aren't sure if Darius is involved or not. The other missing woman, too—the one he brought here."

"Oh…my goodness. That comes as quite a shock to me." She put her curled fingers up to her mouth and stared across the room. Then she lowered her hand. "I just can't believe it. Darius may have done drugs and stole things but he was not a killer."

Many killers had Darius's character...the pride, the reputation. He may have appeared incapable but he wasn't.

"Did he ever steal money?" Reese asked as gently as she could with such a blunt question.

"You mean from a bank or a store? Not that I'm aware, but like I said, Darius didn't share much about himself. I knew he brushed the law with his drugs and stole things from people, but we never discussed it. I suppose he could have had it in him to steal money. He stole other things. When we were in high school he broke into homes. Stealing money would boost his ego and his reputation, wouldn't it? If he had money. He used to talk like he had more than he actually did." She nodded. "Yes, I can see Darius stealing money."

"Would you mind if we had a look around?" Jamie asked. "If he was here, maybe there's something he left behind that will help us find him."

Reese was glad he asked. Maybe they'd find something useful.

"Oh." The woman stood. "There's no need for you to look around. He did leave something behind, from that trip he took all those years ago. Wait here."

Darius's sister returned with an old photograph envelope, torn and worn, and handed it to Reese. "I told him he left them behind but he never came to get them and I didn't think to send them to him. I forgot all about them the last time he came to visit, the last time I saw him." She looked off again.

Jamie moved closer to see the photos with Reese. The first one slammed home the gold mine they'd struck. The picture was of the missing girl with Darius. She'd gone on the road trip with him.

Jamie didn't alarm Reese by telling her he thought someone was watching them. He stood by a front window at the sheriff's office. A man in a car with dark tinted windows had been parked there for about an hour now. He must have noticed Jamie. The car pulled out into the street and passed. Jamie couldn't tell if the driver looked at him, but he didn't move from his post until he could no longer see the vehicle.

He turned and headed back to Reese's desk, the office manager, Margaret, eyeing him as he did. He'd like to know why someone other than Christopher Bishop had shown up. Bishop was still locked in jail. A feeling began to spread that neither Bishop's reason for being here, nor the sudden appearance of this stranger, had anything to do with Eva's murder.

"Something wrong?"

He'd come to a stop at Reese's desk, still in deep thought. "No." He'd tell her when he was sure. Or when he could no longer deny it…

She resumed typing, the sound echoing in the open room. Other than Margaret, they were alone. They had left Durango yesterday. Now they were searching surrounding counties for more murders. Paula was still a missing person, dead or alive. So far nothing had come up.

"I think I may have found something," Reese said.

He perked up and went around to the other side of her desk, leaning his hand on a shallow stack of papers. Reese glanced over at his hand and then her gaze went up his arm to his shoulder and then met his face. She did that a lot—stroked him with hot eyes, albeit involuntary. He moved a little closer to her, lowering his head, testing her. Her eyes widened and she turned to the computer.

Holding back a small chuckle, he looked at her screen.

"This is an email from the Alamosa Police Department."

Jamie read that a woman had been murdered in Alamosa and her body had never been identified. Reese had emailed a copy of a photo of Paula, and the detective confirmed she was his Jane Doe. Paula had been murdered. Cause of death was blunt-force trauma. She'd been stripped of all her clothes and dumped on the side of a road near the Alamosa National Wildlife Refuge. No murder weapon was found, but there was evidence she'd recently had sex. Whether forced or consensual, the coroner couldn't be sure. DNA was on file, but like Ella's case, no match had been found.

"Paula's mother reported her missing. Why didn't the San Diego police find her here?"

"She was murdered forty years ago," Reese said, looking up at him again. "There were no missing persons databases back then."

He still thought that was lazy police work.

"I'll ask him to give us DNA to compare the DNA found at Ella's crime scene," Reese said.

That would take some time.

Hearing the front door open, Jamie looked and saw a man enter and approach the reception desk. In jeans and a white shirt with the jacket open in front, he walked in smooth, slow steps. He had medium brown hair and dark eyes popping out from pocked, dark-complexioned skin.

"Hello," he said to the office manager, Margaret.

"Can I help you?" she asked.

The man pulled out a gun. "Yes. You can stand up and move around the counter."

Margaret inhaled sharply and sat frozen in fear.

Jamie withdrew his gun at the same time Reese did, but neither of them lifted their weapons in time.

The man held up his hand at them, pistol aimed at Margaret's head. "I'll kill her."

"Please…" the woman begged. She looked over at Jamie and Reese.

Jamie's stomach turned with a plummet of dread. He could not allow an innocent woman to die. If he shot him, would he be fast enough? He couldn't take that risk.

"Put your weapons down," the man said.

The man's gun had a silencer on it. "Leave her be," Jamie said, walking around the side of the desk. "You can have me instead."

"Take another step and the lady is dead."

Jamie stopped, hands raised to shoulder height. Reese held her pistol with both hands, but at a downward angle. She'd managed to stand but hadn't raised the gun to aim it.

"Put your weapons down."

When Jamie and Reese didn't move or do as ordered, the man lowered his gun just enough and fired. The office manager screamed as a hole ripped through her shoulder.

Jamie took one automatic step toward Margaret before he stopped again, hearing Reese's strangled sound of alarm.

The woman stumbled backward against the wall, breathing fast and looking down in horror at her shoulder. She put her hand over the wound and looked at Jamie with a silent plea for help.

The gunman eyed him with blatant challenge. Jamie could see he would do whatever it took to get what he'd come for.

"The next one is in her head," he said.

Jamie put his gun on Reese's desk and she did the same, sharing a desperate look with him. He berated himself for not keeping watch for the man. He shouldn't have assumed he'd gone. But how could he have predicted he'd come right into the sheriff's building and take a hostage?

The man walked around the counter and hooked his arm around the woman's neck, pressing the gun to her temple. "If you want to live, you'll do exactly as I say," he said to the woman.

She nodded, grimacing in pain.

"Take me to Christopher Bishop."

He was here to break Bishop out of jail?

The woman walked forward, blood soaking her hand, partially covered by the man's arm.

Jamie followed, making sure Reese stayed behind him. The gunman forced Margaret through the open desk area to a locked door. The other half of the sheriff's building was the jailhouse.

The office manager's fingers trembled as she used the keys she always carried to open the door. Inside, three of the eight cells were occupied, the first containing Christopher Bishop. Dressed in an orange jumpsuit, he sat up from a reclined position on the narrow bed. Smiling, he stood and went to the barred door.

"Unlock the cell," the gunman demanded. He had a military-soldier way about him, only not the reputable kind. He had the eyes and tactics of a mercenary.

Reese looked at Jamie, who nodded once. They had to do as the man said until their circumstances changed.

The office manager trembled as she watched Reese unhook keys from her gear belt. As she unlocked the cell, Bishop's arrogant gaze passed from her to Jamie. When the door clicked, Bishop slid it open.

Jamie pulled back Reese and moved in front of her, making sure he blocked her from the two men. She gripped his arm as she peered around him.

"It's about time you got here, Holcomb," Bishop said to the gunman, stepping out of the cell. "I was beginning to think you forgot the agreement."

"The agreement has not been forgotten." He lifted the hem of his shirt to reveal another gun.

Bishop pulled it free of the waist of his pants and readied it to fire. He aimed it at Jamie's head.

"The keys." Holcomb held out his hand, still pressing the pistol to Margaret's head. "Give them to me."

Reese extended her hand with the keys. Jamie took them from her and handed them to the man.

He snatched them. "Get in the cell."

If he went into the cell he'd be powerless to help anyone.

"I will kill this woman if you don't do what I say."

Bishop stepped forward, the pistol in line with his forehead.

With his gut telling him these men would kill them all if they had to, Jamie fought his urge to fight. He could take Bishop's gun from him and shoot the other man, but probably not before Margaret was shot. The office manager was dispensable to them. She was not dispensable to Jamie.

Taking Reese's hand, he started to pull her ahead of him.

"Not her," Holcomb said.

Jamie stopped, intense dread driving him to take drastic action. No way would he allow them to take Reese.

"She comes with us," Holcomb said.

He moved to face both men. "I'm afraid I can't let you do that."

Holcomb smirked.

"He thinks he's going to stop us," Bishop said, laughing cynically.

"She won't be harmed as long as you do what we tell you."

As if he'd ever believe that. What did Stankovich have planned? Something awful. Torturous. For Jamie. And he'd use Reese to accomplish it. Why the change from attempting to kill them to this, taking Reese alive and leaving him?

"You're going to have to go through me first."

Holcomb pressed on the gun trigger.

The woman squeezed her eyes shut and sobbed. "Please...no."

"It's okay, Jamie." Reese moved out from behind him and paused to look into his eyes. "I'll go."

He saw her boundless strength and confidence and felt love mushroom inside him…now, of all times. He admired her grit, and yes, even her independence. He realized that was the one thing that had drawn him to her. He'd never met any other woman like her.

Silently she communicated what he should have already determined, had he not been so urgently trying to protect her. These men were taking her for a reason. And while Reese didn't know about Stankovich, the men he'd sent would have killed them by now if that had been his intent.

Jamie looked at Holcomb. "What do you want?"

"You will know soon enough."

Bishop took hold of Reese and held the gun to her head, leading her out the door through to the sheriff's office. As soon as the men had their new hostage, Holcomb pushed Margaret into the cell. She cried out in pain as she landed on her hip.

"Is it the money?" Jamie asked, stalling.

"Get in the cell."

Jamie didn't move.

Holcomb's eyes moved in annoyance before meeting his again. "I think we both know how this works." He aimed his pistol at Margaret again.

Jamie had no choice. With one last glance at Reese, seeing her nod in reassurance, he stepped into the cell.

As Holcomb closed and locked the cell, Jamie waited for him to raise his eyes.

"I'm going to kill you."

The man faltered ever so slightly. He must have known the kind of man he faced. Stankovich would have told him all about how he'd stripped him of his power to control him.

Holcomb started to turn away.

"What does Stankovich want?" Jamie hated even speaking the name.

The man paused and met Jamie's gaze. "You know."

Chapter 11

Reese's apprehension mounted as Bishop drove out of Never Summer. From the sheriff's building, no one saw the men put her into the backseat of a sedan with dark windows. People had walked along the sidewalk across the street but hadn't looked her way. And now they drove her along a dirt road just off the highway without covering her eyes. She'd seen them and she'd know where they were taking her. Did that mean they didn't plan on letting her go alive?

Through the windshield she spotted an abandoned mine that appeared to have undergone some renovations. The old wood structure must have been torn down and a new one had been erected to resemble a house. A double front door with two windows on each side almost looked welcoming.

The car stopped and Bishop and Holcomb got out,

Bishop opening the back door with his gun drawn. She got out and he pushed her toward the doors. Her legs felt rubbery as she neared. What awaited her inside? She didn't want to find out.

Stopping abruptly, she grabbed Bishop's gun hand and moved her body to heft him over her shoulder. He landed with a thud on the gravel driveway that extended all the way to the front door. Holcomb swung his gun to hit her but she came up from dumping Bishop to block him with her arm. The impact stung. She ignored the pain and kicked him in the groin. He went down holding his crotch and groaning in agony.

Bishop recovered from his fall, rising to his feet.

Reese bolted. She ran as fast as she could toward the trees. If she could make it to the highway and flag down a car…

Hearing footsteps behind her, she pushed herself harder. She reached the trees and had to slow down to avoid colliding with trunks. Dodging back and forth, weaving her way through the thick understory, she heard a car pass on the highway. A ray of hope soared through her. She jumped over a fallen log. Glancing back, she saw Bishop gaining on her. The look back cost her. She faced forward and barely had time to clear another fallen log. She landed unsteadily and stumbled. Nearly going down, she pushed off a tree and ran harder.

Bishop was right behind her now. She heard his exerted breathing and rapid footfalls. She pushed herself as fast as she could go, but he was faster. She felt him claw at her shirt. Then her arm. He clasped his hand around her wrist and pulled.

Reese lost her balance as Bishop twisted her. She

fell onto her back and tumbled. Rolling foot-over-head, she came down on a deeply buried boulder that dug painfully into her back. She tried to prevent her head from striking but it slammed down, blacking out her vision for a few seconds.

Bishop straddled her on his feet, bending for her arms and yanking her up. She yanked back and his grip slipped. She started to use her legs to trip him off his feet when he swung his fist and hit the side of her face. Her head knocked against the boulder again.

Reese groaned with pain and disorientation. She struggled to stay in the fight but Bishop hauled her up to her feet. She sagged against him, dizzy.

"Start walking." He shoved her.

She stumbled, head swimming, but managed to stay on her feet.

"Try something like that again and I'll just shoot you."

"No, you won't. You're the underling, right?" She looked back to see his sneer.

She faced forward and walked through the forest. "How did a thug like you end up here?"

"Just keep walking."

"Kidnapping could get you life if I'm harmed. Class one felony. Class two will get you eight to twenty-four. You like prison? I hear the food is pretty bad. Nothing like going out whenever you feel like it for Mexican or Chinese. You're talking meat, potatoes and vegetables. Cereal for breakfast. Sandwiches for lunch, probably really dry and tasteless. And forget happy hour with friends. All those fun little things you took for granted will be taken away from you."

"Shut up."

"You hit me back there, so it'll probably be life. Death penalty if you kill me, which you might do, but not now. You'd have done it already." Whoever waited inside the mine house might, though.

"Where are you from?" she asked. Maybe if she got enough information she might be able to do something about it—assuming she escaped alive.

"Not here."

"Who sent you and your idiot friend?"

He didn't respond so she went on.

"How did you wind up on the wrong side of the law? Were your parents criminals? Dad left when you were little? Didn't get enough love from Mommy?"

"I said shut up." He shoved her again. "So shut it, or I'll hit you more than once. Stankovich doesn't care if you're bruised and bleeding, just alive."

"Stankovich, huh?" That came as quite a shock. While she hadn't thought the two of them or the one inside the mine house were related to the Neville case, she would never have connected Jamie's past to them.

Holcomb appeared ahead.

"Thanks for the help," Bishop said.

"That's payback for getting yourself arrested."

Bishop grunted in irritation and Holcomb took up step beside her.

"Try that again and you'll get more than that bruise on your cheek," he said.

"That's what your idiot partner told me."

He eyed her in offense for a bit, as though deciding if he'd give her another bruise, but then faced forward.

As they emerged from the forest and saw the mine house, her unease mounted. Jamie had explained the kind of man Stankovich was. She was a small-town deputy sheriff. She was no match for the leader of a gang of mercenaries.

Holcomb opened one of the doors and Bishop shoved her forward. She found herself standing in a big open area, a kitchen with all the modern conveniences to the left and a living room with a giant television hanging on the wall to the right. Straight back, a hall led into the mountain. She could see doors off the hall and presumed those were the bedrooms.

Who lived here and did they have an obsession with security? The only way in or out was through the doors in front, and she saw those were thick and made of metal. The windows were probably bulletproof.

Holcomb took her from Bishop, grabbing her arm and walking with her to the first door on the right in the hall. The door was open and she spotted a tall, big, lean man sitting behind a huge black desk with four monitors on it. One side of the office was lined with more monitors, each showing varying scenes, none of them of this structure. He looked at her through pale blue eyes. He kept his hair slicked back and wore a giant gold ring and thick chain.

Reese wondered if he was stuck back in the eighties.

He stood. Nothing changed on his face. He seemed to view the world with the same impassive regard. Not glad. Not sad. Not friendly. Not angry. Just...his way.

"You may leave us now," he said to Holcomb in an Eastern European accent.

Holcomb left, shutting the door behind him. The man before her studied her without rushing. His intimidating way threatened her calmness.

"So, this is the woman who captured Jamie Knox's heart."

She decided to play along with his veiled cordiality. Show no fear.

"You appear to know me, but I don't know you," she said.

His brow rose. "Jamie did not tell you of me?"

She didn't reply. Let him think what he would.

"He is very sure of his security. Did he not consider I might not take kindly to his meddling in my affairs?"

What was he talking about? What business did this man have with Jamie? Jamie had left Aesir International. Why would he come after them now? Revenge?

"What do you want from me? Why are you here? Jamie said he no longer works for you." She left out all he'd actually told her.

"So he has told you something of me." He smiled in a calculating way, superior and knowing. "Come." He turned. "Have a seat. We have much to discuss."

She trailed him to a seating area. "Have you lived here long?" She sat on a chair across from him, sure she had little chance of escaping with Bishop and Holcomb in the house.

"I am only staying here. I searched for the perfect place and invited myself in." He looked around. "Quite appropriate, don't you think?"

His accent gave him an air of sophistication, but the look in his eyes told a much darker story. Caution should be exercised when dealing with this man. And his self-invitation must not have been welcome. What happened to the owners?

"It's different." She glanced around. The walls had

been finished but it seemed odd to build into a mountain if national security wasn't at risk.

"Jamie has taken great pains to shield you from the truth of his association with me."

Reese slid her gaze to him, preparing herself for his version of Jamie Knox. Did she want to hear it?

He crossed his legs and elevated his head with an air of superiority. "Did he tell you he left the Army to join my company?"

"Yes."

"Did he tell you why?" He lowered his head, eyes piercing and hard.

"He said you must have viewed his reason as rebellion. He left the Army honorably."

Some of his hardness eased and he leaned back against the chair, uncrossing his legs. "The appearance of honor is of great importance to Jamie. I learned that about him very shortly after hiring him. It's one of his flaws. Jamie had a thirst for danger that was not quenched during his enlistment. He craved third-world chaos. Some soldiers come to me for work because chaos is the only way of life they know. Not Jamie. Jamie came to me so he could unleash the animal inside him."

That didn't sound like Jamie. Jamie had a soft side, a side that liked to charm women, make love and save lives rather than take them.

"What I am certain he left out of his narration is the many missions he participated in where the innocent got in the way. They are what you would call collateral damage in the fight for world peace." He seemed so unruffled, and perhaps arrogant.

"Jamie wouldn't kill innocent people."

"Ask him yourself if you do not believe me. He told you how I framed him, yes?"

She didn't respond but her eyes must have betrayed her.

Stankovich's eyes smiled in affirmation. "He did, I see. It is true. I did frame him, but only for his own good. He struggled with his real identity, the man who needs chaos. He is pretending to have changed. Going to work for that righteous crusader, taking up with you as though he means to begin a family." Stankovich scoffed. "He is fooling himself. I may have been too hard on him, but he will never survive in such a domesticated life."

Some of what he said touched on truth. How well did she really know Jamie? How well did he really know himself? How could he go from such a dangerous profession to an office job that might require occasional travel? He'd always be in an executive management role. He would no longer have to go into the field. Stankovich might have the intentional-violence part wrong, but he may not have the family-man part wrong.

"Jamie worked for me for nearly three years. Toward the end of that time, he participated in missions in Iraq. One mission in particular became challenging from the moment the men landed. The insurgents learned they would arrive and were waiting. They were attacked. My men fought back. Unfortunately, the insurgents used women and children as shields. They were forced to shoot them all to secure the area."

Jamie had shot women and children? "I don't believe you."

He waved out a hand, indicating her belief or disbelief didn't matter. "Ask Jamie. If he is honest, he will tell you he had to shoot women and children to reach the insurgents and stop them from causing more harm."

Reese could no longer hold back her reaction. She put her hand to her mouth and looked away. What this man implied about Jamie was appalling. She couldn't believe it, but it could have happened. He may not have wanted to kill innocents, but he may have been forced.

"I am sorry to have told you this."

Growing angry now, she dropped her hand and turned to him. "Why are you then?"

"You should know the truth."

"A human trafficker worked for you. Do you really expect me to believe you?"

"I make no excuses for who I am."

But Jamie did? "Why did you bring me here?"

"Two reasons. To see if Jamie loves you. And two, to kill him."

He said it so matter-of-factly she had a terrible glimpse into the way this man lived. Criminal. No value for life. Power. Control.

"Why does it matter if he loves me?" *Love?* Did Jamie love her? If she wasn't in this situation the shock would have knocked her off her feet.

"Oh, it matters a great deal." Stankovich's eyes took on a zealous gleam. "You see, the one thing I aspire most to gain from all of this is Jamie Knox's suffering."

"Why did Bishop try to kill us then?"

Stankovich didn't give her an answer, but his eyes narrowed enough to reveal whatever drove him fueled angry emotion.

Jamie had taken from him and now he'd have his vengeance. What would become of her? And Jamie…

Despite reeling from the possibility he could already love her, knowing in her heart he could, an even bigger dilemma presented itself just then.

What if she'd fallen in love with him? What if they'd had all the makings of love from that very first moment they'd seen each other? Spending time with him afterward had only sealed a powerful, undeniable union.

The notion closed in on her even as it enchanted her.

Stankovich stood. "Come. I promise you'll be comfortable during your stay here."

Reese had no choice other than to follow him. He opened the door and Bishop waited.

"Put her with the other one."

Reese glanced back at him as Bishop gripped her arm and began to haul her away. The other one?

A few minutes after Reese had been taken away, the sheriff had returned to find Jamie hollering in the cell and Margaret close to losing consciousness. Now Jamie saw the woman being loaded in an ambulance as he stood outside the sheriff's office and jailhouse. Snow had begun to fall. He forgot that a winter storm had been forecast, which would only hinder his search-and-rescue efforts. He also had the sinking realization that Stankovich wouldn't have taken her without plans to have him join the party. He meant for Jamie to suffer.

He went back into the sheriff's office and began pacing. Where would he have taken her? How long would he make him wait if he couldn't find her first? And what was he doing with Reese? Was she all right? He wasn't accustomed to losing control like this. Nobody ever outsmarted him on a mission. He must have gone a little soft pursuing Reese with those crazy ideas of home and hearth.

What was the matter with him? He batted his forehead a few times.

The sheriff entered, pausing as he saw Jamie beating his own head. Without commenting, he took off his hat with a sigh. "That poor girl's been our office manager for fifteen years. Nothing like this has ever happened to our team."

When Jamie didn't answer, he looked over at him two or three times as he hung up his jacket.

Then he walked over to Jamie. "Reese is a very good deputy."

He didn't want to doubt her ability, but he knew full well the enemy who had her. "Have her parents been notified?"

"I called them just a little bit ago. I'll let them know what happens."

Let them know? That sounded like they hardly cared.

"Are they concerned?"

"Of course they are." The sheriff eyed him peculiarly, as though wondering where that question had come from. "They were both very upset when I told them. They were going to drive in and wait here with us, but I told them not to."

"Reese doesn't seem to be very close to them."

The sheriff looked at him closely some more and walked toward him. "Mr. and Mrs. Harlow are quiet folks. They don't show emotion much. Good people but don't count on a long, stimulating conversation with them at a local barbecue. I imagine Reese has a different relationship with them, though. She was always a good kid, and some day she'll take over as sheriff. You wait and see. The girl's got ambition and she's smart. I couldn't hope for a better successor."

Jamie wasn't so sure. He thought Reese staying and taking over as sheriff might be beneath her capability. Maybe her parents held her back. She had exuberance for life and achievement. She was more like her real father. Trouble was she didn't realize what she was doing, that she was settling for a quieter life than what ran in her veins.

Reese had grown up with few hugs and few displays of affection. No wonder she was so independent. She didn't know how to love. No one had ever taught her. He remembered the way she'd watched Kadin and Penny. Back then he thought it had been fascination. It had, but it had also been more. She soaked in the sight of true love, curious and not understanding the feelings the two had for each other. She could only observe. She had no basis to recognize when she felt it.

Every time she made love with him, every time he touched her, kissed her, she had to feel something. Maybe she tried to subdue it, but it was there. If he found a way to break through her barriers, she might realize what she denied herself. She didn't behave that way intentionally—she had grown up being taught how to be conservative, to not show an overabundance of emotion, or even heightened emotion. Her parents probably only showed that kind of emotion when they were alone. Or maybe even then they both held back, guarded themselves against feeling too much.

"What makes you think her parents don't care?" the sheriff asked.

"I'm sure they do. It's like you said, they're quiet people. It's just… Reese isn't a quiet kind of person." A louder version was trying to burst free every day.

"That's why she's going to make a great Ute County sheriff." The man beamed as though proud to have a part in her transition, as though he'd trained her and groomed her himself.

"Meeting her real father might change that." Kadin would never withhold his emotions from his daughter, not after losing his first so terribly.

The sheriff sobered as he realized what Jamie had said. Kadin had a lot more to offer Reese than anything in Never Summer did. If only she realized that now.

Deputy Miller broke the painful silence when he opened the door and entered with the aroma of warm cinnamon rolls. Jamie lifted his head from his hands, sitting at Reese's desk. Deputy Miller stomped snow off his boots and removed his snow-caked cap. The storm had settled in.

Jamie had spent the entire evening and night going crazy wondering if Reese was all right. He kept hearing Holcomb say, "You know."

Stankovich would make him suffer for as long as it satisfied him, and then he'd call. Jamie would know where to go, where his nemesis had taken Reese. He'd just have to wait in agony. Payback for Watts. For quitting. For being hard to kill. All of it. And then

Stankovich would kill them both. Or was this about something else?

The insurance he'd taken on that whole situation was secret, a card he hadn't played because he hadn't been forced to. Stankovich couldn't possibly know about that. No one but Jamie did.

Foreboding climbed up his chest and into his throat.

What if Stankovich had discovered what Jamie had for insurance on him?

Jamie sprang up from the desk chair and paced from one end of the small office to the other while Deputy Miller stopped in front of Reese's desk and put down the bag of cinnamon rolls. Where was she?

Stankovich could have taken her out of town by now. Jamie had checked all the airports. No private flights had left, and nothing suspicious turned up in any commercial airports. He checked the hotel and all of the other accommodations in the area. No one fitting Stankovich's description had checked in.

Jamie's hope had reached a bleak low by midmorning. He'd even tried calling Stankovich, but he'd changed his number since he and Jamie had last been in contact.

The sheriff came out of his office and stood beside Deputy Miller as he opened the bag of sweetsmelling cinnamon rolls. Jamie stopped pacing behind the desk. The deputy withdrew one for the sheriff and then handed another to Jamie.

Jamie held up his hand and shook his head. All he could think about was Reese, as he fought his imagination over what she might be enduring. And Stankovich's plans...

The sheriff's phone rang. It wasn't the main office line. He took his roll with him and sat down to answer.

"Say again?"

Jamie sat straighter and turned the chair to see him. He wrote something on a pad of paper.

"We'll go check it out."

Deputy Miller stopped chewing his bite as the sheriff walked back to them. "Ray Benson didn't show up for work this morning. Candace over at the bank said he's never late."

Ray could be having a medical emergency. Jamie was about to tell him he'd stay here while the sheriff checked it out when Deputy Miller changed everything.

"Ray lives in that converted mine, doesn't he?"

Converted mine? As in, a remote old mine converted to a house on the outskirts of town?

"Yeah, sure does." The sheriff put on his hat.

Jamie stood. "We should all go, and be prepared for the unexpected."

He couldn't stress that enough. The unexpected could be far more dangerous than making Jamie pay. If his secret insurance ever came out to the wrong people, they'd have more than a corrupt private military company leader to deal with.

Chapter 12

"We're never getting out of here," Ray said.

For a lanky six-foot man nearing seventy, the strain of being locked in his spare room must have been taxing for him. He still had good eyes in that he didn't have to wear glasses, but there were dark circles shadowed beneath and he looked dehydrated. They'd had their unexpected introductions last night. Once Reese had tried to check the hall and found a gunman she didn't recognize standing guard. She and Ray were imprisoned in this room. Built into the mountain, there were no windows in any of the back rooms.

"They will never let us go," Ray said. "We've seen their faces."

"They're not the kind of men who worry about things like that." She put down the TV remote, giving up on finding anything that would take her mind off her situation, or wondering what Jamie and the sheriff were doing. The room was depressing to her, which didn't help. With no light other than that from two three-way lily table lamps on each side of the queen-size bed, the room was dim. Ray had offered her the red-floral quilt-covered bed, but she'd declined.

She had stayed up most the night talking with him. He'd explained how Stankovich and his men had broken into his home and told him his house belonged to them for as long as they were here. They made him a prisoner in his own home.

She hadn't told him everything about Stankovich. She didn't want to frighten him.

"Why haven't they killed us yet? Why haven't they killed me?" he asked.

She'd rather not go there.

He got up from the hardwood-framed Victorian armchair and walked to the dresser, where the television played at a low volume. Reese had stopped channel surfing at an animated movie. Currently it was the most cheerful thing in the room.

"I haven't been myself since my wife died."

He sounded so desperate. Reese hadn't heard him talk about his wife.

"She loved this room." He looked all around, moving to see everything the way his wife might have. "I didn't change a thing in it, but I never come in here. When I do, I can only stand it for a few minutes before I have to leave and shut the door." He walked to the door and then back to where a window ought to have been.

"I'm sorry." Being held in here for an entire night

must have been difficult for him. "How long were you married?"

"Just five years. I never thought I'd find that again, but along she came. I met her online, years after my first wife left me." He drifted off into a dream state, calmer than he'd been in hours.

She knew him through his job at the bank but little else. "Why do you live in a mountain?"

He smiled, the truth shining. "I love geology."

Reese laughed lightly, incredulous that she could at a time like this. Then it dawned on her that Ray was in the right age bracket to possibly have known Eva.

"When did your first wife leave you?"

"When I was twenty-six. We weren't together long, but she was my soul mate. I knew the moment I met her that she was the one." His mouth turned down with the recollection. He wasn't being terribly mournful, just sad. "We met when I was twenty-three."

"How old are you now?"

"Sixty-eight." He lowered his head with raised eyebrows. "I can hardly believe it."

She studied him closer. He could be the man in the photo, but who could tell after aging changed a person so much?

"What was her name?" she asked.

His amicable way faded as he sobered. "I thought I'd never meet another woman I'd love like that. After I married my Beatrice, I promised I'd never say my previous wife's name again. I spoke too much of her when we dated, not realizing I'd fall in love with her. Now that she's gone, too, I still hold my promise."

He wouldn't tell her the woman's name. Was he lying about his promise?

An explosion prevented her from asking any more questions. Gunfire followed.

Ray moved back against the wall, terror paralyzing him. Reese rushed to the door and opened it. No one was in the hall.

She turned back to Ray. "We have to get out of here. Let's go!"

"No." He slithered along the wall to the corner beside a dresser. He was probably afraid to flee because whatever had caused the explosion and gunfire awaited.

"This is our chance!" Jamie was here. She just knew it.

She ran to Ray and took his hand. "Come on!"

"No! No." He resisted.

Reese stopped trying to force him. She let him go and thought for a few seconds.

"If there's a fire, you'll be trapped. That explosion must have caused a fire." Maybe it had only been to break through the door, but a fire would spread, and with no windows, they'd be cooked alive. "We have to go, Ray."

He stared at the partially open door as smoke started to drift in.

"Reese!"

She pivoted to see Jamie standing in the doorway, smoke beginning to fill the hallway. He looked like an apparition, all in black, with gear strapped to his legs and torso and an earpiece for communication.

"We have to leave. Now," he said.

This time Ray didn't resist when she grabbed his hand. They ran from the room.

Jamie led the way. She jumped over a body after he did, Ray doing the same.

Flames quickly engulfed the great room. Reese could barely see the outline of the kitchen counters and pieces of furniture, rooms Ray likely had refitted for himself after losing his wife.

She focused on getting him out alive. Jamie ran through the open double doors. Snow accosted her, stealing her breath. Blinking to see, Reese saw the sheriff and Deputy Miller ready with their guns in case they needed cover. They were behind their vehicles in whipping snow. She ducked her face from a hard gust.

No one else was in the front. Breaking in and taking control had seemingly been easy. She looked at Jamie, in stealth mode and still scanning the surroundings with his weapon ready.

Or had he made it seem easy?

Satisfied they were safe, he lowered his weapon and removed his jacket to drape it over her.

She didn't refuse, clutching it tight.

Deputy Miller took Ray to his vehicle, putting him in the back where he'd be warm and out of the weather.

She and Jamie went to the sheriff, Deputy Miller joining them in a circle.

"Stankovich wasn't here, only a couple of guards," Jamie said, squinting with the sting of snow.

"Holcomb and Bishop," the sheriff said.

"No, not them."

Reese looked toward the house, flames licking out windows and the hole Jamie's team had blown where the front door once had been. "Where did they go?" she asked.

"That's what I'd like to know." Jamie glanced up at the sky. "Let's get out of this storm."

As he took her to Deputy Miller's vehicle, she heard sirens of the town firetruck on the way. She got in first and sat beside Ray. But in her relief to be free, she turned to Jamie.

She saw in his eyes how glad he was to see her, his warrior intensity gone now that they were safe. But he didn't embrace her or show any other sign of his gladness.

She wasn't sure if she liked that, which confused her. Ignoring her conflicting emotions, she let her own happiness free and twisted on the seat to throw her arms around him, pressing her head to his chest.

Jamie chuckled. "You're welcome."

She still had a lot of questions for him, but saving her life counted more right now.

The deputy and the sheriff got into the front of the vehicle.

Leaning back, she introduced her new friend. "This is Ray."

"We know," the sheriff said, turning toward the back. "Candace at the bank called to let us know he didn't show up for work."

Reese turned a sharp look at Jamie.

"Stankovich wasn't planning on us showing up this soon," Jamie said.

"You knew he was here, didn't you?" Reese asked. "That he was the one attacking us?"

"I suspected he sent someone. The attacks were too professional."

"Why didn't you tell me?"

"I didn't want to worry you."

She gave him an admonishing tilt of her head and look in her eyes. "Next time tell me anyway, okay?"

"Deal."

"Do you have a picture of Eva and that man?" she asked.

Ray glanced over at them with the mention of Eva and watched Jamie take a photo out of his inner jacket pocket.

"I don't leave home without it."

She took it from him and showed it to Ray. "Is this your first wife? And is that you with her?"

Ray studied the photo. She wondered if he took longer than normal.

He handed her the photo back. "No. I've never seen that woman before and that isn't me."

Reese looked toward the burning mountain house. If he had any photos from his past in there, they were probably destroyed. The firetruck had arrived, but would it be too late?

The sheriff's cell phone rang and he answered. Almost immediately his eyes widened and he said, "We're on our way."

He disconnected the call. "There's been a robbery at the bank. The money in your safe-deposit boxes has been stolen."

The next day, video showed two masked men stealing Reese's money and a third masked man holding Candace at gunpoint. Stankovich must really want to get him. They'd searched for traces of Stankovich, but he appeared to have vanished. They put notices out statewide and even covered the borders in case he decided to return home overseas.

Jamie closed the file and sat back against the desk chair. At regular intervals, the sound of Deputy Miller's hand going into a bag of cheese puffs joined the low volume of twangy country music coming from the sheriff's office. Reese's mouse clicked every once in a while as she studied the background reports they'd just received on male residents who fit the age bracket of the man in the photos they'd found in Reese's house.

"Hello, Tad," Sheriff Robison said from inside his office.

Jamie opened one of the reports Reese had sent him, as they shared the work of reviewing each.

After a few minutes, the sheriff said, "I keep asking you to come and see your mother and me. You've talked things over with Eddy. He's still pouting over the night the two of you went out and someone else talked to you in a way he didn't like. There's nothing else you can do." The sheriff fell silent for a while and then said, "He's going to have to get over his insecurity. Stop calling him. I bet he'll start coming around real quick then."

Finding the background file on Ray, Jamie began reading.

"Come and see your mother and me. Book a flight." He listened a bit longer. "We love you...Okay...Bye-bye."

Jamie finished searching one of the background reports. "Ray checks out. He's clean. First wife's name was Sandy."

He looked over at Reese when she didn't answer.

"Virgil Church doesn't."

He rolled his chair from the third desk over to hers. "This shows he died thirty years ago, but here he is, alive and well in Never Summer." She clicked on another file Kadin's associate had emailed. "This is the real Virgil Church. Born and raised in Grand Junction. Died of leukemia at fifteen."

They both read the rest. "Back then there were no computers that would make catching the ghosting much easier."

Virgil had assumed the identity of a boy who had not yet acquired a social security number, but whose birthday was close to his.

"He probably never had to explain why he hadn't reported any income for the gap in years from the time the boy died and his age."

"Both he and Eva changed their identities," Jamie said.

"Because of the stolen money?"

"And murder." Could they have found the killer? Excitement made Jamie itch to corroborate all of this.

"If we look up Darius Richardson's tax records, do you think they end thirty years ago?" Reese asked.

"Wouldn't it be startling if they do?"

Yes, because if they could identify Darius as Virgil Church that would mean Darius had lived in Never Summer all this time. Had he done so because of the money? Maybe he'd discovered Eva lied when she'd told him all the money went into buying the house with Jeffrey. And he'd waited ten years to move here. His appearance would have changed enough that no one would have recognized him from the time he visited as a supposed tourist.

"He worked at the hardware store all this time." Reese still sounded incredulous.

"Should we confront him?" Jamie asked.

"No. Let's try to identify him first. We don't have

enough to make an arrest for murder. All we have is identity theft. Best if he doesn't know we're on to him. By now he's got to be pretty confident he got away with murder."

He had to smile at that. "You are your father's daughter."

She looked at him with that uncertainty she always got when something threatened her order. His statement must have conjured up all kinds of future implications. Having Kadin in her life permanently. Joining DAI…

He chuckled. She troubled herself so adorably.

When her brow creased above her nose, he leaned in and kissed her. "Stop worrying so much." She jerked back her head and he kissed her again. He kissed her until he felt her melt, could feel her muscles relaxing, and then her hand went to the side of his face. Then he withdrew. "Let go." He put his mouth on hers for a quick kiss. "Let it be what it is. Don't project the future. Just stay right here, right now, with me."

Her soft eyes didn't flare with tension as he'd seen them do before. She had a protective barrier, a gate locking the love inside. She feared the consequences of opening it, feared the unknown.

When he felt his heart fall deeper into the kind of love he would never escape, he hardened himself. More and more he wondered if he was a fool for putting himself in such a vulnerable situation. He couldn't trust her, not yet.

"Besides, you just cracked a big piece of this case. If all goes well, I'll be out of your hair in no time."

Her eyes revealed she understood what he was

doing. Backing off. When she didn't protest, he knew she still struggled with her feelings.

He rolled his chair back to the other desk, seeing the sheriff watching them with a fond smile.

Deputy Miller, at least, had his back to them.

"What about Stankovich?" Reese asked.

He swiveled the chair to face her. "I guess you're stuck with me until we solve that, too."

"He told me about one of your missions," Reese said.

Hearing a slight accusatory tone, his mind raced to catch up to what Stankovich might have told her. The worst, of course.

"Not my mission. His mission. Did he tell you about the first one? The one in Iraq?"

When she answered with only a wary look, he said, "I thought I was protecting a group of contractors who were supposed to be assigned to do aircraft maintenance. But it wasn't anything close to that. He made a deal with the insurgents for the sale of arms, except he only planned to take their money. I was the only one on the team who didn't know. It was his way of testing me. The team took their money and when no arms were exchanged, we were surrounded. The insurgents anticipated Stankovich would double-cross them."

During his narrative, Deputy Miller had stopped his work on his computer and looked back at him, seeming in awe, or maybe a little apprehensive of a man like him sitting in the Ute County Sheriff's Office.

"I thought he was in the business of private military," Reese said.

"He's in the business of making money however he

can. He has access to arms from many sources. It's part of his business."

"He said you killed women and children."

Did she believe that? Her demeanor suggested maybe not.

"That's a lie," he said, not appreciating that he had to defend himself with her. "I killed men, some of them civilians, who would have killed me. I was forced to shoot or die. The other men with me committed the heinous murders. I avoided them by staying out of the line of fire until I could escape them."

"They had guns?"

"Some of them, yes. Young boys. Women. Others the insurgents used as shields."

She grimaced with the awfulness the imagery brought up.

"That mission, that lie, opened my eyes to the kind of man Stankovich was. I quit as soon as I returned. But by then I knew too much according to him, so he set me up."

She studied him for long seconds.

"He's a good man, Reese."

Jamie and Reese both looked into the sheriff's office. Sheriff Robison wore a fatherly look.

"Like he said," Deputy Miller added, "he got out after he was fooled into thinking the mission was legit." He had the bag of crunchy cheese snacks out again. He dug in for a handful and started munching away.

"Why don't you gain weight eating like that?" Reese asked.

"I run ten miles a day." He put more cheese snacks in his mouth. "And I've always had a fast metabolism."

Deputy Miller did have a lean body, a runner's body. In his forties, he was healthy—if the junk food wasn't affecting him—and had no lack of energy.

"Just wait till you're my age," Sheriff Robison said, facing his computer again.

"Enough chitchat." Reese stood up. "Do you want to go see if we can find anything in Virgil's house?"

"Sure." He rose from the chair and followed her through the front door. The storm had passed and left the streets icy and well over a foot of snow on the ground.

"Aren't you going to have to compete against Miller if you run for sheriff?" he asked.

She glanced at him, slight affronted. "He's never said he wants to be sheriff."

"He's older than you and has more experience. Do you really think he'll want to remain deputy his entire career?"

She must have considered that before now, but she didn't appear to like talking about it. "He's not the one who's going to solve the Neville case."

"Never Summer's only cold case." She'd get bored without any other challenges. Did she honestly believe she'd be fulfilled here? As soon as she'd learned of the cold case, she'd picked it up and run with it. Reese had ambition, and not your everyday ordinary ambition. To him, she didn't just think, "I'm going to go to college and get my X degree and then I'm going to get a job I love." Her ambition consumed her.

"That's right. Great leverage for campaigning."

Didn't she hear herself? She would get that college degree and the job and rise to the top in record time. Deputy Miller was more suited for the kind of work she'd encounter here. He liked sitting at his desk eating junk food. Desk time. He doubted Reese sat at her desk very often.

"And then it's back to splitting up drunken bar fights." Not much else could go on in this small town. "Not very exciting."

She stopped at Jamie's rental truck. "Are you trying to talk me into joining DAI?"

He unlocked the door. "No. Just saying…not very exciting." Seeing her baffled look, he realized she didn't know what he was talking about. She had clear goals she intended to go after but she didn't see how they fell short. Maybe she spent too much time protecting her dream rather than recognizing what the dream meant to her.

Without stoking those coals, he opened the door for her.

She didn't move, but put her hands on her hips just above her gear belt. "Are you saying you think I need excitement?"

"Independent woman like you?" He nodded. "Hell yeah."

Leaving her to mull over his comment, he walked around to the driver's side, all but choking back a laugh.

Chapter 13

Reese went with Jamie to Virgil and Lavinia's house on the off chance Virgil had kept something that would identify him as Darius. They'd parked at a trailhead pull-off along the highway that was close to the driveway. She wouldn't have to work out tonight after walking the distance they'd cover today.

She noticed Jamie taking in the scenery, sun melting snow from pine trees and south-facing slopes. Jagged peaks in the distance would take longer to melt.

"I never thought I'd say this, but I like the wilderness almost as much as I like the city."

"What is it you like about cities?" She didn't understand how anyone could think this was worse. "There's so much noise and pollution."

He thought awhile as they hiked up the snowy, icy incline toward Virgil and Lavinia's house. "I guess I have trouble being still and quiet."

In the city he could walk to a variety of things to do. After working for Aesir, the ride down from all that excitement must have contributed to his geographical choice when he returned to the States.

"Are you turning into a quiet man?" she asked in fun, her tactical boots crunching on snow.

"I joined an investigation agency named Dark Alley, so I kind of doubt that."

She laughed softly. He would not get bored working there.

Neither would she...

She caught his playful half grin. He knew what she was thinking.

Reese walked faster, her boots getting good traction on the icy patches in the shade. "I hope Virgil doesn't see us."

"Nice way to change the subject. We'll hear a car and get in the woods before he does."

They reached the clearing in front of the Church residence and paused by a tree.

"It doesn't look like anyone is home," Jamie said.

"They parked their car in the garage last time."

"Let's stick to the woods and look for a better place to approach."

Reese hiked with him through snow until they reached a clearing where the sun had melted to the ground in places, exposing branches and pine needles. The smell wafted up to her nose and she closed her eyes for an inhale. When she opened them, she saw Jamie watching with heating eyes.

They left the cover of the woods and ran to the side of the garage. Jamie peeked into the window.

"No car."

She walked with him to the front door. There, they found the door unlocked.

Reese drew her weapon and pushed the door open. Jamie covered her and she covered him as they entered. The house seemed devoid of life. No sounds indicated any movement. It smelled like bacon grease.

Reese pointed two fingers toward the hall for Jamie and then pointed to herself before aiming toward the garage.

He nodded once and headed for the hall.

She moved through the living room, stepping around a magazine-cluttered coffee table with a half-full cup on top of one. A three-quarters-empty bottle of beer sat on a side table.

At the garage door, she opened it a crack. She pushed it wide open. Nothing else had been disturbed. Going back to the living room, she spotted Jamie coming back down the hall and inquired with her eyes if he'd found anything.

"Nothing." He glanced over the room, seeming distracted.

"Garage, either. No sign of a previous life, although I didn't expect to get that lucky." She glanced at the beer bottle. "Should we ask him to give us a DNA sample?"

"Yes." He turned to her and then sighed. "Don't you think it's strange the bank was robbed by three men in masks when Virgil appears to be the man in the photos with Eva?"

"You think they worked together?" How? And, especially, why?

"I think Bishop or Holcomb broke into your house. They knew about the money. What if Virgil heard them talking, say, over a few beers one night? He may have gone to them or even Stankovich."

"Heard them talking about the money I found and struck up a conversation that led to the revelation Virgil, aka Darius Richardson, stole a quarter million more than forty years ago?" That seemed like quite a stretch to Reese.

"It's a small town."

Reese considered his statement for a moment. Then she nodded lopsidedly. "Virgil could have asked questions about me. Then Holcomb and Bishop could have revealed you worked for Stankovich and he was in town to collect a debt."

"Then Virgil, with a keen eye for criminals, felt safe in mentioning there could be more money to be found, that maybe Eva hid it all over the house."

She could see how Virgil might make that assumption. Jeffrey hadn't lived like a man whose wife had that much money. "Why risk including a stranger, especially one as dangerous as Stankovich?"

"You saw him with Lavinia. Despite their fighting, he loves her. If he killed Eva, he isn't afraid of men like Stankovich. And remember, he has no criminal record. He'd do anything to prevent exposure. Stankovich assures success and removes scrutiny from him. He could have negotiated a percentage in exchange for the location."

She believed it was possible. Virgil, if he was indeed Darius, would do anything to avoid having to leave Never Summer. But a quarter of a million dollars—or even a percentage of it—made the risk worthwhile for a man like him, a man of average, if not meager, means.

Just then, the sound of the garage door opening alerted them. Reese hurriedly followed Jamie to the front door.

Carefully going out the door, Reese could hear Lavinia laughing.

"What a lovely day. I'm a little concerned over the money you spent, but it was like we were young again."

"Anything for my love."

Those two had a strange relationship. Reese looked up at Jamie, who stood close behind her on the front porch. Lavinia and Virgil stood at the trunk of the car, lifting out bags. They were partially concealed by the house and slightly recessed garage, while a tall juniper tree hid Reese and Jamie. Reese watched through the branches.

When Lavinia followed Virgil to the inner garage door, Jamie took Reese's hand and they ran down the dirt road still snow-packed in places until the forest hid them from view. Then Reese walked with Jamie, who didn't let go of her hand.

"I used to hike all the time," he said.

She noticed him looking all over their surroundings.

"I used to breathe in the fresh air the way you do. I don't know why I didn't think of that until now."

"You've been too busy facing down insurgents and living in big cities."

He grunted a half laugh. "One big city. I thought that was what I needed."

"To acclimate to a new life without danger in it?"

"There will always be some amount of danger. But yes. Acclimate."

She watched where she stepped as she imagined him hiking through woods like this as a young man. "Didn't you say you were from Whitman Park?"

"I did. But we went camping in the Appalachian Mountains, and when I was stationed at Fort Carson, I spent as much time as I could in the mountains."

Just when she thought she had him figured out, he surprised her. "You're not a city boy, after all."

"I was a city boy. It took meeting Kadin, and then you, to realize I wasn't a city man anymore. I forgot how much I loved the mountains."

"And here you are trying to coerce me to move to Wyoming."

"There are mountains in Wyoming."

He didn't deny he'd tried to coerce her. How did he make her feel so safe when her mind kept telling her he'd be her ruin if she continued to fall for him? He'd take all she'd worked for and all she planned to achieve if she let him have his way with her. And yet, when he talked with her like this she felt such a deep and satisfying connection. They could talk about anything and she'd feel connected. Maybe because they thought the same and had similar emotional needs.

They reached the road, most of the ice melted except in the shady areas, and ended up closer to the truck than she thought. She walked beside him along the road, trying to ignore how her hand felt in his and his big body moving beside her, taking in the clear day with her.

At the truck, Jamie tugged her away from the door handle and pulled her against him.

She inhaled sharply, startled but instantly aroused.

"We're close to Slumgullion Pass from here," Jamie said. "There's an overlook I want you to see."

Like the wild horses, his enthusiasm infected her. "Windy Point Overlook?"

"I don't remember the name. I only remember the view, and the history."

History? She was about to ask what history when he bent for a quick kiss.

During the few minutes he drove along Highway 149, Jamie watched with a glance every now and then as Reese recovered from the kiss. He'd kept it deliberately brief, just enough to remind her they had something special. She responded instantaneously to him. Her reaction only intensified his.

He also kept an eye on the road, especially behind. He had to stay on the lookout for Stankovich. His nemesis wasn't finished with Jamie yet. In fact, Jamie wouldn't be surprised if Stankovich had planned for him to rescue Reese, a perfect distraction while he robbed the bank. Phase one. Phase two…?

Parking on Windy Point Overlook, he sat back and soaked in the sight—and the memories from so long ago. He'd been such a dreamer back then, believing only good things could happen to him. He'd never considered anything negative would come his way, nothing like Stankovich. Weren't all young people that way? He'd been a young man full of blind ambition. Invincible. Caution hadn't mattered until life changed him from a fool to a grown man.

"I never get tired of it, either," Reese said.

She leaned back, her eyes drooping as though she was bathing in warm water at the end of a long day.

He opened the door and got out, walking to the edge of the lookout. Lake San Cristobal glistened in bright sunlight, the blue-green water shimmering like diamonds.

"In the right sunlight you can see clouds reflected on the surface," Reese said. "The Slumgullion Slide formed this lake."

"I know. I read all about this area after coming here."

"You never told me you've been here before."

"I am now." He smiled over at her and then turned back to the view. "You can see where the slide broke and changed the landscape, including creating Lake San Cristobal." He turned and pointed to the peaks. "That's Uncompahgre Peak. The Wetterhorn was probably a large volcano at one time. It's an intrusion with radial dikes."

She drew her head back with a breathy, "What? How do you know all of that?"

"I studied it."

"Geology?"

"I read a lot. I like to read about things like that."

"Do you now…?"

"Sunshine and Redcloud Peaks sit in a caldera." He pointed again. "They're comprised of volcanic rock, but the west and south rim of the caldera is Precambrian rock uplifted to form the San Juans."

"Are you sure you didn't want to become a geologist instead of a soldier?"

"I think I would have wanted both. It's a hobby, that's all."

"I like to read nonfiction, too, but I don't study it the way you do."

"If you like listening to me talk about it I'd be happy to oblige." The breeze picked up into heftier gusts, living up to the lookout's name.

"I never knew most of this about my hometown. I mean, I knew there were volcanoes and about the caldera, but not in any detail."

"Now you do." He hoped she enjoyed hearing him talk like this, or showing her things like the wild horses.

He stood behind her and looped his arm across her abdomen, tucking his head close to hers. "It's getting windy."

She didn't resist or try to pull away, just stood with him and took in the view. After a few moments, he lifted his head enough to see her profile. Beautiful golden-brown eyes, soft with contentment, drooped as they had before. Then they rose to look up at him. Caught by the window of light and vibrancy that was Reese, he lowered his head. Her lips were positioned at just the right angle for a kiss.

He felt her indrawn breath and the brush of her lips as they parted to receive him. She responded almost automatically, as though her body knew exactly what to do once he touched her.

Still in the moment the view and geologic history had enchanted them into, he kissed her softly. Turning in his arms, she put her hands on his face as he continued to kiss her.

When he began to react in a way that would necessitate more privacy, he ended the kiss.

"A rock might be uncomfortable," she quipped.

"Even these rocks." As much as he admired them…

* * *

Reese woke slowly, warm and snuggled in softness. No, some of it was hard. Her hand moved over softness and felt hardness beneath. The remnants of a dream about rocks and sex accompanied her as she came fully awake. She opened her eyes to her hand on a sturdy chest, fingers spanning over a nipple that rose and fell in a restful rhythm. She looked up to see Jamie's handsome face still slack in sleep.

With her thigh draped over his hip, she reacted as she always did. Instant heat coursed through her. She didn't let her conscience interfere. She put her finger over his full lips and traced their outline. His kisses felt so good.

Because she preferred denial over self-gratification right now, she pushed up onto her hand and knee and slid on top of him. His eyes cracked open. Then his hands went to her thighs and slid up to her hips. He pulled her up a bit, and she felt him growing hard as his eyes opened more.

Reese bent to kiss him. He sank his fingers in her hair and kept her firmly there, kissing her back.

She moved against his erection and then reached for the hem of her nightgown. He stopped her with his hands.

He rolled her onto her back and crawled on top of her. Excitement raced in her veins and fired up her mind. Yes.

But instead of continuing to make magic with her, he simply gazed down at her.

She grew confused. What was he doing?

"Do you need some help?" She took the waistband of his underwear in her hands.

He grasped her wrists and put them down on the mattress beside her head. "I want more than sex to bring you close to me."

Stunned, she watched him climb off the bed and go into the bathroom, shutting and locking the door.

Reese propped herself up on her elbows and stared at the closed door, battling with feelings of bewildered rejection. He hadn't minded using sex before. What had changed?

He must have stronger feelings for her.

While a deeper part of her melted with the idea and told her to go to him now, right now, another more familiar part prevented her. She was in real danger of being forced to end another relationship she knew wouldn't last. She didn't want to hurt Jamie. She didn't want to hurt anyone. That's why she had to be careful.

If Jamie was no longer willing to engage in a casual affair, then she had to end it before it got any more serious.

No matter how difficult it would be to sever their ties, she had to think of him more than herself. She liked Jamie. She liked his strength and resolve. She liked his mind. She liked so many things about him.

The word *love* kept echoing in her head. She dismissed its significance.

She got off the bed and put on her robe. Going into the kitchen, she waited for him to finish in the bathroom. She had coffee made and half of her first cup finished by the time he emerged showered and fully dressed.

She resisted the left-out feeling she got seeing him. He hadn't invited her in the shower. He'd locked her out.

"Jamie, we need to talk."

He took a cup from the tray beside the television on the cabinet.

"Your reaction in there tells me it's time."

With steaming cup in hand, he leaned against the counter. "My reaction?"

He hadn't let their passion get out of hand. "Why did you withdraw?"

When he didn't respond, she wondered if he was getting too serious.

"You have to admit, up until now you've been playing me," she said. "Not *me*. My attraction to you."

He sipped his coffee, too calm and too calculating. "I'm courting you. I've been courting you on faith that you'll come around."

Come around to marriage and babies and suburbia and…shared bank accounts. "I'm not saying you are, but I feel like you're trying to…to…trap me into something I'm not ready for."

"I haven't asked you to marry me."

Anger was subtly laced into his tone. No, he hadn't asked her to marry him. Maybe she was overreacting. Maybe she shouldn't have any expectations about them. They had sex. They were seeing each other. That didn't mean she had to stay with him for good. A familiar apprehension came over her. She'd been with men who wanted her, knowing she wouldn't reciprocate. The breakups had been messy. Uncomfortable. She'd been riddled with guilt.

"I had plans before I met you."

"Have I asked you to change them?"

"No." She began to wonder if she'd overreacted. Still, things needed to be said. Clarified and understood by both of them. "But it's more than just that. Eventually our differing paths will drive us apart— me apart…from you." How else could she say it? A man would derail her plans. Period.

"I'm not the same as those other guys, Reese, so don't even go there." His stern face and tone couldn't be denied. This man didn't do anything without confidence.

"I know you're not the same." She would never make the comparison. "It's only the situation that has similarities. I have dreamed of being sheriff of Never Summer for years."

"And I would never ask you to give that up." Although he would hope she could see she was made for more, for DAI.

"In a way you are. You just took a job for my father, who lives in Wyoming. You can't live here and work there. Besides that, I don't ever want to hurt you the way I've hurt others, so maybe it is time to cool things off."

Now he strode over to her, intense, masculine and full of outrage. She had to stop herself from stepping backward.

Standing close, he put his hand on her chin, cupping it with his thumb and palm. She met his fiery eyes, but they didn't show anger. It was determination.

"Don't be mistaken," he said in a low, gravelly voice. "There may come a time when you convince me you'll never accept what we have together. You're a woman who doesn't know her own heart. I'm still here because I haven't given up hope you'll decide to learn." He dropped his hand and stepped back. "You're not the only one with a decision to make, Reese."

Each well-planted word sliced through her with lancing truth. She could only stand there frozen in singed shock as he turned and left.

Chapter 14

Kadin asked them to stop by his cabin. He hadn't explained why and Jamie suspected it was to get Reese to come and see him again. Jamie walked toward the front door a little ahead of Reese.

She wasn't as tense as she had been the first time she'd been here. She was quiet for another reason. He didn't feel like talking to her right now, anyway. Finding out her stubbornness would stand in the way of their happiness really got to him. When he'd come to Never Summer, he didn't think anything Reese could say or do would either deter him or make him mad. Well, she had.

She didn't want to hurt him. She'd hurt others before him. And she'd rather let him go than alter her course. Right or wrong.

He wasn't sure if he was angrier with himself or

her. She chose to stay blind to the love the two of them were building. He hadn't experienced betrayal from a woman before. He hadn't been around long enough, nor did he go into a relationship without being completely honest about the time he could and couldn't offer. But he had experienced betrayal. He trusted Stankovich when he shouldn't have. Reese made him feel like that again, like he should have known better than to trust her, trust that she'd outgrow her stubbornness or lack of insight to change. She didn't want to change and there was nothing he could do about it.

Jamie rang the bell. In his peripheral vision, he saw Reese glance at him once. His mood might trouble her, but he didn't care unless she had more to offer than sex.

Kadin let them in. He was cleanly shaven but with stubble showing, and wore jeans with a big belt buckle and flannel shirt. No hat.

He eyed them as they passed. "Lovers' quarrel?"

Jamie ignored him and greeted Penny, who held the baby in one arm and a bottle with the other. She wore leggings and a black ruffle-sleeve kimono over a white-and-black patterned T-shirt. The baby was in a blue-and-black outfit with Mom's Home Run printed on the front of the long-sleeved T-shirt.

The moss rock wall and fireplace dominated the living room and the gold furnishings and wood floor gave it warmth. The kitchen was a little brighter with a rock base island and lighter granite countertops, but the dark cabinetry carried the aura of romantic lighting.

Penny took a seat at the dining room table adjacent to the living room. Jamie went there with Kadin, Reese joining them last, sitting on the last chair.

"How's the investigation coming?" Kadin looked at Reese. "You haven't called."

Her eyes lowered before meeting his. "We think we know who killed Ella Neville, aka Eva."

Jamie listened as she narrated all they knew. Virgil's falsified identity and the timing of the change. The not-so-coincidental robbery by masked men.

When she finished, Kadin looked at Jamie. "Anything else?"

Jamie shook his head.

"Your home was burglarized in Rock Springs," Kadin said.

While that didn't come as a shock to Jamie, it did come with a good dose of dread. His suspicion was right.

"What aren't you telling me?" Kadin asked, his wife looking up from feeding the baby.

Stankovich was looking for Jamie's insurance. But Kadin suspecting something else was at work didn't change Jamie's reason for not telling anyone.

"Telling you will put more than myself in extreme danger," he said.

"At the risk of sounding arrogant, look who you're talking to," Kadin said. "Nobody is going to hurt me or anyone close to me."

Jamie looked at Reese. He hadn't exactly been referring to Kadin.

Reese lifted her brow at him, a dare to say what she must know was on his mind.

She lightened his mood. He grinned at her sass.

"Just tell us, Jamie," she said impatiently.

He leaned back against the chair. "Back when I cleared my name and wiped any false evidence Stankovich had on me, I also planned to get something dirty on him, sort of as an insurance policy if he ever decided to get at me again. I didn't think he would. I'd caused him enough grief. And by then he should have known I wouldn't tolerate any of his control tactics." He stopped. Revealing more would put them all in jeopardy. He looked at Reese, and then at Penny and the baby. He could never live with himself if anything happened to the innocent.

"Go on," Kadin said.

Maybe it was too late for secrets. Maybe not. "First you have to understand this isn't only information on Stankovich. It involves someone else, an entire organization. A big, scary one. Stankovich is a tiny flea compared to this raptor."

Kadin sat still a moment, now comprehending the purpose of extreme secrecy. He turned to Penny, who narrowed her eyes and said, "Don't even ask me to leave the room. If someone could come after my husband I want to be armed with all the information so I can fight if I have to." The baby made mewling sounds and reached his tiny hand toward his mother. She bent down and kissed his fingers, eliciting laughter and abandonment of the bottle.

"I'm an officer of the law," Reese said. "Stankovich committed a crime in my county. I should know everything I'm up against."

Jamie turned to Kadin and they exchanged a look that showed their mutual sense of defeat.

At last, Jamie said, "All right. But no names. To get what I have on Stankovich, I had to talk to a few people to find out about his latest activities. I knew he'd have some dirty ones. That's how he operates. If he can make money, he takes opportunities, no matter the cost, innocent or not. I followed a couple of his closest men and heard they planned to travel to Crimea for an arms deal. I trailed them and took photos of them stealing arms from a warehouse. I then learned of a plan to take the arms to Syria and sell them. I trailed them there, too, and took photos of them selling the stolen arms to rebels. I later learned who owned the weapons—a Russian mob leader."

"He sounds like a real charmer." Penny stood with the baby, who'd begun to fuss. She moved over to Kadin and bent to kiss him. "Catch him, honey."

Kadin kissed her back. "We will."

Jamie watched how the easy exchange of love once again captivated Reese. She must not have seen her adoptive parents kiss like that, much less look at each other the way these two did.

He could feel her thoughts. Did she kiss Jamie that way? Did she look at him that way? Was she looking at him that way now? He began to smolder with stirring desire. She looked at him the way Penny looked at Kadin. Did that mean she loved him?

"How did Stankovich find out you had photos?" Kadin asked.

Reese jerked her gaze away.

Jamie turned his focus to Kadin's question. "My inside man must have told him I knew about the arms." He wouldn't have to be told there was evidence. He knew Jamie wouldn't have intercepted them without recording something. And the man who'd kept him informed wouldn't have willingly talked. He must have been forced and, presumably, was now dead.

"So now Stankovich wants the photos." Reese stated the obvious. "Is that why he kidnapped me?"

"If we hadn't rescued you before he could carry out his plan, yes, I don't doubt that's what he'd have done. My first phone call would have been a demand for the photos in exchange for you."

He watched Penny walking the room with a slight bounce that had rocked Clayton to sleep.

"Virgil might have capitalized on making a chance deal with Stankovich, but he's the least of our concerns," Kadin said. "We have to find Stankovich."

Reese saw a stack of file folders on the table and noticed they weren't the Neville case.

"Are you working on another investigation?"

Kadin leaned forward and slid the files closer to her. "It's a serial murder case. No DNA. No prints. No fibers."

Reese opened the file and flipped through the pages and photographs.

"All the women are assaulted and then stabbed to death, presumably with the same weapon. No witnesses. This killer is meticulous and knows how to avoid leaving forensic evidence. He's been on the loose for an estimated six years."

A killer who had to be stopped. A deep urge expanded in her to catch the sicko. Her fascination didn't help, either. Ever since her college criminal justice classes she'd discovered a talent and a natural interest in not only what makes a person cross the line into murder, but also the lives of their victims and the legal process to deliver a well-deserved punishment. Being part of that process gave her purpose. Was Jamie right when he said her job as sheriff wouldn't be exciting?

Kadin's cell phone rang. The cabins were close enough to the highway and a cellular tower to provide service.

He answered and Reese waited while he listened briefly. Penny disappeared to go put the baby down.

"Thanks." Kadin disconnected and then said, "The DNA we got from Eva is a match in Paula Kowalski's case. She was killed by the same person. Jeffrey's DNA didn't match."

Reese expected Jeffrey's test to come back with those results. She felt glad he'd be put back to rest with his reputation intact. But Virgil... Could he be the killer? He seemed an unlikely suspect, but more than forty years had passed.

She barely listened as Kadin and Jamie moved on to a discussion on the candidates Jamie had interviewed and which ones to hire. They'd already hired some, and they all sounded like fearsome soldiers.

She stood when they finished and went in for Kadin's hug. She almost didn't want to leave. If she stayed she could talk more with him, and not about murder cases. The hug made her stiffen. So did her desire to stay.

"Call more often. Stop by whenever you want."

"Okay." She put her arms around him and hugged back.

This was an alien thing for Reese. She didn't hug anyone. But the embrace with her real father began to warm into something she'd never felt before. She relaxed a little while she picked apart the gesture. He held her like a dad would. She felt his good intentions, his growth in getting accustomed to the fact that he had a living daughter.

He must have his own struggles in that process. This hug was a milestone for him as much as it was for her.

What had only been seconds felt more like minutes before he finally withdrew. He planted a kiss on her cheek and stepped back.

"Say goodbye to my baby brother." She beamed a smile she genuinely felt.

"I'll do better than that. I'll give him a kiss for you."

This felt so like a family. She started to turn.

"Hey."

Reese looked back at her father.

"I almost forgot. I wanted to ask you if you have any pictures of when you were growing up. When you were a baby. Your first birthday. Holidays. That sort of thing. And anything else you have. Videos. Maybe when your case is solved you could tell me all about your life up until now. I've missed out on a lot."

She had to hand it to him. He'd waited until now to make such a request. He'd allowed her time to get used to him as her real father. And while they had a long way to go before either of them could say they knew each other well, they were off to a healthy start.

"Yeah. Sure. Of course." She nodded, that invisible space of hers threatened. Except now her resistance seemed kind of silly. Why wouldn't she want to get to know her father? So it was different than what she'd had so far. What was wrong with different?

"Take good care of her," Kadin said to Jamie.

"Always."

"And Reese?" She braced herself for some fatherly advice. "He's not a bad guy. Give him a chance."

Reese could only gape at him.

"I'm just trying to give my approval," Kadin said.

"Thanks, boss." Jamie chuckled and guided Reese out the door.

Reese smiled, having to make herself somewhat, but not willing to let go of the magic. "Dad."

His smile broadened and he lifted his hand for a wave.

Outside, Reese walked in a daze toward Jamie's truck, not sure what had just happened to her. Something significant.

"Good job in there," Jamie said.

"What?" Good job? As in, good job hugging your dad?

"You actually hugged your father." He opened the passenger door for her. "It's okay if you feel a connection with your dad, Reese. Don't be so hard on yourself."

Reese didn't get into the truck. "I'm hard on myself?"

"You keep what you feel locked away. Just then, you let some of it out and it was amazing. Maybe you should try letting it go more often. Let what you feel out."

Didn't she already?

Virgil arrived at work on time the next day. He got out of the car with a paper cup of coffee.

"We can use that if he doesn't agree to a sample," Reese said.

"All right." They'd reveal how close they were to catching him. What if he ran? Jamie didn't think he would, not without his wife. And if she didn't know about Eva's murder...

He approached Virgil with Reese.

"Good morning, Virgil," Reese said.

Virgil stopped, looking wary of why they were there and talking to him.

"Mind if we ask you a few questions? We'd like to bring you to the sheriff's office if you don't mind."

"For what?"

"Eva Sinclair's murder," Reese said calmly, in a friendly tone.

Virgil flinched ever so slightly. "Eva?"

"Yes. If you'll come with us?"

"I can't. I have to work."

Screw process. "We discovered you assumed someone else's identity, Mr. Church," Jamie said. "And the timing fits that of Eva's murder. Paula Kowlowski's, too. We have matching DNA on both crime scenes and would like to eliminate you as a suspect."

Virgil looked stunned at first and then a cool mask slid into place. "And if I refuse?"

"We'll consider you a suspect in both women's murders," Reese said. "I can arrest you for identity theft right now. But we just want to ask you some questions and get a DNA sample."

"I don't have to talk to you." Virgil started walking toward the hardware store. Turning his head over his shoulder, he added, "I didn't kill anyone and I don't know anyone named Eva or Paula."

Jamie stood with Reese and watched him go into the hardware store.

"I was afraid it would go like that," Reese said. "He seems guilty."

"He doesn't want to talk. He must have something to hide."

"It's almost sad," she said. "He's a much older man with a new life. He probably regrets what he did. He doesn't have a criminal record."

"He killed two women. I hope they haunted him every day."

"I wasn't saying what he did is all right. He lost control of weak emotions that turned violent and now he'll have to pay the consequences."

Jamie could see through the front window and watched Virgil disappear toward the back of the hardware store. "Let's go in when the store opens and see what he does with that coffee cup."

Fifteen minutes later, the owner unlocked the doors. He and Reese got out and crossed the street.

"Morning, Reese," the owner called from behind the counter. "I thought you were all finished with your renovations."

"Just a few touch-ups left."

Jamie walked with her through the hardware store, searching for Virgil and his coffee cup. She pretended to look over some curtain rods. Down the next aisle, they spotted him. He was putting containers of windshield washer fluid onto a display near the front window.

He paused and drank from the cup, draining its contents and putting it on a nearby shelf. When he glanced their way, Jamie picked up a light fixture and showed it to Reese. Virgil looked at them again, with severe consternation. But he kept on working, seemingly secure that they weren't going to make an arrest for murder. Not today.

He and Reese stayed at the light fixtures awhile longer. Virgil finished stacking the containers and took his cup with him as he headed for the back. Jamie went to the end of the aisle and then walked to the last aisle closest to the back. As he approached the entrance, Virgil appeared abruptly, stepping to the corner of a countertop and tossing the coffee cup into a nearly full bag of trash.

Jamie veered into the aisle and checked out a row of shovels. Virgil eyed him for a while and then walked back out into the hardware store. He walked toward the front, seeing Reese paying for a light fixture. The hardware store owner rang up her purchase and casually bade her goodbye.

Back in his truck, he drove to the back of the store, where a Dumpster was enclosed by a wood fence.

"This might take a while," Jamie said.

"Yup." Reese sighed and reclined her seat a little, closing her eyes.

"How did it feel hugging your dad?" Jamie asked.

She opened one eye and rolled it toward him. "You're asking me that now?" She closed both eyes again.

While they were tracking a suspect? "Why not? It's something to talk about. Pass the time."

"Not something I want to talk about."

"Did it scare you?"

Both eyes came open, dark lashes accentuating their striking beauty. She sat up, her blond hair swinging as she turned to look at him fully. "Why do you think that?"

"You hold back with me out of fear. Fear of the unknown. You have set plans and nothing will deter you from them, but what you haven't paid attention to is

I'm not the one who'll steal your dreams. You'll do that all on your own. You'll rob yourself of opportunities by not being open to them."

"Are you still mad about before?"

"I'm not mad at you. I'm mad at myself for trusting you."

Her eyes lowered at that comment. He watched her swallow as though the truth had gotten stuck in her throat.

"I told you I wasn't ready for a serious relationship," she finally said.

She'd cling to that excuse until she lost him. No one could show her the way. She had to find it on her own.

"Nobody plans on when they meet someone who could be their soul mate." He already knew she was his. "Plans can change. Life is about change. If you can't change with it, you'll be stuck in the same place your entire life. Just look at your parents if you don't believe me." He didn't have to meet them in person to know they were those kind of people.

Slowly her head lifted and she looked at him.

"Hugging your father felt good." He didn't need her to tell him. He hoped she'd have the courage to admit it. She didn't. "You also know deep down inside that you'd love working for him. The light in your eyes gave you away when he showed you that case."

Her eyes began to mist. "Don't."

"Do you think he left those files on the table by accident?"

"Jamie…"

He couldn't believe he'd breached her iron wall. "He knows that part of you better than you know it yourself. You're his daughter. Look at him. A born detective, just like you."

A tear slid down her cheek. Inside she must be cracking. Everything she'd originally believed no longer held up to this new reality.

"I have a life here." She sounded choked.

"You have a life with your father, too. Forget about me. Kadin wants you in his life, Reese. Are you going to shut him out? Why did you find him if you didn't plan on that?"

A tiny sob broke from her. "I don't know." She banged her fist on her thigh. "I don't know, okay?" She turned her tear-streaked face to him. "I don't know."

The woman had some serious soul-searching to do. She thought she knew herself but the act of reaching out to find her biological parents without deciding whether to have them involved in her life said she didn't, not wholly and completely. She only knew the independent her, the part of her that had come out being raised by aloof parents.

"I don't want to hurt you." Jamie felt as though he had to rip out who she really was to make her see what she missed.

She sniffled a few times without responding. But finally he heard her quietly say, "It felt good."

He dug behind the passenger seat for a box of tissues.

"The hug did?" He handed her a few tissues.

She nodded as she took them, dropping most in her lap and using one to wipe her eyes and blow her nose.

"It felt real," she continued. "Like he meant it. Like it came from his heart."

Touched beyond measure, thrilled that she'd poked

her stubborn head out for this glimpse of true love, Jamie put his fingers beneath her chin and lifted.

Her teary eyes met his.

"Do you mean it when you kiss me?"

Her soft inhale, a sign of warming passion, gave her away before she said, "Yes."

"Do you feel that I mean it when I kiss you? Do you feel it coming from my heart?"

She closed her eyes for several seconds. Then opened them. "I don't know."

Jamie fought his disappointment. She cut herself off to love so stoutly that he had no way in. But her wall was down right now.

Putting his face closer to hers, he said, "Relax and let me in, Reese. Close your eyes and let me in. Just for one kiss."

She met his eyes and didn't pull back.

He touched his lips to hers. Their quickening breaths filled the cab of the truck. He restrained himself from devouring her. He kissed her with a message. A sweet, pure message.

In her vulnerable state, he felt her sink into the kiss a lot softer than before. Rather than passion leading the way, their hearts did. He felt closer to her now than ever, and rejuvenated that she met him as an equal, even if just this once.

Her hand came to his chest and upward, to the back of his neck. He moved his hand down to the middle of her back. This wasn't about sex. He kissed her only with his heart, drawing hers out, keeping her wall open to loving light. Fighting for her love. He'd fought many battles, but this one would be the toughest one. She had him thinking tender notes that had never before entered his mind. He wouldn't call himself soft, but right now, he felt as light and feathery as a cloud.

At last he pulled back. Her eyes fluttered open and peered up at him with naked emotion, skin flushed and breathing heavy.

"I love you." The words tumbled out unbidden, too late to take them back and keep them to himself until he was more certain of her. "I've loved you since that first night."

"Oh, Jamie." Another tear slid down. She put her hand on his face.

Would it be enough to bring her home with him? She had a life in Never Summer. And her desire to become sheriff couldn't be easily dismissed. Would she be able to embrace a change as big as coming to live with her new family?

When she didn't say she felt the same as him, doubt engulfed all hope.

Chapter 15

After digging in the trash and finding the coffee cup, Reese gave the sample to Kadin, who would rush testing. Now she and Jamie could concentrate on finding Stankovich before he made his next move. They began searching the remains of the burned mine house, which had been nearly destroyed by the fire.

Reese picked through the rubble inside on the off chance they'd find a clue. They had lost the trail on Stankovich. Shadow Mountain Ranch reported he'd stayed there one night, but then left. No one had seen him in town and he hadn't traveled by plane from any of the nearby airports, private or public.

The weather had turned sour overnight, bringing in colder air and gray clouds. The forecast called for more than a foot of snow by tomorrow. Snow fell heavier as flakes sprinkled down through the giant hole in the roof and slanted outside through the sections of walls.

She looked over at Jamie going through what had once been Ray's office. She was still disconcerted over the things Jamie had said, the things he'd made her consider. She didn't want to face them right now. She wasn't sure she ever would.

"I doubt he would leave without finishing his business with me," Jamie said. "That isn't like him. He'd never pass up an opportunity to make money, which he did through Virgil, and he wouldn't leave while I still breathe."

"Where could he have gone?"

"Somewhere strategic. Somewhere he could safely draw me out. And you, probably." He said the last in disgust.

Reese thought of what Stankovich might have done if his first attempt to lure Jamie hadn't failed. She stopped searching through charred debris and arched her aching back, looking around. Where the mine tunneled into the mountain was dark. The door that had once been there was gone, burned to a pile of ash and pieces of blackened wood.

To think she'd once been locked in a room near there made her shudder. Her gaze went back to the opening of the mine shaft.

"Ray said he was working on turning his house into a museum. The mine should still be intact." She started to walk over there.

After removing her flashlight from her gear belt, Reese switched it on. Shining the beam over jagged rock drilled out of the mountain, she stepped into a bulbous kind of space and saw an opening to the right, flanked by metal stairs leading up to a machine.

Jamie appeared beside her. "Mine elevator shaft." He climbed the stairs to the hydraulic drum and moments later the elevator rumbled to life.

He came back down the stairs to her.

"Ray was going to make a museum of this?" she asked, watching the cables move as the elevator lifted.

The metal elevator car came to a clanking stop.

She glanced at Jamie. "Why was the car at the bottom?"

"Let's find out." He removed his gun as he opened the metal door and stepped into the car. Reese stepped on after him, taking out her gun, as well. After closing the gate, he reached for the car control panel and started them lowering.

Light from the opening disappeared as rock surrounded them on all sides. Only Reese's flashlight provided illumination.

"Maybe Ray came back," she said.

"Maybe."

Through the darkness she saw him turn to her. The way he looked at her said he didn't think so and he probably wished he could tell her to stay up top.

The rock wall opened at the bottom, the elevator coming to a noisy stop. No lights were on. Reese shined her flashlight into a mostly square space where miners used to load ore onto the elevator. Old railroad tracks still ran from the elevator opening and branched off to vanish into the darkness of three tunnels.

Ray had begun to set up a display, a mannequin dressed as a miner standing beside an ore cart. Another stood beside another cart inside the opening of one of the tunnels, eerily lifelike. They gave her an impression of the lonesome, hard-living miners they represented, ghosts from the past. Nothing stirred. The mine was utterly silent and dark.

Reese put her pistol away and went to the mannequin at the tunnel, having to tip her head up to look at the marvelously realistic replica. The mannequin's blue work pants with suspenders and tan shirt were dirty.

A sound carried from somewhere down the adjacent tunnel. She looked there and saw only darkness.

"What was that?"

Jamie was looking toward the tunnel, too. "I don't know."

"It sounded like...moaning."

"We'll—"

Something moved in the tunnel where Reese stood at its threshold. Alarm snapped her into action. She turned the light in that direction and reached for her gun, but before she could draw it, a man sprang up from behind the cart with the barrel of his weapon aimed at her. He moved in front of her and pressed the pistol to her forehead. She found herself staring up at a tall, lean man with pale blue eyes shadowed by the rim of a baseball hat, holding the same impassiveness she remembered from the last time they'd met.

Stankovich.

"Drop your weapon," he said, looking past her at Jamie.

With dread and terrible foreboding churning, she turned her head just enough to see Holcomb and Bishop had emerged from another tunnel and had him at gunpoint. He hadn't put his gun away and must have seen Stankovich before she did, because he aimed his pistol right at him.

Stankovich slid her gun from its holster and tucked it into the waist of his pants.

"Do it now or I will kill her."

"Then you'll never get the photos I have of you doing business with the Russians," Jamie said.

"I will have all I require, one way or another."

What would he do? Torture Jamie until he talked? Kill him and take the chance the evidence he had would never surface?

"Not from me you won't," Jamie said with a dark, certain curve to his mouth.

Stankovich grunted cynically. "Oh, yes I will. Unless you prefer to have the death of your boss's son on your conscience?"

Reese drew in a startled breath. He'd kidnapped her half brother? "He's just a baby!"

"Then I suggest you talk your lover into dropping his weapon."

Unable to stop the sting of tears, she saw Jamie looked equally bleak and disgusted. Stankovich would go to any lengths now.

"How do I know you kidnapped Clayton? Kadin would never allow anyone to take his son."

"He wasn't there when we broke into his rented cabin. His wife put up a valiant fight but she was outnumbered and outgunned."

"I swear if you hurt her or anyone—"

"No one has been harmed and no one will be as long as you do as I say."

Jamie's cell phone began to ring. That had to be Kadin.

Still holding his gun, Jamie pulled out the phone.

"Do not answer," Stankovich said.

Jamie pressed something on the phone and put it away. "How do I know you kidnapped Clayton? I demand proof of life."

Stankovich nodded once to Bishop, who took out his phone and showed Jamie what must have been a video clip. Next, he called a number and held the phone to Jamie's ear. When Jamie closed his eyes in dismay, Reese knew it was the baby. And now they also knew there was more than these three in Never Summer. Stankovich had a team.

Jamie dropped his gun. "I'm not the monster you are. In that you'll always come out ahead. Men like you are cowards. You use the innocent because you're no match against men like me and Kadin."

"Enough talk. You know what I require for the safe return of the boy and the woman." He gripped Reese's arm painfully.

Craning her neck, she watched Jamie turn to Bishop and Holcomb, no doubt weighing his odds. They didn't look very good from her vantage point.

"Come with me." Stankovich forced her into the tunnel.

She held her flashlight and Stankovich turned on the one he had clipped to his hat. Deeper into the tunnel, thick log trunks formed supports for the rock ceiling and walls. Jagged edges of rock cast eerie shadows, the darkness ahead an abyss. She craned her neck to try to see Jamie, but the path behind her was also complete blackness.

Where the tunnel widened, Stankovich shoved her toward one of the log supports. She stumbled and stopped herself from bashing face-first into the hard wood. She dropped her flashlight and it illuminated a roll of duct tape on the ground.

"Sit down," he ordered.

She hesitated. The idea of being bound and helpless disquieted her.

He pressed the gun against her temple. "My patience wore thin after you escaped my first attempts to rid Knox from my life. Do not attempt to escape again."

Seeing intense menace in his eyes, she listened to the veiled threat and sat on the hard ground. He picked up the duct tape and handed it to her.

"Put that around your ankles."

She slowly unwound some of the tape.

"And do a good job or I'll shoot you where the tape should go. You won't be able to walk."

She could do without gunshot wounds to her ankles. Reese wrapped two layers of tape around her ankles.

"Now put your hands around the log."

Reese scooted so she could fit her arms around the log pole. Her elbow rubbed against the rock wall and she sat on her hip with her legs bent.

Holding the gun, he wrapped her wrists.

She tested her bonds as he straightened. She'd have a difficult time getting free. At least he hadn't gagged her.

"Now. You will wait here for me."

"What are you going to do?"

He walked back down the tunnel without answering.

* * *

Jamie could kick himself for not remaining more vigilant. Stankovich had what he wanted. With Reese, he'd force Jamie to do his bidding. Jamie felt the same as he had when he'd worked for the heartless criminal. Watching Reese disappear into the tunnel had taken a few years off his life. He had to restrain himself from engaging in a fight with these two goons and going after her and severing his ties with Stankovich permanently.

Stay calm. Stankovich may have the upper hand now, but he wouldn't for long. Jamie would die before he allowed anything to happen to Reese. As it happened, he wouldn't have to. He'd sent a message to Kadin, one he'd written prior to coming to the mine. Unbelievably he had cell service down here. Though an old mine, it was close to the highway. Plan B. If Stankovich did happen to be hiding somewhere at the mine, all he had to do was press Send. The video Bishop had shown him showed Clayton in a car seat somewhere in this mine. The sound he'd heard must have been him.

"You," Stankovich said to Holcomb. "Go watch the woman."

Holcomb strode off into the tunnel, disappearing in darkness until he flipped on his flashlight. But he quickly vanished as he rounded the turn in the tunnel.

"I do not think I have to tell you how this is going to go," Stankovich said. "I shudder to think what might have happened had I not learned what you had on me and I executed you too soon. You have cleaned yourself of anything I have on you. Do you not think it is only fair that I have the same allowance?"

"You don't know the meaning of the word *fair*. So my answer to your question is no."

"Brave, bold words for a man who will lose the woman he loves as a consequence of such foolishness."

Jamie didn't doubt Stankovich would kill Reese. If he believed Jamie would never hand over his evidence, he would kill her. He operated in the cut-and-dried. If there was no evidence, then he would view it as having nothing to lose by killing someone important to Jamie. That way he still won a part of his warped plan.

"You have twenty-four hours." Stankovich walked to the elevator car and opened the metal gate. "Don't make me stay down in this hole any longer than that."

Jamie went into the elevator car and started the lift upward. At the top, he left the mine shaft and took out his phone. Stankovich was slipping in his evil ways. Why hadn't he taken his phone from him? So he could stay in contact with him?

As soon as he stepped out into the rubble of the charred house, Jamie heard and saw several black SUVs slide to a halt on the snow-packed driveway, clouds of snow billowing up.

As soon as his son had been taken, Kadin had called in the cavalry. How had he gotten them here so fast?

Kadin jumped out of one SUV, his wife out of the passenger side.

"You move fast."

"You helped. All the operatives you've been hiring agreed to meet and stay in Never Summer until this situation is resolved."

Penny rushed toward them from around the SUV. "Where's Clayton?"

Jamie got down to business, explaining to everyone where Reese was being held and who guarded her and where Clayton was. He drew the layout of the mine in the snow with a stick.

"They're going to hear the elevator," Jamie said.

"We'll go down silently." One of Kadin's men lifted his hand and gave his finger a twirl, which must be code for rappelling equipment.

"I'm going with you," Jamie said.

"We're all going." Kadin turned to Penny. "Except you. We need someone to stay topside as a lookout for more of Stankovich's men."

Penny didn't respond right away—a mother intent on getting her child back safely had taken her over.

Kadin stepped closer, putting his hands on her arms. "I *will* bring him back to you."

With that she blinked and pressed her forehead to his chest. Then she lifted her head and Kadin kissed her.

"Stay out of sight just in case," he said as he backed away. When she nodded, he said to the team, "Let's gear up!"

In his harness, Jamie rappelled down after Kadin. The team had set up a pulley to lift them out. If he had his way, Stankovich and his cohorts would be stuck down in the mine. If they survived this raid.

Jamie's headlamp shone on the volcanic rock that had been drilled out to install the elevator. He lowered down the middle of the shaft and probably moved faster than the elevator had. He saw Kadin's headlamp and looked up before his feet touched the top of the elevator car. Kadin aimed his high-powered automatic rifle into the open area where Jamie had last seen Stankovich.

Dots of moving headlamps showed the progress of the rest of their team. Quite an impressive feat, how the man mobilized rescuers, how he predicted the need for them.

He stepped out of the way as the other men reached the elevator, joining Kadin in standing guard.

When all the men stood on the elevator car, Kadin pointed to himself and then two other men and then the tunnel where his son had been taken. Then to Jamie and the remaining two down the tunnel where Reese had been taken.

Jamie jumped down from the top of the elevator car and started toward the tunnel where he'd last seen Reese. Kadin stopped him with his hand on his shoulder. "Bring my daughter back."

"I will." His certainty of that met no bounds.

Jogging to the tunnel, Jamie stopped in the darkness with his two special operatives. Ahead he could make out the outline of the rock walls and some of the ribbing of timbering supporting the tunnel from collapse. He heard talking but couldn't discern what was being said. Two voices. No others had joined her since he'd left.

One of the operatives moved forward and put his back to the wall, rifle raised and ready to fire. The second operative tapped Jamie's shoulder.

Jamie turned and saw the operative looking down the dark tunnel. He saw nothing, but heard the approach of several men. In seconds they'd be upon them. Stankovich must have had them waiting in the third tunnel, just out of sight in case Jamie planned a return like this.

The second operative had caught on to what was coming and just as a half-dozen armed men emerged from blackness, he jumped out and fired at Reese's guard. Moving behind one of the large log supports, Jamie saw the other operative do the same.

He started firing at the group and the operative across from him did the same. The men took what cover they could in the open tunnel and fired back. Bullets hit the log trunk. The operative across from him moved to fire. Jamie fired with him and the second operative's rifle began to go off between them. Their automatic weapons overpowered the men who'd approached. Jamie ran up the tunnel, making it around the turn and putting his back to the wall behind another log support. He saw Reese bound and sitting on the ground, Holcomb shot and either dead or unconscious, sprawled on the ground a few feet from her.

"Hurry," Reese said, stretching her neck to try to see around the curve in the tunnel.

While the operatives finished fighting off the attackers, he went to her, going down on one knee. "You're safe now." There was no time to express his great relief to find her unharmed.

He slid out a knife from a strap at his thigh and cut the tape from her wrists. She sat away from the log, wincing from being tied at an unnatural angle for too long. He removed the tape at her ankles and helped her to her feet. The two operatives came to stand before them.

"The tunnel is clear, sir."

"Jamie," he corrected the man.

Gunfire and shouts from the other tunnel brought them all turning. Kadin's fight couldn't be heard over theirs, but now that they'd taken the tunnel, it became clear that it wasn't over.

Reese ignored her aching muscles when she heard the gunfire. She ran after Jamie and the two strangers—where had they come from? She followed the sound of their running feet to the open area, but slowed as they entered the next tunnel. She was not armed. She walked to a log beam, more timber forming a rib here, as well. She peered into the tunnel, gunshots ringing out along with shouts, some in pain.

Carefully, she moved forward. The ribbed log structure ended at a wider section of the tunnel. Men fought beneath strings of lights that had been hung, illuminating long tables with white linens and candles, bowls of fruit and platters of cheese. Bottles and glasses of wine, some empty and some partially full, sat abandoned, as though a party had been interrupted. A refrigerator and a television fastened to a rock wall ran off humming generators. A veritable food court had been set up here. Cots lined the tunnel beyond. She heard a crying baby and spotted the outline of a baby in a blanket on one of the cots.

Tucking herself behind a log, she watched as Jamie and the men quickly subdued Stankovich's soldiers, sending one crashing into a log support. The log gave way, falling to the ground. She heard the wood above crack and break, as crumbling rock sagged and a few fine granules fell.

Stankovich was not among the captured. Seeing a gun lying near a fallen man's hand, she took it up. Just before she turned to go in search of him, she caught sight of another fallen man.

Kadin?

"Dad?" She jumped over bodies as she ran past tables.

Reaching the edge of the cot where Clayton lay crying, she flew to Kadin's side. He lay unconscious, bleeding from a wound to his head and oozing from a gunshot wound to his back. He'd been compromised in his determination to reach his son.

One of the men went to the cot and lifted Clayton. "Jamie!"

"Someone call for help!" Jamie yelled.

"Already radioed," one of the men answered.

Crouching beside Reese and checking on Kadin, he pressed a hard kiss to Reese. "I'm going to find Stankovich."

But as he straightened, two men were roughly man-handling Stankovich, who eyed Jamie in contempt.

Jamie walked to him and punched him in the face. Stankovich's head rocked backward.

Reese felt the unprovoked punishment justified and inwardly cheered, but she was more concerned with Kadin. *Her father.*

She kept pressure on Kadin's wound. "Wake up." She couldn't lose him now, not when she'd only just begun to understand what it meant to have found him.

A piece of wood crashed down from the timbering, loose rocks tumbling down after it. Their only way out had begun to crumble.

When Jamie paused to look, Stankovich rammed his elbow back into one of his captors and shoved the other. He bent to produce a knife from his boot.

"You think you can take me down?" Stankovich growled.

More rocks fell from where the log ribbing had failed.

"You'll do that on your own." Jamie blocked a swipe of the knife and then used his pistol to hit Stankovich.

"We have to get out of here!" Reese shouted.

Stankovich stumbled back as timber cracked, explosions of breaking wood creating a domino effect. Rock began to fall in a roar.

Two of the men lifted Kadin and began running with him through the tunnel, dust and dirt flowing after them. Reese ran beside them, seeing Clayton ahead in the arms of another man.

She glanced back to see Stankovich lunge for Jamie again. She stopped. But Jamie blocked that attempt as well and then knocked the man in the head, sending him down to the ground.

More beams failed. Bigger rocks crashed down.

Jamie started to go for Stankovich, but the ceiling began to fail. Stankovich yelled with his arm raised as though that would protect him from the boulder that crashed down on top of him, silencing him forever.

The ceiling above Jamie began to crumble. Smaller rocks sprinkled down.

"Jamie!" Reese screamed. They had to get out of there.

He ran toward her. More rocks and boulders fell from the matrix of mined earth, splintering the big logs as though they were twigs. When Jamie reached her, she ran with him hand in hand toward the elevator.

Someone had lowered the elevator car. Reese heard it along with the roar of caving rocks behind them.

Dust engulfed them as they all ran onto the lifesaving lift.

The men carrying Kadin put him down on the floor and the elevator began to ascend. She coughed along with others as dust filled the elevator car, barely audible along with crashing rocks. But the car raised and the air began to clear. Light from above grew brighter.

Endless moments ticked painfully by as she looked at Kadin's still slack face. How could such a powerful man be taken down this way?

All of Stankovich's men had certainly perished in the mine. Stankovich was dead. She, Jamie, Kadin and Penny had nothing more to fear from him, and yet it seemed so awful that so much life had ended.

Kadin's couldn't.

The elevator stopped and the metal door creaked and clanked open.

Penny rushed in with a wail, seeing her baby was all right in the arms of one of DAI's newest security officers. She fell to Kadin's side and pleaded for him to wake up.

Reese leaned against the side of the elevator, meeting Jamie's eyes. He knew what losing Kadin would do to her.

Chapter 16

Reese sat beside Jamie in the ICU waiting room. Kadin had been flown to the Montrose hospital and was now in surgery. The room had framed photographs of beaches that seemed out of place and inappropriate. Who could think of something as pleasant as being on a beach when someone close might die? Magazines cluttered tables and it smelled stale, like many people had come and gone and left only their germs and bad breath behind. It was an awful room. Even with new furniture and clean walls and floors, what it represented made it awful.

Penny paced from one end of the room to the other, rocking Clayton to sleep. She held herself together amazingly well, but Reese had no illusion what not knowing whether her husband would survive did to her on the inside.

Jamie gave her hand a squeeze, as he had a few times already.

The shock of her biological father facing death had shaken her foundation. She sat in a daze, unable to think of anything else other than he could die and what would she do if he did. The realization struck that she did want him in her life. That hug he'd given her had mattered. Jamie had worked his magic, as well. He'd loosened her rigid resolve regarding the course she'd chosen. It had all seemed so simple before. Go to college. Get a job as deputy sheriff. Get promoted. Be sheriff someday. She had not once included anything personal in those plans, and now she could see her mistake.

Being raised by distant parents who'd provided well for her and had taught her to provide for herself and function socially had brought her success, but little else. There had been acts of affection and caring but not what she'd call genuine love. Knowing Jamie and meeting Kadin had shown her what she was missing, and that it was all right to include a personal life in her plans. There was nothing wrong with including Kadin, Penny and Clayton in her circle. In fact, they would enrich her life, make it much more fulfilling with love.

She wanted the chance to experience that.

What about Jamie? She liked looking at him, but the zing that came with it set her off balance. She didn't know what to do with all the feelings he brewed. Was it love? She didn't know. But she needed to. She couldn't give herself completely to him until she decided what she would do. Stay with him or end the relationship? Maybe she just needed a little more time. She didn't have to plan on when she'd find a man to share her life with, but she needed to understand her feelings.

Jamie caught her next glance his way and his eyes conveyed care and concern, which he didn't verbalize.

If only he could read her thoughts.

A doctor emerged into the waiting room.

Penny's softly said, "Oh."

Reese stood and went to her side, imagining the sheer panic shooting through her right now. Little Clayton began having his own conversation, staring up at his mother, tiny brow going low with the basic understanding that she was upset.

Jamie came to stand beside Reese as the doctor reached them.

"He's going to be all right," he said right off. A Native American with John Lennon glasses and thick, short dark hair, he was on the tall side and lean.

Penny's shoulders shuddered and she let out another, longer "Oh," then leaned down and kissed Clayton's forehead.

Reese shared her relief.

"The bullet passed all the way through above his heart and lung. He's very lucky that way. Actually, the blow to his head had me more concerned. Being unconscious for so long, I wasn't sure of the extent of his injury. But he woke up before we started surgery, angry over where he was. He'll have a concussion for a while and a few stitches, but that's it."

"My husband doesn't like to be a victim," Penny said, brushing her auburn hair behind one ear.

"He's no victim, I assure you." The doctor laughed. "For a moment I thought he'd perform the surgery himself."

Penny smiled.

"He was shot in the back," Jamie pointed out, leather jacket draped over his arm, taller and younger than Doc. His stubbly face and blue eyes confiscated her gaze again.

"He'll awaken soon. A man like him, sooner than most. You can go and see him now."

Walking alongside Jamie, Reese followed Penny into an elevator. On the way up to the floor where Kadin now recovered, she moved closer to Jamie when he put his arm around her waist. Penny didn't even notice. She bounced up and down as she rocked the child and was clearly trying to relieve her anxiety.

She walked the fastest down the sterile hall, arriving at the door and bursting inside.

Holding the door, Jamie let Reese in before him. She stopped and waited for Penny to have a moment. Holding her son with one arm, she touched Kadin's face.

He opened his eyes.

"Kadin." Penny cried and leaned over to kiss him.

When she straightened, he reached up and put his hand on his son's head, intense love glowing from his weary eyes as they traveled up to Penny.

After a touching reunion, Kadin looked at Jamie. "I will never be able to repay you."

Jamie and the men had saved Kadin and his son.

"It wasn't just me."

Penny moved away when Clayton began to fuss. She went to a chair on the other side of the bed and sat. Kadin watched for a moment and then turned to Reese.

She went forward, going to the bed. When he opened his hand to her, she put hers there.

"Our family is whole again," he said.

"What kind of drugs do they have you on?" she quipped, and not very successfully.

"I mean it," Kadin said. "You're my daughter. I'd like us to spend as much time together as we can."

She wasn't a kid anymore, but the lightness in her heart told her the truth. "I'd like that, too. And someday I'd like to call you my father." She just wasn't ready yet.

"Take all the time you need. Is when I'm released from the hospital long enough?"

He was better at joking than her. "You won't be in here long. The doctor says you're feisty."

"Kind of like you?"

She smiled and glanced at Jamie, who grinned crookedly. "I can be rather stubborn."

More than a week later, the DNA results came back, confirming Darius Richardson was indeed Virgil Church and the man responsible for killing Eva and Paula. Jamie went with Reese to the Church residence to inform Lavinia of Virgil's arrest. When they arrived, Lavinia invited them in for tea and told them Virgil had left her and she had no idea where he'd gone.

She appeared distracted, as though confused over why they had shown up when she hadn't called for help. And perhaps she was a bit out of sorts with the abruptness of Virgil's abandonment. She wore a flowing floral robe over her nightgown and it was late afternoon. Had sadness kept her in her pajamas all day?

"Why did he leave?" Reese asked as Lavinia handed her a steaming cup.

"He left me a letter." Lavinia sat on a kitchen table

chair and chewed on her thumbnail. "I knew I should have never married him. No wonder I always called for help. He wasn't who I thought. He lied to me."

Could they be so lucky as to get a written confession—at least for the identity theft?

Jamie pulled out a chair for Reese, who eyed him as though he was too old-fashioned. He didn't care. He'd do things like that for her until he was old and gray. If she ever let him.

He also sat down, with Reese closer to Lavinia at the round table.

"Can we see the letter?" Reese asked. "It might contain evidence."

Lavinia frowned. "Evidence?" Then she waved her hand with the roll of her bright blue eyes like beautiful crystals glittering out from their wrinkly nest. "He assumed another man's identity."

Getting up from the chair, she went to a built-in desk in the kitchen and lifted a folded letter. Returning, she placed it in front of Reese.

"All a crock of lies." Lavinia sat down. "All this time I believed him when he was hiding who he really was." She shook her head. "It's had me locked up in here for days, trying to get my head to figure out how he got away with it for so long."

"Many people have a sixth sense," Jamie said. "You seemed to have picked up that something wasn't right with him."

"Oh, yes I did. In my younger years nobody could pull wool over my eyes. I didn't live to make others happy. But you get on in age and certain things don't matter the way they used to."

"'Dear Lavinia,'" Reese began to read. "'I can find

no words to describe how sorry I am to have to tell you this. There is something I have never told you, something I have never told anyone. Long before I met you, I lived in San Diego and met a girl I fell in love with. I was young and anxious to make a lot of money. Back then, I stole things and probably would have followed a lifetime of crime if I hadn't met you."'

Reese looked up at Lavinia, who'd put her fingers to her mouth and listened. "'I would have kept this a secret to my grave, and especially to preserve the life we've built together. But the police found me. They went to see my sister in Durango and asked me for a DNA sample. I have to assume they've made the connection between me and the man I used to be, Darius Richardson. I can't tell you the rest. It pains me too much. You'll find out soon enough, I'm guessing. Police will come looking for me and I have to be long gone by the time they do."'

"What is he talking about with police? We had our trouble but he sounds as though he'll be arrested. What for? Stealing an identity?"

"No," Jamie said. "Murder."

Lavinia inhaled sharply.

"Darius Richardson is the man who killed Ella Neville, who also assumed a false identity," Reese said. "The money I found in my house was stolen. Darius Richardson robbed a bank and Ella, who is really Eva Sinclair, drove the getaway car. Eva hid the money but Darius came for her and killed her before she could do anything with it."

Lavinia flattened her hand to her heart. "Oh, my Lord, this is much worse than I ever dreamed. I was married to a murderer?" Her eyes rounded and her mouth stayed open in her shock.

"We're sorry to have to tell you," Jamie said. "He's already been arrested."

Lavinia looked stunned. "I wish I would have learned this when I was several years younger. It's not as though I'll be able to attract a new man. I'll be forced to live alone now. Die alone." She averted her eyes as she stared off, contemplating her fate. "I suppose I could write him while he's in prison for the rest of his miserable life. I could tell him what an ass he was for lying to me."

"You could." Jamie smiled. The woman had spunk.

"How did you arrest him?" Lavinia asked.

"His sister called police and told them where he'd gone. US Marshals picked him up in Tijuana. He was transported back to Colorado and during questioning, confessed to everything."

He'd gotten nervous when Reese began investigating Eva's case, particularly since the man who'd come to town to help her was from such an elite agency. He'd found out who Jamie was and his past, that he'd worked for Aesir International. When he'd seen Stankovich in town, he'd recognized him as the owner of Aesir. He'd approached him after learning Reese had found the money he thought Eva had spent buying the house with Jeffrey. He'd broken into Jeffrey's house after he killed Eva just to be sure she hadn't lied. He'd thought she told the truth up until Reese found money hidden in the floorboards. He'd struck a deal with Stankovich, suspecting Eva had hidden the rest of the money somewhere else in the house. He hoped

Stankovich would take care of Reese and Jamie before they figured out he was Darius Richardson.

As to Eva's and Paula's murders, he claimed he'd followed Eva to Never Summer because she had stolen his money. When he found out she married another man, he'd lost control of his temper. He'd loved her despite her deception. She'd loved him, too, but he had issues with his temper back then. After she told him all the money had gone "into the house" she'd purchased with Jeffrey, he'd killed her. He was forced to kill Paula because she witnessed him strangle Eva and thought she'd go to the police, even though she kept promising she wouldn't.

Darius Richardson's DNA would match that of the bloodstained fiber and he would go to prison. Case closed.

Jamie opened the door for her at the grange. Reese entered in a skirt and country blouse and boots. A town celebration honoring her achievement had been arranged. She couldn't have solved the forty-year-old case without her father and Jamie, and wouldn't have been promoted to assistant sheriff, either. But she couldn't refuse the town's kindness. The sheriff had insisted on celebrating.

Jamie had gone mysteriously quiet since learning she'd be promoted. Of course the news made her happy, but she was still so mixed up about him—what to do about him.

The podium had been removed in the grange and tables arranged into more of a reception-like configuration. White tablecloths spiffed up the place and someone had added vases. The DJ was where he always was, chewing gum, bobbing his head to A Florida Georgia Line song and tapping the edge of the platform with an old-school pencil.

Betsy and Horace Milton danced with more exuberance than the only other, much younger, couple swinging it up on the dance floor. In jeans tucked into a pair of cowboy boots and a flannel shirt, Betsy smiled big with sparkling eyes as she kicked out one of her feet. Horace smiled with her, twirling her and bending her back over his arm.

"I'm going to be like that when I'm their age," Jamie said.

"It's all about movement." She'd go along with that.

Catching herself thinking in terms of being with Jamie when she reached that age, Reese turned to scan the gathering crowd. Many residents had shown up. She spotted Candace, whose face lit with a smile. She waved as she approached.

"Congratulations, Reese!" She hugged her briefly. "You solved the cold case. That's so awesome!"

"Thanks. I had help."

Candace gave a small swat with her hand. "You're too humble. Is she always that way?"

"She's humble but there are other words that describe her better," Jamie said.

"He thinks I'm stubborn."

"You two are together now, right? Sheriff said he saw you kissing." She wiggled her eyebrows. "You going to take our celebrity away from us now? You live in Wyoming, right? You work for that famous detective. The one who was shot?"

"Yes, and if I can I'll seduce Reese into moving there with me." He turned a challenging but flirtatious look her way. When she lifted her eyebrows in answer to his challenge, he added, "Her father would like her to come and work for him, too."

What a well-placed dangling carrot.

"Oh, how romantic!" Candace put her hand by her mouth and leaned closer to Reese. "I won't tell the sheriff."

"What won't you tell me?"

Reese turned to see him approach, mortified that he might think she'd leave her job now that she'd gotten a promotion.

"I'm trying to steal her away from you," Jamie said.

She glared at him in warning but he only grinned and pecked a kiss to her lips.

"He's joking," she said.

Sheriff Robison took her in for a hug. "You deserve this promotion, Reese. You're a good detective."

"Excuse us." Jamie took her hand and led her to the dance floor. A slow country Western song had begun.

"I'm not coercing you. I'm teasing. You need time to decide. I'm going to give that to you."

"What do you mean?"

"I'm going back to Wyoming tomorrow morning. After this dance, I'll go to my hotel room."

"You're not even staying for the party?"

"I'm happy for your achievement but I won't celebrate something that will take you away from me. You have to decide if I'm worth a change in your lifestyle."

She stopped dancing with him. "You're asking me to leave my hometown."

He lowered his arms. "Yes. I am. You have more than me waiting for you in Wyoming."

Her father. She had family there, a real family. "You'll wait for me?"

"I believe in us, in this, in what we have together." He touched the side of her face. "I can only hope you come to believe the same."

Without the certainty he clearly had, she couldn't promise him anything. Not only did she have to decide what was best for her and her future, but she also had to be sure if her feelings were strong enough to justify picking up her life and moving it somewhere else. She'd just gotten a big promotion. Would she pass it by for a chance to prove herself at Dark Alley Investigations?

Chapter 17

"So you just left her there."

"Would you rather I begged?" Jamie stepped outside to the bite of a late February wind, seeing a flashy red Ferrari pull into a parking space at the edge of the sidewalk.

He and one of the detectives at DAI had decided to go out for lunch at the Spicy Habanero. Jasper Roesch had joined DAI shortly after Kadin had opened the doors to his investigation agency. A big Swiss man with thick blond hair and blue eyes, he had a lumbering gait and a taste for spicy food diametric to his fair heritage.

"No, but if I met a lady like that, I wouldn't have given up." Jasper paused to watch the Ferrari.

"Who says I've given up?"

Jasper chuckled just as a woman got out of the expensive sports car. "Take a look at *that*."

A leggy dark Spanish beauty rose from the car. Long, wavy black hair framed olive skin and full lips. Her eyes were hidden behind dark sunglasses but Jamie bet they were as striking as the rest of her. She looked at them as she shut the car door. Holding a black clutch with glittering stones along the top, she wore a figure-fitting black dress that revealed some cleavage and her legs from midthigh down.

"Holy mother…" Jasper said in a low voice.

If Jamie hadn't already fallen in love with his soul mate, his jaw would have dropped, too. She was Jasper's polar opposite. Dark where he was light. But they both had the looks to attract each other.

"Are either one of you Kadin Tandy?" She held a hint of an accent, but must have been raised in the United States.

"He's on leave for several weeks," Jasper said.

Penny had ordered her husband to take some time off to be with his family. They, including Jamie, hoped that would include Reese very soon.

"Can I help you?" Jasper asked.

The woman hesitated, glancing at her car as though contemplating leaving, and looked back at Jasper. Then she began to walk around the car.

A vehicle slowed while it passed. Jamie turned just as a man lowered the dark windows of a black sedan and stuck out a gun. He fired, and Jasper bolted for the woman while Jamie pulled out his pistol.

The woman went down. The driver of the sedan sped away as Jamie fired his pistol several times. He thought he saw the silhouette of the passenger slump in his seat, but the driver must have been unharmed. The sedan disappeared from sight.

"Call 911!" Jasper yelled.

People from inside stores poured out into the street, several with cell phones to their ears. Someone had already called for help.

The woman lay on the sidewalk in front of DAI, one leg bent, one arm above her head. Blood began to spread beneath her. She'd been shot in the chest.

Jasper ripped open her dress to reveal the gunshot wound. He pressed hard against the bloody hole and leaned down to test for breathing.

Jamie knelt on the other side of her, taking her pulse. He felt one but it was faint. He looked up for signs of an emergency vehicle. He heard it before he saw it swing around a corner.

Seconds later, paramedics went to work on the woman. Hooked to an IV, she was placed onto the gurney. Jasper climbed into the ambulance with her.

After watching the ambulance race away, he grew aware of people asking him questions.

"What happened?"

He ignored the woman who asked and went to the Ferrari. The passenger door was locked but he hadn't seen the woman lock the driver's side. He went to that door and it opened. He leaned inside and searched for some identification. There was no registration or insurance papers. Jasper had taken her purse with him in the ambulance. He'd have to wait to find out who the woman was. And hopefully she survived to tell them why someone had tried to kill her.

The next day, Reese parked her Jeep in front of DAI. The building looked different than it had the last time she'd been here. She hadn't noticed its historic architecture and tinted windows. And the size. This was no one-man private investigation agency.

She got out of her Jeep. No longer in a uniform, she'd opted for a skirt and jacket. The chilly air touched her legs as she approached the building.

She entered to find a smiling receptionist. "May I help you?"

"I'm here to see Jamie Knox. Would you tell him Reese Harlow is here to see him?"

"No need. He said if you showed up to let you in." She stood and went to the secured doorway, using her badge to release the lock.

"Thank you." Reese stepped into the busy work area. Detectives talked on phones and among themselves. Someone laughed. She reached the end of the hall and headed for Jamie's office. The door was open.

Her heart drummed a nervous beat. At the door, she slowed as the sight of her lover gave her that familiar electric shock of attraction. She went inside and closed the door, making sure she switched the lock with enough verve that he would hear. He looked up from whatever had him riveted on his computer screen.

He stared at her, at first blankly and then with heating eyes and an emerging grin of pure satisfaction.

She laughed lightly, the joy of this moment stimulating her, too. The rightness of it assured her she'd made the right decision.

She walked fast to him as he got up from his chair. Around his desk, she threw her arms over his shoulders and he lifted her against him as he kissed her.

"Oh, Jamie," she breathed against his mouth. "I was heartbroken from the moment you walked out of the grange." She planted kisses on his mouth and face. "I've been so lonely. So lost without you." She kissed his mouth longer. Then drew back and put her hands on each side of his face. "I'm not whole without you."

He looked into her eyes for a while, obviously basking in the light of their love, as she was.

"What took you so long?" he asked.

"I had to be sure. I had a long talk with my mother. My real mother." Giselle had tentatively talked at first, seeming as unsure as Reese had been up to this point, but soon they opened up.

"You'll be seeing her again?"

"Yes. She helped me to see the right path."

His mouth curved. "And here you are."

"Here I am." She laughed lightly again. "And I couldn't be happier."

"Marry me."

"Just say when."

"After this." He reached for her skirt and pulled it up.

"Jamie." She glanced back at the door. She had locked it…

"You're all I've been thinking about." He kissed her as he tugged down her underwear. "I can't wait to take you home."

His fingers brushing her removed any hesitation she had about where they were. With the view of the butte, she unfastened his pants and pushed him down onto the office chair. He held her as she straddled the chair, the arms spreading her legs wide. Hanging onto his shoulders, she eased down on his erection, his strong hands steadying her. Then she moved up and down, slowly at first, then going into a bounce as they ended the drought of having each other.

"There's something I have to tell you," she said.

"Shoot."

"I've loved you since that day we spent together, too."

He chuckled. "I know, but thanks for telling me."

She ran her finger down his nose, smiling on the inside and out.

A knock on the door drew her back up, and she went rigid. "Jamie?"

"Hold on," Jamie said loudly, then to her he whispered, "That's a detective." Jamie lifted Reese off him. She found her footing and smoothed her skirt while he pulled up his pants and fastened and belted them.

"He must have news about a woman who was shot yesterday."

She looked over at him as he strode to the door. "Shot?"

Unlocking the door, Jamie stood aside as another man stepped in, eyeing the door and then Jamie before looking at Reese.

"Reese, Jasper Roesch. Jasper, Reese Harlow, my fiancée."

Jasper swung his gaze to him.

He grinned lopsidedly. "I told you."

"You didn't tell me anything." Jasper walked toward her.

Remembering her panties, Reese looked for them. Seeing them on the floor near her foot, she kicked them under the desk just as Jasper stopped beside her.

"A pleasure."

She shook his hand. "Likewise."

Jasper turned to Jamie. "The woman woke up. She's got a long recovery but the doctors think she'll be all right. I was just heading out to go talk to her. You want to go with me?"

Jamie looked at Reese. "No. I have to help Reese move in with me." He went to stand beside her and took her hand. "Did you ever get her name?"

"No. She had no identification on her. Just some makeup and money in her purse—a lot of money."

"I've had enough mystery for a while. I'm going to concentrate on running security operations and leave the mystery solving to you guys." He put his arm around Reese. "And maybe start working on growing a family."

Reese gaped at him. They hadn't talked about *that*. How did she feel about having babies? As confused as she had been about opening her heart to love, she hadn't even considered having children with him.

"You're going to have to work pretty darn hard."

"If I can woo you into being with me, I can woo you into having my baby."

Amazed he'd picked up on what she'd really meant, she answered his teasing tone. "Your baby?"

"Doesn't that have a romantic ring to it?"

"It has a ring to it. I'm not sure about romantic." A painful ring—when she gave birth. A trying ring—when she thought of all the times the baby would cry and keep her from doing what she wanted.

"You weren't sure about me, either." He kissed her cheek.

"All right, this sounds like a personal conversation." Jasper headed for the door. "I'll leave you two lovebirds alone." He shook his head. "Some men just lose their heads over women."

"You should try it sometime," Jamie said.

"No thanks." He closed the door behind him.

"He'll learn someday," Reese said. "If I did, anyone can."

* * * * *

If you loved this novel, don't miss other
suspenseful titles by Jennifer Morey:

COLD CASE RECRUIT
JUSTICE HUNTER
A WANTED MAN
THE MARINE'S TEMPTATION
THE ELIGIBLE SUSPECT
ONE SECRET NIGHT

Available now from Mills & Boon Romantic Suspense!

MILLS & BOON®

INTRIGUE
Romantic Suspense

A SEDUCTIVE COMBINATION OF DANGER AND DESIRE

MILLS & BOON®

Why shop at millsandboon.co.uk?

Each year, thousands of romance readers find their perfect read at millsandboon.co.uk. That's because we're passionate about bringing you the very best romantic fiction. Here are some of the advantages of shopping at www.millsandboon.co.uk:

* **Get new books first**—you'll be able to buy your favourite books one month before they hit the shops

* **Get exclusive discounts**—you'll also be able to buy our specially created monthly collections, with up to 50% off the RRP

* **Find your favourite authors**—latest news, interviews and new releases for all your favourite authors and series on our website, plus ideas for what to try next

* **Join in**—once you've bought your favourite books, don't forget to register with us to rate, review and join in the discussions

Visit **www.millsandboon.co.uk**
for all this and more today!

MILLS_WEB